I have always been able to count on a highly emotional and enjoyable read from Andrea Boeshaar. Once again she comes through in *Unexpected Love*. She has skillfully captured the essence of nineteenth-century Chicago with characters who gripped my heart.

—DEBBY MAYNE
AUTHOR OF *LOVE FINDS YOU IN TREASURE ISLAND, FLORIDA*
AND *SWEET BAKLAVA*

An enchanting tale of redemption and love that transported me back to the nineteenth century, where another place and time came alive in my imagination. This book had me thinking about the characters even when I had to set it down to go to work. It's a wonderful read!

—JENNIFER HUDSON TAYLOR
AUTHOR OF *HIGHLAND BLESSINGS*

Andrea Boeshaar pens a sweet, heart-tugging romance that will stay with the reader for a long time. Renna is every woman, and her captain every woman's dream. Don't miss this one!

—GINNY AIKEN
AUTHOR OF THE *SILVER HILLS TRILOGY*
AND THE *WOMEN OF HOPE SERIES*

*Unexpected Love* is a tale of friendship and faith, love amidst tragedy, and a rascal given a second chance at life. It's the heart-tugging story of a man who can have any woman he wants and a woman no man has ever wanted.

—VICKIE MCDONOUGH
AWARD-WINNING AUTHOR OF
THE *TEXAS BOARDINGHOUSE BRIDES* series

# UNEXPECTED
## LOVE

*Seasons of Redemption*

BOOK THREE

# UNEXPECTED
# LOVE

*Seasons of Redemption*

BOOK THREE

# ANDREA KUHN
# BOESHAAR

REALMS
A STRANG COMPANY

Most STRANG COMMUNICATIONS BOOK GROUP products are available at special quantity discounts for bulk purchase for sales promotions, premiums, fund-raising, and educational needs. For details, write Strang Communications Book Group, 600 Rinehart Road, Lake Mary, Florida 32746, or telephone (407) 333-0600.

UNEXPECTED LOVE by Andrea Kuhn Boeshaar
Published by Realms
A Strang Company
600 Rinehart Road
Lake Mary, Florida 32746
www.strangbookgroup.com

The characters portrayed in this book are fictitious unless they are historical figures explicitly named. Otherwise, any resemblance to actual people, whether living or dead, is coincidental.

All Scripture quotations are from the King James Version of the Bible.

Cover design by Bill Johnson

Visit the author's website at www.andreaboeshaar.com.

Library of Congress Cataloging-in-Publication Data
Boeshaar, Andrea.
  Unexpected love / by Andrea Boeshaar.
     p. cm.
  ISBN 978-1-61638-192-9
  1. Nurses--Fiction. 2. Amnesia--Fiction. 3. Shipwrecks--Fiction. I. Title.
  PS3552.O4257U54 2011
  813'.54--dc22
                                        2010039332
E-book ISBN: 978-1-61638-408-1
First Edition
11 12 13 14 15 — 987654321
Printed in the United States of America

To Sally, Gloria, and DiAnn—critique buddies from days gone by. Thank you for encouraging me, challenging me, and pointing out all my typos when I first began writing this story. I often think of you three ladies when the fax machine rings. Love you always.

Also…to my youngest son, Brian. May you find a love to last a lifetime. Thank you for allowing me to use your name.

## ONE

*Chicago, Illinois, September 4, 1866*

D o you think he'll live, Dr. Hamilton?"

The gray-haired man with bushy whiskers pondered the question for several moments, chewing on his thick lips as he weighed his reply. "Yes, I think he will," he finally said. "Of course, he's not out of the woods yet, but it seems he's coming around."

Lorenna Fields breathed a sigh of relief. It had been two whole days with nary a sign of life from this half-drowned man, but finally—*finally*—he showed signs of improvement.

"You've done a good job with this patient, Nurse Fields." The physician drew himself up to his full height, which barely met Renna's five feet six inches. "I don't think he'd be alive today if you hadn't given him such extraordinary care."

"Thank you, Dr. Hamilton, but it was the Lord who spared this man and the Lord who gave me the strength and skill to nurse him."

The old physician snorted in disgust. "Yes, well, it might have had something to do with the fact that you've got a brain in your head, Nurse Fields, and the fact that you used it too, I might add!"

Renna smiled inwardly. Dr. Hamilton always disliked it when she gave God the credit for any medical advancement, especially the miracles. Yet Renna's intelligence and experience weren't typical of women her age, and she determined to use them to God's glory.

The patient moaned, his head moving from side to side.

"Easy now, Mr. Blackeyes." Renna placed a hand on the man's muscular shoulder. "It's all right." She picked up the fever rag from out of the cold water, wrung it once, and set it on the patient's burning brow.

Dr. Hamilton snorted again, only this time in amusement. "*Mr. Blackeyes?* How in the world did you come by that name, Nurse Fields?"

She blushed but replied in all honesty. "It's his eyes, Doctor. They're as black as pitch and as shiny as polished stones. And since we don't know his true identity, I've named him Mr. Blackeyes."

"I see." Dr. Hamilton could barely contain his laughter.

"Well, I had to call him *something* now, didn't I?" She wrung the fever cloth more tightly.

"Ah, yes, I suppose you did." Dr. Hamilton gathered his instruments and put them into his black leather medical bag. "Well, carry on, Nurse Fields." He sounded tired. "If your patient's fever doesn't break by morning, send for me at once. However, I think it will, especially since we got some medicine and chicken broth into him tonight."

Renna nodded while the old man waved over his shoulder as he left the hospital ward.

Returning her attention to her patient, Renna saw that he slept for the moment. His blue-black hair, which had just a slight wave to it, shone beneath the dampness of the fever. The stifling late summer heat of the room threatened to bring his temperature even higher.

Wiping a sleeve across her own beaded brow, Renna continued to sponge down her patient. Poor Mr. Blackeyes had been found floating in Lake Michigan after a terrible storm the past Sunday. The crew of the passing ship that found him had thought he was dead at first. But they pulled him aboard anyway. The ship's doctor immediately examined him and detected a heartbeat, so he cared for him until the ship docked in Chicago's harbor. As soon as the sailors could manage it, Mr. Blackeyes was deposited at Mercy Hospital and admitted to the second floor and into Renna's care. Now, two days later, he finally showed some improvement.

Pulling the fever rag from the round porcelain bowl filled with cool water, Renna replaced it carefully across Mr. Blackeyes's forehead. She could tell this man was different from the usual "unknowns" that the hospital acquired. His dark features somehow implied sophistication, even through several days' growth of beard. And his powerful broad shoulders and muscular arms indicated the strength of a man accustomed to lifting or hoisting. And he was handsome, all right. A lady's man, no doubt.

"But who are you, Mr. Blackeyes?" Renna murmured, gazing down at him.

As if in reply, the man groaned.

Renna settled him once more and then slowly stood. She forced her mind to dwell on her other patients as she made her rounds through the sick ward, a large room with whitewashed walls and a polished marble floor. Eight beds, four on each side, were neatly lined in rows, leaving a wide area in the center of the ward.

Moving from bed to bed, Renna checked each patient, thankful that this ward wasn't full: only Mr. Anderson, suffering from a farming accident in which he lost his left arm; Mr. Taylor, who had had pneumonia but had recovered and would soon be released; and, finally, young John Webster, who had been accidentally shot in the chest by his brother. It appeared the wounded young man wouldn't live through the night, and his family had gathered around him, his mother weeping.

Taking pity on the Webster family, Renna set up several wooden screens to allow them some privacy. Then she checked on John. She could see death settling in. She was somewhat accustomed to the sight, as she'd trained in a Union military hospital in Richmond, Virginia, during the Civil War. Still, watching a life slip away never got easier. But in this case Renna took heart that the Websters were people with a strong faith. Young John would soon go home to be with his Savior.

"Can I get anything for you, Mrs. Webster?" Renna asked the boy's mother now.

A tall, very capable-looking woman, she shook her head. Several brunette curls tumbled from their bun.

Renna asked the same thing of the boy's brother and father, but both declined.

"I didn't mean ter shoot 'im, Ma!" the brother declared. He suddenly began to sob.

"Aw, I know ya didn't mean it, son," Mrs. Webster replied through her own tears. "It was an accident. That anyone can see!"

"Tell it to Jesus, boy." His father's eyes were red, his jaw grizzled. "Give the matter to Christ, just like we done gave John over to Him."

Renna's heart was with the family, but she suddenly felt like an intruder. The Websters needed their privacy. Stepping back, she gave them each a sympathetic smile before moving away.

Walking to the other side of the room now, Renna sat down on the edge of Mr. Blackeyes's bed and sponged him down again. Afterward, she checked his head wound—nearly a three-inch gash above his left ear. It had needed to be sutured, and Dr. Hamilton had seen to that when Mr. Blackeyes was first admitted. "Unknown Male" was the name on his chart. Most "unknowns" didn't survive, so Renna was heartened that Mr. Blackeyes's prognosis seemed promising.

Now if only his fever would break. If only he'd regain consciousness and pneumonia wouldn't set in.

Momentarily closing her eyes, Renna prayed for God's healing of this man. She had been praying earnestly for the last week. Why she felt so burdened for him, she couldn't say, but she was.

Suddenly an abrupt command broke her thoughts. "Nurse Fields? Nurse Fields, you may go. I'm on duty now."

Renna glanced at the doorway where Nurse Rutledge, the night nurse who was also her supervisor, stood. A large woman with beady, dark eyes, she had a no-nonsense way about her. That same stern disposition kept her lips in a perpetual frown.

"As usual, your charts are in order."

Was that a hint of a smile? Renna guessed not.

"You're excused."

Renna replied with a nod. She didn't dislike the night supervisor, although she wasn't fond of the woman's overbearing manner. Still, Nurse Rutledge was in charge. "Thank you, ma'am. I'll just finish up here, and then I'll be on my way."

The older woman came up alongside her. "The first rule in nursing is, do not get emotionally attached to your patients. You know that."

Renna rinsed the fever rag once more and draped it across Mr. Blackeyes's forehead. "I'm not getting emotionally attached." Renna felt her conscience prick. "I'm just... well, I'm burdened for this man. In the spiritual sense."

"Humph! Call it what you will, Nurse Fields, but I happen to think you're much too emotional and far too sensitive. It's a wonder you've lasted in nursing this long. Why, I heard from the other nurses on duty today that you were crying with the Webster family over their boy." She sniffed in what seemed like disgust. "A nurse must never let her emotions get in the way of her duty, Nurse Fields."

"Yes, ma'am." Renna endured the rebuke. She'd heard it many times before.

Nurse Rutledge squared her wide shoulders. "Now, may I suggest that you leave your burden right here in this hospital bed

5

and go home and get some rest? You're due back here at six a.m., and I'll expect you promptly!"

Renna nodded. Then, with a backward glance at Mr. Blackeyes, she left the sick ward. She gathered her things and made her way to the hospital's main entrance. Outside, she paused and breathed deeply. The air was thick and humid, but it was free from the chloroform and antiseptics that she'd smelled all day.

She spied a hired hackney, and within minutes, Renna rode the mile to the home she shared with her parents. She was the oldest child in the family, but at the age of thirty, Renna was what society termed "a spinster." Her two younger sisters were married and producing children galore, and her one younger brother and his wife were now expecting their first baby.

Renna loved all her nieces and nephews. They filled her empty arms when she wasn't nursing, and Jesus filled her heart. Time and time again, however, Renna was asked by a young niece or nephew, "Why didn't you ever get married, Auntie Renna?" And her reply was always, "I never fell in love."

But the truth of the matter was no man would have her—even if she had fallen in love. The large purplish birthmark on the left side of her face deterred every eligible bachelor. The unsightly thing came down her otherwise flawless cheek to the side of her nose and then around down to her jaw, like an ugly purple horseshoe branded into her face. One would think she'd be accustomed to the gawks, stares, and pitying glances sent her way at social functions, but they unnerved her. All dressed up and looking her prettiest, Renna still felt marred and uncomely under the scrutiny of her peers—especially when she was in the company of eligible men to whom she was supposed to be attractive and charming. Renna never felt she was either of those.

Nursing, however, was different. In the hospital Renna felt confident of her abilities. Moreover, her patients were usually too sick or in too much pain to be concerned with her ugly birthmark.

Rather, they just wanted her care and sensitivity, and that's what Renna thought she did best…in spite of what Nurse Rutledge said about her being too emotional and too sensitive. God in all His grace had given Renna a wondrous work in nursing, and it pleased her to be used in that way. What more could she want? And yet lately—lately Renna desired something more. Was it a sin to feel discontented after so many happy years of nursing?

The carriage stopped in front of Renna's house. She climbed out, paid the driver, and then turned to open the little white gate of the matching picket fence around the front yard. A slight breeze blew, and Renna thought it felt marvelous after her sweltering day on the second floor of the hospital.

"Well, there you are, dear." Her mother, Johanna Fields, stood with a pair of shears in her hand. She had obviously been pruning the flowers that graced the edge of the wide front porch. "You're late tonight, Renna." She studied her daughter. "Mr. Blackeyes? Is he…?"

"He's still alive." She stepped toward her mother. "Dr. Hamilton thinks he may even live, except he has an awful fever now. We're hoping it breaks by morning and that pneumonia doesn't set in."

"Oh, dear…" Mum shook her head sadly. "Well, we'll keep praying, won't we?"

Renna gave a nod before Mum hooked arms and led her into the house.

"I've made a light dinner tonight, Renna. Help yourself."

"I appreciate it, but I'm too tired to eat."

"But you need some nourishment." Mum fixed a plate of cold beef, sliced tomatoes, and a crusty roll. "Here, sit down at the table."

Renna allowed her mother to help her into the chair. After one bite she realized how ravenous she was and cleaned the plate.

Minutes later her sister Elizabeth walked in with her twin

daughters, Mary and Helena. Delight spread through Renna as the girls toddled into the kitchen.

"Hello, darlings." She gave each a hug before smiling up at her younger sister.

"Renna, you look exhausted." Elizabeth shook her head vehemently, causing strands of her light brown hair to escape their pinning. "You'll be old before your time."

"And what would you have me do? Sit around the house all day, twiddling my thumbs?" Seeing her sister's injured expression, she softened her voice. "I'm sorry. I guess I'm more tired than I thought."

Elizabeth smiled. "All's forgiven."

Renna struggled to her feet. Her entire body ached from her long shift. "I'll have to visit another time. I'm going up to bed."

After bidding everyone a good night, Renna climbed the steps leading to the second floor. In her small bedroom she poured water from the large pitcher on her bureau into the chamber basin and then washed away the day's heat. She pulled her cool, cotton nightgown over her head then took her Bible off the nightstand and continued her reading in John chapter 9. Renna realized as she read that physical ailments allowed God to show His glory, and she marveled as she read about the blind man who by simple faith and obedience regained his sight.

She bowed her head. *Oh, Lord, that You might heal Mr. Blackeyes. That You might show Your power to those who don't believe by healing him.* Renna paused to remember her other patients then. *And please rain down Your peace that passeth all understanding on the Websters tonight.*

Despite the fact her eyelids threatened to close, Renna finished her Bible reading. She turned down the lamp as a breeze ruffled the curtains. Somehow Renna knew that John Webster would not be in her sick ward tomorrow morning. Nor would his family be there. Somehow Renna knew that John was with the Savior already.

But Mr. Blackeyes…why, he might not be a believer. It pained Renna to think of him spending an eternity apart from God.

*Please heal him, Lord,* she prayed as she crawled into bed. She allowed her eyes to finally shut, and the darkly handsome stranger who lay fighting for his life was the last person on Renna's thoughts as she drifted off to sleep.

# Two

RENNA TOOK PURPOSEFUL STRIDES DOWN THE HALLWAY TO the ward the next morning, taking care that she didn't slip on the polished brown tiled floor. In Ward Two she checked on her patients and was pleased to learn from Dr. Hamilton that Mr. Blackeyes's fever had broken.

"His thrashing has ceased," the doctor said, "and he seems to be emerging from his delirium."

Renna was speechless. Answered prayer to be sure!

"Close the shades, Nurse Fields," Dr. Hamilton barked. "The sun is shining right in the poor fellow's eyes."

Renna went to do as she was told when Mr. Blackeyes weakly said, "The sun...what do you mean it's shining in my eyes?"

His voice sounded dry and hoarse, but his words alone stopped Renna in her tracks. With eyes wide, she looked to Dr. Hamilton.

"You can't see the sun shining in your eyes?" he asked the patient.

"No, and I would venture to say it's the middle of the night." The man turned his head toward the sound of Dr. Hamilton's voice. "Why are you questioning me in the dark, man? Are we in the bowels of a ship?"

"No, no, you're at Mercy Hospital in Chicago." Dr. Hamilton waved his hand in front of the patient's eyes. Then he looked at Renna and mouthed, "Blind."

Her heart sank.

"What's your name, my dear fellow?" Dr. Hamilton pulled various gadgets from his medical bag, waving them in front of the patient. No reaction.

"My name?" The question seemed to stump him.

"Your name…what is it?"

"I–I don't know…"

"Oh, come now," Dr. Hamilton said on a note of impatience. "Everyone has a name. What is yours?"

The dark-featured patient seemed to grope for a reply. Finally all he said was, "I–I really don't know."

Renna's jaw momentarily slacked as she realized the implication. Looking to Dr. Hamilton, she mouthed, "Amnesia?"

He nodded. Clearing his throat, he ordered her to fetch some salve and bandages from the supply cabinet. Renna hurried to get them. When she returned to the sick ward, Dr. Hamilton was in the midst of explaining the situation to Mr. Blackeyes.

"It's a result of your head injury, I'm afraid. Now the blindness may or may not be temporary. However, I'm inclined to believe that your memory will come back within a relatively short period of time."

Renna assisted Dr. Hamilton in applying the salve to his eyes. Next they bandaged them tightly.

"Since you can't see sunshine in your eyes, you won't be able to see other harmful things either," Dr. Hamilton explained. "The bandages will protect your eyes until your sight comes back." He paused before adding, "If it does."

Mr. Blackeyes fell back against the bed, seemingly exhausted by this news.

"He'll sleep now, Nurse Fields." Dr. Hamilton sent her a look from beneath his bushy brows. "But when he awakens, feed him and clean him up. See if you can jog his memory loose too."

"Yes, Doctor."

Renna stepped away from Mr. Blackeyes's bed. As she went about her business, she noted he slept all day. It wasn't until the end of Renna's shift when he finally felt strong enough to eat something. A coddled egg and milk toast were on the menu tonight, and Mr. Blackeyes grimaced at every spoonful Renna slipped into his mouth.

"Roast beef and potatoes would suit me just fine," he complained.

"Then you must be feeling much better." Renna spooned in another bite.

He grimaced and swallowed. "What is your name?"

"I'm Nurse Fields."

"Are you Miss or Missus?"

A smile toyed on her lips. "I'm Nurse Fields, and that's all you need to know."

A sardonic grin curved Mr. Blackeyes's mouth. "You've got some spirit, Nurse Fields. I like a spirited woman."

"You remember that much, do you?" Renna retorted.

Before he could reply, she spooned the last bit of his supper into his mouth.

He nearly gagged. "See here! That's not fair, Nurse Fields. I couldn't see that coming."

Renna laughed inwardly and moved off the side of the bed where she'd been sitting.

"Nurse Fields?" He managed to grab hold of her white smock. "Would you stay and talk with me awhile?" The dark brows above his bandaged eyes drew together in earnestness. "Tell me what you know of me and my condition. Will you? No one's told me a thing. It's quite aggravating."

Renna unloosed her apron and considered the request. "All right." She supposed she had time to do that much. "But I have to finish writing up my charts and check on my other patients. Then I'm off duty and can sit with you."

Mr. Blackeyes grinned. "Your husband won't mind?"

Renna expelled a weary sigh. She was glad her patient felt better, although she, herself, was wilted from the heat and exhausted from twelve hours of working. She certainly couldn't muster the energy to play cat and mouse.

"I am not married, sir," she said, sounding a little too harsh to her own ears. She forced herself to soften her tone. "Now let me go and finish up, and I'll sit with you awhile."

Strolling from bed to bed, Renna quickly wrote up her charts, checking on each patient as she did so. John Webster's cot had been, as she suspected, empty this morning. He had died during the night. Mr. Taylor was much better and would go home tomorrow, and Mr. Anderson...

Renna felt his forehead and realized the man burned with fever! Quickly she ran from the room and fetched some cool water along with a fever rag.

"What is it, Nurse Fields?" Nurse Rutledge asked as Renna whizzed by.

"It's Mr. Anderson. He's fevering from his wounds."

"The man who lost his arm in a farming accident?"

"Yes, that's the one."

"You'll have to stay until that fever is down, Nurse Fields. I'm short of nurses tonight."

Renna nodded, figuring that would be the case. With Mr. Blackeyes momentarily forgotten, she set out to sponge down Mr. Anderson.

He moaned and protested having the cool water on his body, but Renna fought to do her job.

Hours later Nurse Rutledge summoned Dr. Hamilton. Upon examining the wound, the aging physician shook his head, his expression grave. "It's a blood infection."

"No..." Renna's heart sank. "I kept the wound clean, Doctor."

"Well, at times, Nurse Fields, that's not enough."

Renna tried to think of what more she could have done but thought of nothing.

"Don't blame yourself," Dr. Hamilton said as if divining her thoughts. "You did what you could. So did I." He lowered his gaze and pressed his lips together. "Give him a spoonful of this if he's in pain."

Renna accepted the brown bottle filled with an opium elixir.

Dr. Hamilton packed his medical bag and left for home. Renna resigned herself to sponging off her patient and keeping him comfortable—until death set in.

She dabbed the man's forehead, wondering if he had family. He wasn't an old man. Did he have a wife? Certainly someone should be called. Taking a few minutes, Renna scoured his chart, but no one else had been named in case of emergency.

"I'm dying, ain't I?"

*He's conscious.* Renna set down the clipped paperwork and hurried to Mr. Anderson's bedside. His eyes were bright, and she could only soothe his burning brow and try to smile. "It's God who controls life and death. Not me." She thought for a long while then asked, "Is there anyone you want me to send for? A wife? Children?"

"No one. Just me on the farm…along with a few hired hands."

Renna thought it so sad that he should die alone.

"My wife left me years ago."

"That's a shame, Mr. Anderson." Renna continued sponging his forehead.

"She said I was a no-account drunk, and I suspect she was right. I left her alone far too much of the time."

"I'm sorry to hear it." Renna rinsed the fever rag again, and her heart grew burdened for this man. He'd apparently alienated everyone in his life. "Is there a minister I can call?"

"I said there's no one," he ground out. Then he muttered more, but Renna couldn't discern it.

"Do you know the Lord, Mr. Anderson? Do you know Jesus

Christ?" Renna normally wasn't so bold, but the words seemed to tumble from her mouth.

He nodded. "He's the One who hung on a tree and died." Mr. Anderson turned his fever-bright eyes toward Renna. "I heard a preacher man say that…once."

"It's true." She began to sing softly, a song she knew that was set to the biblical verse John 3:16. "God so loved the world that He sent His only Son. Only begotten Son. That whosoever believeth in Him should not perish, but have everlasting life. Everlasting life." She set the cool rag on his forehead.

Mr. Anderson closed his eyes. "Who wants everlastin' life? Mine has been nothing but drunkenness, heartache, and pain."

"But, to the contrary, everlasting life with God will be free from all that we suffer in this world."

"I'd like that. Living free from sufferin'." The little smile on his lips suddenly turned downward. He began to thrash and moan. "The pain…from the accident…"

Renna administered a dose of the elixir, and within minutes Mr. Anderson settled down.

"There. That's better." Renna set the fever rag on his forehead and resumed her song. "For God sent not His Son into the world to condemn the world, but that through Him the whole world might be saved."

"You think God'll save a drunk like me?"

"We're all sinners, Mr. Anderson. Just some of us are sinners saved by grace. God's grace."

His eyes fluttered closed, and then he grew quiet for a long while.

Rinsing the rag in the bowl beside her, Renna continued to sponge his face, neck, chest, and arms. She hummed the same song and tried not to think of how tired she was. She ignored her aching feet and the pain in the small of her back from bending over her patients all day.

"Oh, Christ, I'm sorry for the bad things I done!" Mr. Anderson's shout echoed through the ward and scared Renna so that she pushed to her feet. When she realized Mr. Anderson's deliriousness, she soothed him.

"Shh..." Renna thought he'd awaken the others.

"I'm sorry...take me to heaven. Take me..."

The poor man writhed in pain, and his body burned so badly from the fever that Renna couldn't keep the rag cool no matter how many times she rinsed it. She spooned more elixir into his mouth. His breathing slowed. Renna held his hand.

By morning Mr. Anderson was dead.

As Renna pulled the sheet over his head, her legs wobbled, partly from the sadness she felt but mostly from exhaustion. *Lord, I can only hope that Mr. Anderson met You as his Savior.*

Nurse Rutledge suddenly stood beside her. "I'll tell the orderlies to take care of the body. In the meantime, Nurse Fields, you're going home. I'm replacing you with Nurse Thatcher."

"Yes, ma'am."

Feeling so weary, Renna scarcely remembered the ride home in the hired hackney. She hardly felt the cool breeze against her hot skin as it blew in through the carriage window, and she was only vaguely aware of the towering masts of the vessels moored in the Chicago River. Normally Renna liked to watch for them as they peaked and dipped above many of the city's buildings. But this morning she didn't even think of them as she leaned her tired head back against the leather seat.

And it wasn't until later, after she arrived home, ate, washed, and had crawled into bed, that she remembered Mr. Blackeyes and his request that she sit with him awhile.

She bolted upright in her bed and moaned. He had wanted to talk. Guilt assailed her, and she massaged her temples.

Settling back against her pillows once more, Renna realized that she'd done what she needed to do. Mr. Anderson had needed her immediate attention, while Mr. Blackeyes was well enough to wait.

*I'll make it up to him*, Renna thought with a yawn. Perhaps she'd even bring him some of Mum's apple pie...

On that thought she closed her eyes and slept.

# THREE

Renna slept most of Thursday, rising only to accept a light supper from Mum. Then she fell soundly asleep once more and didn't awaken until the next morning.

She yawned and stretched, seeing the pinks of dawn beyond her open windows. A cool breeze blew into her bedroom, and the sun steadily rose in the eastern sky. Birds began chirping, and suddenly Renna couldn't stay in a bed a moment longer.

Feeling refreshed, she washed and dressed, and, as she did, she caught a glimpse of herself in the mirror. She paused to examine her attire, the dark gray dress with white collar and cuffs. Once at Mercy Hospital she'd don her long white apron. Renna gave her reddish-brown hair a pat. She had pinned it up to fit under the frilly white cap she wore to work, another piece of her uniform.

Next her gaze scrutinized her birthmark. How ugly she thought it was, that purplish horseshoe-shaped mark, as though someone had taken a hot iron and branded the side of her face. Renna had tried everything from creams to powders, soaps, and herbal teas. Nothing but nothing made the thing fade even slightly.

On a small sigh of despair, Renna turned away from the mirror. She took a few more minutes with her appearance and then took time for prayer. Leaving her bedroom, Renna made her way downstairs. She ate some breakfast and then packed up the remaining half of her mother's apple pie to take to the hospital with her. Renna wasn't about to forget Mr. Blackeyes today. She also took a jar of milk, a napkin, and a fork along with the pie. It looked like a small picnic lunch.

Renna kissed her mother's cheek. "Bye, Mum."

"Don't work too hard today, darling."

"Oh, I'll work plenty hard. That's for sure." Renna strode through the parlor.

Her father was just descending the stairs for breakfast. "On your way out already, are you?" His voice held a hint of a brogue, as Grandma Fields was full-blooded Irish. She married Grandpa Fields, an Englishman, and together they had made their way to America. Da had been born in the "New Country," but he picked up the Irish accent, and it never seemed to go away. Mum said that was what drew her to him—that charming brogue and Da's strong faith.

"Good morning, Da."

"And the best to you, Renn—my little wren." His hazel eyes twinkled just as they did each time he used her childhood moniker, wren—a derivative, of sorts, of her given name.

"Have a good day." Renna blew him a kiss.

"I shall." Wendell Fields sent her an affectionate wink as he straightened his tie.

Still smiling, Renna left the house and walked the nine blocks to the hospital. As she planned, she arrived early for duty and crept silently into the sick ward. Two new patients had been added sometime yesterday, but Renna hadn't met them yet. She checked on Mr. Blackeyes and suspected that he wasn't sleeping.

"Are you awake?" she whispered.

He turned his head. "Who's there?"

"It's Nurse Fields."

"Nurse Fields." Mr. Blackeyes grinned rather wryly. "I had thought you fell off the face of the earth. You haven't been around for days."

Renna smiled, although her patient couldn't see it. "I went home yesterday morning and had the day off. A girl's got to sleep sometime, you know."

"Feels like you've been gone for years."

Renna shook her head at the man, although he couldn't see the gesture.

"Nurse Hatchet has the coldest hands I've ever felt!"

"Nurse Thatcher," Renna corrected.

"Hatchet suits her perfectly."

Renna pressed her lips together in an effort not to smile. However, his complaints told Renna that he was feeling better.

"And Nurse Ruthless."

"Rutledge."

"I beg to differ! Why, I'd go so far as to say that…person isn't even human."

"Now, now, I'll have none of that. Both Nurse Thatcher and Nurse Rutledge are accomplished women." Renna set down the basket and began to unpack.

"And the food is awful!"

Renna thought she might agree with at least that much. "Well, I brought you some of my mother's apple pie for breakfast. How would that do? A special treat because I didn't get a chance to talk with you the other night." She paused in all seriousness now. "Mr. Anderson was, as you might know, deathly ill. In fact, he died the following morning."

"I heard it all," Mr. Blackeyes said in a somber tone. He turned momentarily silent then asked, "Was that all true what you told him? About God and salvation?"

"Yes." Renna sent him a curious look. "I spoke of the gospel, straight from the Holy Bible."

Another pause. "I prayed to God that night, right along with Mr. Anderson." Mr. Blackeyes's voice was but a whisper. "I somehow knew you spoke the truth because Richard used to tell me about salvation and my need for it."

"Richard? Why, that's wonderful!" Gladness soared inside of Renna. Her patient's memory was returning. And that he accepted

Jesus Christ the other night was as much a thrill to hear as it was a miracle! "And who's Richard?"

She waited for Mr. Blackeyes to continue, but he didn't immediately. Finally he just said, "I don't know who Richard is. But I can see his face right now in my mind's eye. He's fair-headed and wears spectacles sometimes...when he does my books."

"He's your bookkeeper?" Renna sat down on the side of his bed, totally absorbed in this man's puzzle of a past. "You must have some kind of business if you have a bookkeeper. Do you remember your name and where you're from?"

"No. And it's most infuriating too!"

"Be patient with yourself, Mr. Blackeyes."

He drew his chin back in surprise, and Renna laughed. "While you were unconscious," she explained, "I felt I had to call you something. So I made up the name Mr. Blackeyes. It's because of the color of your eyes. They're the deepest black I've ever seen."

Another hint of a smile shone through the man's dark beard. "I wish they worked."

Renna smiled sympathetically. "Perhaps in time they will. In fact, we'll ask God to heal them, all right?"

"Do you think He'd do that?"

"He might. God is all-powerful, and He can do anything. He created you, after all, so who would know better how to heal you than God?"

"He didn't let me drown."

"No, He didn't."

"I could have died in that frigid water during the storm..."

Renna chewed her lower lip in thought. "Do you think you were a believer before but just can't remember it now?"

Mr. Blackeyes rolled his head from side to side. "No. I laughed at Richard. And Sarah too. She went to church with the children..."

"You're remembering. How marvelous!" Renna stopped to think it over. "And do you think Sarah is your wife?"

Mr. Blackeyes was momentarily pensive. "I...I don't know," he admitted at last. "I feel something for her. Something special."

"Love?"

"Not exactly."

"Hmm...well, I'm sure you'll remember soon enough." Renna felt certain the man was married with children. But why should she feel so disappointed at the news?

She gave herself a mental shake and stood. Finding a fork and a napkin, along with the pie, she made her way back to her patient's bedside. "I'm not on duty for another half hour. Would you like your apple pie now? And I can stay and talk with you, if you're up to it."

"I've been longing for someone to talk to." Mr. Blackeyes worked himself into a sitting position.

"Well, all right, then."

Renna allowed him to feed himself. In spite of his blindness he did rather well, using his fork and napkin in a mannerly way that suggested proper training. And the way he spoke too—Mr. Blackeyes was obviously a learned man. There was an air of sophistication about him.

"How about a good strong cup of coffee to wash that down?" Mr. Blackeyes dabbed the corners of his mouth.

Renna grinned. "How about a cup of milk instead? It's all I brought with me." She looked at the pie tin. He'd scarcely eaten even a quarter of the portion she'd brought.

"Milk will do nicely, thank you." He seemed tired now.

Renna gave him the jar of milk, and he took a few long swallows; however, he didn't finish even half of it.

"I'll save the rest of this for you," she promised. "There's a good deal of pie and milk left."

Renna cleaned up and prepared to put the food in the icebox

downstairs. She could keep it there for the day without a problem.

"Nurse Fields?" Mr. Blackeyes's tone sounded both pleading and commanding. "Could I get a shave? I simply abhor wearing a beard."

"Of course," Renna replied easily. "I'm quite good at shaving a man's face. I shaved so many faces during the war that some say I put the local barber to shame." She smiled.

"I was on the Mississippi River during the war," Mr. Blackeyes stated. "I was on a gunner..."

"You're remembering!" Renna's voice reverberated through the ward, and she had to remind herself to quiet down.

But Mr. Blackeyes only sighed. "That's all I remember. This is most frustrating!"

Renna set her hand on his shoulder. "It'll come. Give yourself some time."

"Thank you." He suddenly captured her hand in his, and something strange and powerful zinged through Renna, all the way up her arm and straight to her heart.

Confused, she pulled from his grasp. "I need to clean this up. I'll be back soon to give you a shave."

Not waiting to hear the reply, Renna took purposeful strides from the sick ward. She ran down the stairs to the storage room and set Mr. Blackeyes's pie and milk in the icebox. Next she reported for work.

At the centralized nurses' station on the second floor, to which she was always assigned, she charted everything Mr. Blackeyes had told her, hoping that all the slices of remembrances would somehow come together as a whole.

Minutes later Dr. Hamilton came through on his rounds, and Renna followed him. It was then she was introduced to her latest charges. One man, Mr. Baker, suffered from cholera. Another outbreak had recently struck the city.

"Make sure the man gets plenty to drink," Dr. Hamilton said.

"He has severe cramps but an unquenchable thirst. And look at his skin...it's gray and wrinkling. An indication, I'd say, of poor circulation."

Renna took the matter seriously. "Do you think he'll live?"

"I'm not sure." Dr. Hamilton's tone sounded uncertain and heavy. "Time will tell." He sighed. "Thank goodness it's not contagious from contact. But mind yourself just the same."

"Yes, Doctor." Renna began cleaning the man up. She managed to change his bed sheets, depositing them in the incinerator on the lower level. Afterward she scrubbed her own hands thoroughly. The water was cool and refreshing, and the air downstairs was mild. However, by the time Renna returned to the second floor sick ward, she was perspiring again. Although it was September, it was still summer, and these last days were hot and humid. The unbearable weather made Renna long for fall and cooler weather.

Mr. Blackeyes suddenly hailed her. "Nurse Fields? Is that you?"

"It is. What do you need?" Before he replied, she recalled. "Oh, yes, about your shave..."

She fetched the necessary supplies and a good, sharp razor before returning to Mr. Blackeyes's bedside. She felt more in control of her feelings again, more like herself.

"You've been very patient." Renna lowered herself onto the side of his bed.

"I've got no pressing engagements." A hint of a smile peeked through his thick beard. "Tell me as you shave me. What do I look like?"

"Well," Renna began, "you have dark, thick black hair." A frown weighed on her brow. "Do you remember what the color black looks like?" She had to wonder.

"Yes, I know black. I'm in it constantly."

"Of course..." She took off a good patch of beard before continuing. "You've got black eyes, as I've told you before. But they're not mean or menacing. They're like polished stones. Like the kind you can find on the beach."

"You're a romantic, Nurse Fields," Mr. Blackeyes said with a grin.

Renna blushed, glad her patient couldn't see it. She continued shaving. "No more talking now," she warned facetiously, "or I'm likely to slit your throat, and then Doctor Hamilton will have to forgo his lunch to stitch you up."

"A bit of medical humor, I presume?"

She smiled. "Hush."

He complied, but only for several long moments.

"Please go on with your description of me."

"All right. You seem to be a tall man, and I would guess that you do some sort of lifting or pulling because you have well-developed shoulders and arms."

The corners of Mr. Blackeyes's mouth lifted sardonically. "And do you like tall men with well-developed shoulders and arms?"

Taken aback, Renna gasped, and the movement nearly sent the basin of water toppling off her lap. She hadn't meant to get so personal. She was merely trying to do the man a favor and tell him what he looked like to jog his memory.

Breathing hard from the rescue of the water, she eyed her patient. "Mr. Blackeyes, you are quite fresh. I believe I'll stop shaving your face right now and you can just wear half a beard for the rest of the day."

She moved to get up off the side of the bed and make good on her threat when he suddenly caught her arm.

"I apologize, Nurse Fields." His voice was smooth and sincere. "I shouldn't have embarrassed you that way. I couldn't seem to help it." He cleared his throat and then smirked. "You must admit that I am in somewhat of a compromising position here. And you...well, you smell...very soft and pretty."

"Hardly. I'm hot and sticky. I doubt I smell very good at all."

"On the contrary, Nurse Fields. You smell far better than this sick room and one hundred times better than the food in this hospital."

"I'm sure you mean that as a compliment, sir." Renna couldn't help teasing him now.

Mr. Blackeyes grinned. "I do, indeed."

Renna shifted uncomfortably then, thinking about her patient's "compromising position." She had taken care of hundreds of men throughout her nursing career and had never thought of her role with any of them as compromising. She was a nurse. They needed medical care. That was all there was to it.

But this man was very, very different. He made her feel sensations she'd never felt before—

And put ideas in her head that ought not be there!

"Perhaps you're a pirate," she murmured, studying his face now. He had a very straight nose and a rugged-looking jawline. He looked darkly handsome—even with only half a beard.

Mr. Blackeyes laughed. "Like Edward Teach, perhaps? Are you familiar with him? He was an English pirate in the 1700s, also known as Blackbeard."

Renna grew wary, but his next remark disarmed her.

"I used to tell my two sons pirate stories all the time...before they went to bed."

"You have two sons? See, you are remembering." She resumed his shave. "Can you think of their names?"

Mr. Blackeyes fell silent for quite some time, and it wasn't until Renna had finished with the razor that he replied. "I can't think of either one's name, but I see their faces in my mind's eye. I can see them...and two little girls. My daughters, I think. We're at a funeral..."

His voice trailed off in a way that let Renna know he got lost somewhere in his past. She quietly cleaned up and straightened his bedcovers. *Children. Four of them. And a wife.*

Renna bit back another onslaught of disappointment, wondering why she should feel anything but concern for the man.

"Nurse Fields? Are you still there?"

"I'm here." She smoothed the folds from her apron. "I was just thinking that your family must be terribly worried about you."

"No, I don't think so." A derisive note edged Mr. Blackeyes's tone. "And I believe you may be right. I am more of a pirate than I ever was a husband and father."

# FOUR

H E COULD PICTURE THE WHOLE SCENE IN HIS MIND. THE beautiful woman laid to rest in the casket, the children hovering around their governess's knees. He could hear the organ music as they all stood in the large sanctuary. Somehow he knew that the beautiful woman was his wife, but he couldn't recall her name. He knew their relationship had been strained, if nonexistent, since he'd returned from the war, but he couldn't remember why. Was he sad that the beautiful woman had died?

No.

He remembered feeling apathetic, even annoyed at having to leave his business for this much overdone funeral! Thank heaven Richard had taken the time to plan everything.

The service, replaying so vividly in his mind, ended, and he remembered calling for the children's governess. He recalled that she was one of many who had come and gone throughout the years.

Yes, that's right. He and his wife sported a very demanding lifestyle.

And then he remembered more...the elegant dinners in lavishly furnished mansions, the parties and fine affairs. Was that what killed her? The beautiful woman? His wife?

No. No. He remembered that she'd frequently been ill.

In his mind's eye, then, he watched as the middle-aged governess prepared to take the children away. He remembered it was close to Christmas, and he had promised the kids he'd come home for dinner. They could open a present early. In memory of their mother.

However, he never made it home that night. He rarely did. Business took precedence in his life, especially during the off-season, and attending social functions was essential to his economic success.

But what exactly was his business?

He saw himself at his wife's funeral again, the vision unfolding like a scene from a play. He stood conversing with several prominent citizens who had come to pay their respects. They were important people in the community, he remembered—

Except he couldn't think of their names or which community!

"Mr. Pirate Blackeyes?"

He recognized Nurse Fields's voice at once, and its soft timbre swung him back to the present. He wished he could see her. She sounded so beautiful. Amusement frequently laced her tone, and he imagined that she stood over him now, smiling at the new nickname. *Mr. Pirate Blackeyes.*

He felt her warm hand come to rest upon his arm. Her touch reassured him somehow. This darkness could be so frightening at times, irritating at others. But Nurse Fields had become his fragile link to the world beyond this blackness and the images that taxed his memory.

"Are you awake?" she asked.

"Yes, of course I'm awake."

A pause. "You've been sleeping for most of the day, you know."

"I have?" He felt puzzled. "But you were just giving me a shave—"

Her palm gave his arm a comforting pat. "That was this morning, Mr. Blackeyes. It's suppertime now, and I brought you a tray. It's beef stew...I think."

"You mean you don't know for sure?" He grimaced.

She laughed, a light and delicate sound. "Try it and let me know."

The challenging note hung between them. She helped him into a sitting position before placing the tray on his lap.

"On your right, at one o'clock, is your coffee—I managed to get you a cup."

"You're most kind, Nurse Fields." Sarcasm dripped from each word.

He felt her closeness and smelled the increasingly familiar scent of the soap she used, like roses and soft powder. He inhaled deeply. She was like a breath of fresh air compared to those women he knew who doused themselves with French perfume.

"And at about three o'clock are your utensils." He had to force himself to pay attention. "At nine o'clock is your napkin, and at eleven o'clock is a slice of the apple pie from your breakfast."

"I'll eat that first. At least I know it's safe—and delicious. Compliment your mother for me, will you? My own cook, Isabelle, couldn't even match that, I'm sure."

"Isabelle!" Nurse Fields gasped in what sounded like delight. "You've remembered someone else! Very good!"

He heard the rustle of her skirts now as she moved away. "Are you leaving?" He hoped she'd stay. This darkness could be so very lonely.

"Yes. I am expected at home, and I've already stayed here too long. But if you wouldn't mind, I'd like to ask my father to come back and visit you tonight. He works at the Chamber of Commerce in the exchange room where they sample grains, and he is a very faithful man in our local church. Perhaps it would be beneficial for you to speak with someone as dedicated in both faith and business as my father."

"I'd like that." Somehow he sensed that she was smiling at him from where she stood at the side of his bed.

"You may have come into this hospital a pirate," she said on a teasing note, "but you'll leave here a man of God!"

That seemed doubtful, but he pushed out a polite smile. What might such a conversion entail? It sounded drastic. From pirate to parson? Surely not! But something vague came to mind when Nurse Fields mentioned the grain exchange.

"Yes, please. Ask your father to come. I'm desperate for the company anyway."

"So I've gathered."

A little laugh, and then he heard her heels clicking on the tiled floor as she walked away.

~~~✦~~~

Renna couldn't help smiling as she left the hospital. The late summer sun shone from the sky but the wind had shifted, and now cool breezes blew off Lake Michigan. It suddenly felt a bit like fall here in Chicago.

As she walked the near mile home, Renna held her grin. Da would be the perfect companion for Mr. Blackeyes this evening. Da would likely read to him from the Bible—assuming Mr. Blackeyes agreed to it. Hearing the Word of God was exactly what that handsome pirate of a man needed in order to grow in his new faith.

The memory of him telling her how pretty she smelled this morning still lingered. Renna had felt awkward around him all day. He had a virile way about him that frightened Renna, for his manner implied he knew women very well. And of course he would, since he was a married man.

*He's married.* Renna tried to shake the man from her thoughts. She shouldn't think about him as anything other than a patient. And yet he spoke to her in such a personal manner. How could he with a wife and children? It didn't say much for his character.

But things were different now. The pirate claimed to be saved by grace.

*A fact that should please his wife greatly.*

Renna continued with her walk home. She inhaled deeply, reviving her senses after the hours she'd spent in the sick ward.

She admired the well-maintained lawns and white picket fences of her city neighborhood not far from the downtown area. It was by far the most exciting part of Chicago. This side of town had the stores, hotels, and other public buildings, such as the Chamber of Commerce building—where her father worked—and the courthouse.

She nodded politely as she strolled past those with whom she was acquainted, keeping a hand on her bonnet so it concealed the birthmark and didn't fly away on the wind.

Finally she reached her block, where homes were slightly better than average. But Renna didn't care about mansions and wealth. She was happy with her common existence...

Wasn't she?

She suddenly spied her father climbing down from his buggy.

"Well, well, it's about time you fluttered home, my little wren."

Renna grinned, knowing he meant to tease her for arriving home as late as he did.

"I suppose you're going to tell me that a man can work from sun to sun, but a woman's work is never done."

Nibbling her lower lip, Renna couldn't contain her laugh. "You're so poetic, Da," she teased right back.

He tethered his horse to the hitching post. Then he and Renna walked arm in arm through the gate and up the walk to the front porch stairs.

"You work too hard, my little wren." They reached the front door. "It isn't right. You'll grow old before your time."

"Oh, Da, please...don't start on that subject."

"I don't like to see you looking haggard."

Renna brought her chin back. "My appearance is so bad?"

"No, no..."

Da opened the door and motioned for Renna to enter ahead of him. Stepping into the small front hall, she pulled off her gloves and removed her bonnet.

"Don't be insulted. I'm merely trying to protect you."

Renna swallowed an exasperated sigh. She and her father—and all her family—discussed her occupation numerous times before. As a dedicated nurse, she worked long hours and sometimes odd shifts at the hospital. And, although she'd admit that her back ached and her limbs felt weary, she couldn't just quit. What would she do? Society deemed her a spinster, so without a family of her own, she had to bide her time somehow. At least she was needed at the hospital.

Which reminded Renna of her pirate.

"Da, are you busy tonight?"

He looked a bit surprised, as she'd changed the subject rather quickly. "Why do you ask, Ren?"

"Well, it's my patient. You know, the one you, Mum, and I have been praying for. Mr. Blackeyes."

"Ah, yes. And what about him?"

"He needs some fellowship, Da." Renna smoothed the folds of her skirt. "He's so lonely. I try to keep him company when time permits, but what bothers me is that..." Renna tried not to blush as she confided in her father this way. "Well, from what Mr. Blackeyes has remembered, it's quite apparent that he's married. And, well, he's...he's all too familiar with me, Da. I believe he's probably been something of a lady's man, and some of his words and gestures make me terribly uncomfortable."

"I see." A heavy frown settled on Da's graying-blond brow. "I take it that nursing Mr. Blackeyes was easier when he was unconscious, eh?"

"I'm afraid so." Renna let a grin slip.

"Well, then, let's see what your mother has planned for me tonight, and if there's nothing pending, I'll visit with Mr. Blackeyes for a while." He cocked a brow and added, "It would be my pleasure."

"Now, Da…" Renna shook her head at him. "I'm an adult, not sixteen. You don't have to protect me."

"Your age doesn't prevent me from being your father, and without a husband—"

"All right, Da. I appreciate your willingness to visit with Mr. Blackeyes." Renna stifled a groan. Would she ever live a single day without being reminded of her spinsterhood?

Well, no matter. The important thing was, pending Mum's approval, Mr. Blackeyes would have some good company tonight.

~~uellcllee~~

Hours later Renna paced the parlor. As it happened, Mum had nothing planned for Da tonight, so after supper he climbed into his carriage and went over to the hospital. Now Renna anxiously awaited her father's return. She hoped that Mr. Blackeyes would somehow remember more of his past. But, most of all, she prayed that he would get a taste of God's Word and want to take his faith seriously.

"Renna, what about tomorrow night?"

Her mother's soft voice interrupted Renna's thoughts of Mr. Blackeyes. "Tomorrow night?" She turned her attention to Mum.

"Dinner." Mum sat in a nearby armchair with mending in her lap. "Everything's all planned."

"But I work all day."

"Could you, perhaps, ask off early?"

Renna shook her head and Mum sighed. "I must finish my shift or else the hospital will be short-staffed."

Mum seemed disappointed.

"What's happening that you need me here at home?"

"Your father invited his associate, Matthew Benchley, to have dinner with us."

Renna had heard of Da's young, unmarried associate before.

"Mum, I don't want to meet Mr. Benchley. I know he is an eligible bachelor, but—"

"And Mr. Benchley is the right age for you too, Renna," Mum added. "He's not too old. It's hard to find an unmarried man over thirty and under fifty."

Renna cringed inwardly. "Why do you and Da insist upon finding me a husband? I'm too old to be a bride. In fact, I don't think I want to marry."

"Oh, now, Renna…you don't mean that. Every woman wants to get married." Mum tipped her head, and several coppery tresses fell onto her forehead. "Clyde Montgomery was rather nice."

Renna replied with a half-smile and a shrug. She supposed Mr. Montgomery had been nice enough, although he'd been fifteen years her senior. But his age hadn't bothered Renna. Even the man's ill-mannered fourteen-year-old son hadn't discouraged Renna completely. It was Mr. Montgomery's habit of addressing Renna as if he spoke to a very slow child and not a woman with a brain in her head that she found most infuriating. What's more, Clyde Montgomery had claimed to know the Lord in a personal way; however, Renna didn't see any evidence of his faith in his life. The latter had been the deciding factor.

"I understand, though, why you didn't marry him," Mum continued. She slipped her needle in and out as she darned socks. "But your father said Mr. Benchley is quite different. He's not a widower. He has never been married, and Abigail Hoffmann told me that he's very charming."

Already warning bells went off in Renna's head. Abigail Hoffmann was not a good judge of character, bless her heart anyway.

"So why do you suppose Mr. Benchley never got married?" Renna ceased her pacing and took a seat on the rose-colored divan.

Johanna Fields smiled, but her gaze remained on her sewing. "Perhaps he's waiting to meet you, dear."

Renna rolled her eyes.

"I'll ask your father to send a message to him. We'll dine later in the day so you can join us."

Renna resigned herself to the fact she wouldn't easily get out of tomorrow's dinner arrangement. She would just have to attend and do her best to have a good spirit about it.

———ˡˡˢ⳩ˡˡˡˡ———

The tall grandfather's clock in the parlor chimed ten o'clock as the front door opened. Renna quickly stood and watched as her father entered the house. Mum had already gone to bed, but as exhausted as Renna was, she forced herself to stay awake until Da came home.

"How did it go with Mr. Blackeyes tonight?"

"Very well, my dear." He stepped farther into the parlor. "The nurses allowed me to stay past visiting hours. Of course, they know that you're my daughter. I suspect they did me a special favor."

Renna grinned. "I'll be sure to thank them tomorrow."

"We spoke quietly. I'm sure that helped."

Impatience got the better of her. "So what happened?"

"Well…" Da inhaled deeply, and the chest of his tan waistcoat puffed out. "I began with reading the Bible, starting with the book of Genesis. I figured that would be a good place. With God's creation. And, oh, Mr. Blackeyes had the questions!" Da smiled and shrugged out of his dark brown suit jacket. "My, my…"

Renna smiled. "Anything else?"

"I got as far as chapter twenty, just after the destruction of Sodom and Gomorrah."

"That's good."

"But I didn't want to give Mr. Blackeyes too much too soon."

"Very wise."

"So, we talked for a while."

"What about?"

"Things in general."

"And?"

Da gave her a little grin. "And he's a widower, my little wren."

Renna averted her gaze. "A widower?" Why did she suddenly feel so hopeful?

"Yes. He remembers that his wife died, around Christmastime last year, but he can't recall her name. He remembers, however, that he has children. Gabriel, Michael, Elizabeth, and Rachel."

"He remembered their names," Renna whispered in awe. "His memory is returning."

"Indeed." Da cleared his throat now. "And I have a vague sense that I've met this man somewhere, but I can't place him." He shrugged. "I'm sure it'll come back to me eventually."

"You think you might have met him before..." Renna's voice trailed off. She strode to the cold limestone hearth and toyed with a few knickknacks on the mantel. "And what about his...well, you know...his—"

"Getting too familiar with you?"

Renna blushed but nodded.

"I spoke to him about the matter, and he has promised to apologize in the morning. I believe him. He does nothing but sing your praises, Renna."

"Well, he should be singing praises to God, not me!"

Da chuckled again. "In due time, daughter. I'm going to visit him again tomorrow afternoon—if your mother doesn't object, that is."

Disappointment flooded her being. "Mr. Benchley is coming to dinner tomorrow."

Wendell Fields snapped his stubby fingers. "That's right. How could I forget?" He smiled.

An idea formed. Renna arched a brow. "We could cancel it."

"Yes, but—"

"Postpone it then?" Renna sent him a pleading look.

Da seemed to guess what she was up to and wagged his graying head. "You don't want to meet Matthew Benchley?"

She shook her head. "I'll meet him if you want me to, I guess."

Da sighed. "Renn, we've had this conversation before—about your birthmark. That's what this is all about, isn't it? The reason you don't want to meet Matthew?"

"No, I…it's just…" She gestured helplessly. "Oh, I don't know."

"I would have thought you'd gotten over that. My dear, one scarcely notices it at all. Now, then…" Da came toward her and put his arm about her shoulders. "You must overcome this fear you have of meeting new people."

"I'm not afraid, exactly."

"No one notices the birthmark, Renna. Just you." Da hugged her before moving away slightly. "Let's remember, vanity is a sin. And it's vain to be so self-conscious."

Renna squared her shoulders. "Da, how can you say I'm vain? Have you ever experienced the look of horror on people's faces when they first meet you? No, of course you haven't. But I have!"

"Renna, it's not horror on their faces; it's just surprise. They're surprised to see the birthmark on your cheek—just at first." Da lifted one of his bushy brows. "I hope you're not harboring an unforgiving spirit, Renna, toward those who might have hurt you in the past."

She clenched her jaw and turned around without another word. Exhaustion weighed heavily upon her, affecting both her mind and tongue. She didn't trust herself to reply. Of course she wasn't vain or unforgiving. How could Da insinuate such a thing?

"Good night," she said in a clipped tone as she headed for the stairs.

"Good night to you too, little wren."

Da's gentle tone did nothing to sooth her temper, which soured all the more as she thought about dinner tomorrow evening. She traipsed down the dark hallway to her bedroom, loathing the very thought of meeting Da's associate.

But she would. She loved her father and knew he wanted only the best for her. With a deep sigh she resigned herself to his matchmaking schemes yet once more.

# FIVE

S O TELL ME...AM I FORGIVEN?"
Renna was gathering the razor, basin of water, and towels
after she'd given Mr. Blackeyes his morning shave. She still had
two other men waiting for her. Then those who were able would
have a bath today and clean shirts and drawers. Today promised
to be a busy one.

"Pirates aren't well versed in the way of propriety," Mr. Blackeyes was saying, and Renna forced herself to concentrate. After
all, he was trying to apologize. "I realized some things last night,
after talking with your father and, well...I...well...I'm trying to
be less of a pirate. All right?"

Renna felt heartened. "Yes, of course you're forgiven. And I
believe you when you say you're trying. I think it's commendable."

"Commendable for a pirate. Is that what you mean?"

He smiled, displaying large, even white teeth, and Renna could
well imagine him aboard a tall-masted ship, surrounded by his
crew, counting the booty.

"Are you still there, Nurse Fields?"

"Yes, I'm still here."

"You don't appreciate my humor this morning, is that it?"

"No, that's not it at all. I guess I'm just tired." Balancing the
basin on her knees, she massaged her throbbing temples.

Today the hospital was near to capacity, what with the cholera
epidemic. The warm temperatures outside made conditions here
on the second floor uncomfortable. Already Renna's clothes were

damp with perspiration—and she had nine more hours of nursing ahead of her.

And then dinner tonight. The obligation weighed heavily on Renna.

"I'll be back shortly to draw your bath," she promised Mr. Blackeyes as she crossed the room to where young Mr. Adams lay. He had been brought in after a fire. Unconscious for days, he seemed to be recovering nicely now. Complaints about the food always indicated better health.

"Yer an angel of mercy, is what you are." Bandages covered the burns on his arms and hands.

Renna smiled. "I'm just doing my job."

"Well, I'm here to say, ya do it a lot better than some of the other nurses on this floor." Mr. Adams smiled. "Them women are downright mean!"

"Oh, now, they're not really mean at all. They're just busy. In any case, don't let it spoil your day. And guess what? The orderlies are bringing up the bathtubs. You'll have a good soaking soon—and have some clean clothes." Renna wrinkled her nose. "You still smell a bit like smoke."

"A good soaking will feel real good, 'specially on my burned foot."

"I'll bet." Renna smiled as she finished with his shave. Most of the other nurses would never allow time for their patients to have such luxuries as a shave. But Renna thought keeping up one's appearance was conducive to the healing process. Most of her patients agreed, although she'd have to move quickly if she hoped to get to everyone this morning. As it was, she had to juggle several tasks.

Hours later two large tubs were brought into the ward and filled with hot water. Patients with cleaner hygiene went first.

"All right, Mr. Blackeyes, it's your turn."

The orderlies helped him into the tub while Renna stripped his bed.

"And I'm sure I don't have to tell you to use the soap," Renna called over the wooden screen.

"Are you sure it's safe? It smells strong enough to take my skin off!"

Renna had to grin as she made up his bed with fresh linens. Judging by the amount of complaints, it seemed her pirate was definitely on the mend.

~~uulℓxℓℓu~~

By midafternoon things quieted in Renna's wards. All the other nurses said she was daft for taking on such a monumental project as bathing patients on a day as warm and sticky as today. But Renna had thought her patients would feel better if they were clean and cool and if their beds were changed. And it seemed she was right. There were no complaints being shouted out from her sick wards, as there were from the others.

A satisfied feeling enveloped her as she walked by, checking on her patients.

"Nurse Fields?" Mr. Blackeyes hailed her.

She came to his bedside. "You're supposed to be napping."

"Would you talk to me for a few minutes?"

Renna thought it over then decided she could spare him a few minutes. She knew he felt disappointed since Dr. Hamilton had come in and changed the bandages on his eyes. Afterward he wound a white strip around Mr. Blackeyes's head to keep the bandages in place. But the news came hard and fast. No change. Mr. Blackeyes still couldn't see.

His head wound, on the other hand, had healed almost completely. Dr. Hamilton said his lungs sounded clear, but because of his memory loss and weakened condition, Mr. Blackeyes would be staying in the hospital for a while.

After all, he had nowhere else to go.

"Your father told me your first name is Renna," he began. He was sitting up in his bed, although the exertion of taking a bath had exhausted him, and it showed on his expression. "Renna," he said again. "That's a most unusual name."

She smiled, thinking her name sounded differently, somehow, coming from his lips. As though he didn't speak her name—he caressed it.

Renna cleared her throat, wondering how she could think such things. Perhaps exhausting herself had made her a bit daft after all. In any case, she forced herself to reply. "My given name is Lorenna. Lorenna Jane, after my father's grandmother."

"Lorenna. It's beautiful." A smile formed on Mr. Blackeyes's full mouth. "Renna is a nickname then?"

"Yes."

"Renna." Four times now he'd said her name, sending a tiny shiver up her spine. What was it about this man, anyway?

"And if I roll the R with my tongue," Mr. Blackeyes continued, "it sounds Spanish, don't you think? Renna."

She laughed while lowering herself into the chair beside his bed. She had found a fan to cool herself and waved it back and forth as she conversed. It was a nice break.

"Do you think you're Spanish, Mr. Pirate Blackeyes?" Renna couldn't seem to help teasing him. "I might think you are because of your dark features, although you have more of a European look about you."

"Hmm…" The comment had Mr. Blackeyes thinking for a few moments. Then he shrugged. "I don't know."

"It'll come. You've remembered a lot so far."

"And I'm learning more. My present state of mind seems sharp anyway." He paused. "I'm looking forward to another of your father's visits. He said he'd return tonight."

Renna grimaced. "No, he can't come. He forgot about a dinner engagement. I'm sorry. I should have told you earlier."

"I'm disappointed."

Two disappointments in one day. Renna's heart went out to him. "What sort of dinner engagement is it?" Mr. Blackeyes wanted to know.

"Oh." She sighed. "My father is entertaining an associate at our home."

"I can recall some very fine dinners that my wife and I hosted. She was very beautiful...Louisa." He sat up a little straighter. "That was her name!" Mr. Blackeyes snapped his fingers. "Louisa!"

Renna smiled. "You're remembering!"

"Yes..." Again he exhaled audibly, sitting back against the metal headboard of his bed. "She's dead. My wife, Louisa. She was ill ever since the birth of our youngest child."

"I'm so sorry. I'm sure you loved her very much."

"I suppose I did. She was the mother of my children, after all. That warranted some affection."

Renna fell stone silent. His marriage sounded loveless in her opinion.

"Did I shock you? Does my honesty disturb you? I suppose it would, and I apologize. You probably believe in falling in love and living happily ever after. Like in the fairy tales. But when you grow up a bit, you'll see that love is—"

"When I grow up a bit?" She sat forward in her chair. "And just how old...or should I say, how young do you think I am?"

Frown lines creased Mr. Blackeyes's brow. "I assumed that you were...well...young. You're spirited, unmarried—"

Cynicism gripped her. "I'm thirty years old, Mr. Blackeyes."

Her patient was speechless.

Immediately Renna regretted her harsh tone. God made her this way, with a purple horseshoe stain on her cheek, and He had called her to nurse the sick. "Now it's my turn to apologize,

Mr. Blackeyes. While I might be what the neighbor boy called me—an old maid—I have enough wherewithal to enjoy my work. What's more, I have a family who loves me." Her gaze dropped to her now-folded hands. Wasn't that enough? What more could she ask for? "I'm really not ungrateful for my lot in life."

"I...I would have never guessed that you're a—"

"A spinster? Yes. But I'm not a nun with the Sisters of Mercy order as many nurses here are. I'm just unmarried, and I like to take care of people. I went to a finishing school for two years, and I was always interested in medicine. Then I got my nursing training in a military hospital, and that's where I served during the war.

"You see," she continued, "God never sent me a husband and children to take care of, but instead He sent me hundreds and hundreds of patients. And I have loved them all. Some just needed a kind word. Some have needed a tender heart and much understanding. Some needed a hand to hold and someone to cry with. Some"—Renna paused, her heart aching as memories flashed across her mind—"some as they lay dying needed me to write to their wives and mothers. And many have needed to hear about salvation through Jesus Christ."

"I'm sure that's right." Mr. Blackeyes had found his voice.

Renna shook off the heaviness and smiled. "Like you."

"Like me." His voice trailed off, and Mr. Blackeyes seemed to retreat inside himself somewhere.

Their visit had obviously come to an end.

Renna stood, thinking she'd likely alienated Mr. Blackeyes with her honesty. And here he thought he had shocked her by his.

Nurse Rutledge called for her, and Renna squared her shoulders. While her wards were quiet, the others were not, and she would likely have to help the less-efficient nurses this afternoon. And she couldn't dally. She had her own assignments to complete before she could leave for the day.

As the afternoon wore on, Renna kept insanely busy. When the clock in the nurses' station chimed five o'clock, she realized she still had to update her patients' charts before she could leave. Sitting down at one of the large walnut desks, she began to pen in Mr. Baker's chart. She forced her hand to hurry. She didn't want her parents to be miffed if she showed up late to dinner.

"Good evening, my little wren."

Renna's head popped up, and seeing her father, her eyes widened in surprise. "What are you doing here?"

He removed his hat. "I thought I'd come for you and give you a ride home."

"Thank you. I'll be done in about an hour. Can you wait?" She remembered. "Oh, but you can't leave your dinner guest waiting."

"Actually, Matt asked to postpone it. Evidently something pressing came up."

*Oh, thank You, God!*

"He sends his regrets, and we've rescheduled for next week. Your mother is aware. I sent a message to her earlier today."

Renna couldn't contain her sigh of relief while straightening her paperwork.

Da chuckled at her reaction. "So how's my friend Mr. Blackeyes?"

"Fine for the most part. But he's very disappointed. Dr. Hamilton changed his bandages today, and there's no change. He's still blind."

Da gave a sad wag of his head. "That's a shame." He glanced at his watch. "Tell you what. You finish up here, and I'll chat with Mr. Blackeyes. Then I'll take you home."

"And Mum won't mind us both coming in late…again?"

"I believe she's used to it by now."

"Yes, I believe you're right." Renna smiled. "Thank you, Da. Mr. Blackeyes said he was disappointed when he learned you wouldn't be visiting tonight. I think the change of plans is exactly what he needs."

"God works in mysterious ways, Renn."

"That he does." Smiling, she watched her father amble down the tiled hallway toward her pirate's ward.

# Six

BLACKEYES, MY DEAR FELLOW, ARE YOU AWAKE?"
He knew the voice. "Wendell Fields?"

"'Tis I."

Surprising. "I thought you had a dinner party tonight."

"Oh, not a party exactly. One guest." Sounds of the wooden chair legs scraping against the tile let him know Renna's father had seated himself. "He had to cancel."

"A pity." He couldn't help a grin. "But apparently it worked to my advantage."

"You'd welcome a visit, then?"

"Absolutely." He tried to sit up straighter in his bed. Curiosity gnawed at him. "Tell me...how is it that your daughter is yet unmarried? She told me herself. She said she's thirty years old and a spinster. I could hardly believe it."

There was no reply for many long moments, and he thought perhaps the question was offensive.

"Forgive me," he said at last. "I didn't mean to pry. It's just that—"

"Renna is a beautiful person," Mr. Fields answered at last. "That's what you mean, isn't it? And it's so true. She is a blessing to her mother and me. But the fact of the matter is Renna is also intelligent. Smarter than most of the eligible men her mother and I have tried to pair her with over the years." The man chuckled. "You must admit, Mr. Blackeyes, that there isn't a man alive who wants his wife to be smarter than he is!"

He grinned. "An intelligent woman such as your daughter would make a far better companion, I think, than, say, my deceased wife, Louisa."

"Oh?"

"I don't mean to speak ill of the dead. Louisa bore my children, for which I will always be grateful. She had sense about decorating and fashion, but she had been sorely lacking on issues of real importance. Issues that mattered." More memories surfaced. "I wouldn't have married Louisa if not for my mother. She had been determined that I marry into a wealthy family—and I did."

"What was your mother like?"

"I remembered just now. I can see her in my mind's eye. She was a very beautiful but very eccentric woman. She insisted that I call her by her first name during all my growing-up years. And my children called her by her first name also." He felt a rueful smile curve his lips. "She disliked being a mother and abhorred the idea of being a grandmother."

"Pardon my saying so, but that's rather strange. However, you did say that your mother is an eccentric. Can you remember her first name?"

"No." Despair settled over him.

"What about your father?"

"He was a mariner and died shortly after I was born." He searched his mind. "I don't recall the reason for his death. My mother remarried, but something happened to my stepfather when I was young...an accident of some sort. He was killed." He clenched his jaw. Why couldn't he remember the details?

"No father figure to speak of, then?"

He heard the note of pity in Wendell Fields's voice. "Plenty of father figures, although none you'd approve of. All leathery old seadogs who somehow wound up on the Great Lakes." He tried to come up with the name of the barrel-chested man on the docks who taught him to tie a bowline knot while schooling him on women's wiles, but it eluded him like so much else. "My mother sent me off to boarding school when I was twelve, fearing I'd end up like them or my...*my father.*" A flash of remembrance. "My father had been a drunk."

"His name? Can you recall it?"

"No." Clenching his fists he tried not to groan aloud. "Oh, this memory loss and blindness are maddening!"

"Easy there, Mr. Blackeyes. It'll come. Be patient."

His new friend's voice reassured him somehow.

"What about other family members?"

"No. I'm an only child." There! He'd come up with that much. Suddenly he remembered something more. A hard right to his jaw. His trusted steward, Richard, had delivered the blow...because of Sarah.

More of his past came rushing back. Richard found out that he'd been trifling with Sarah, but not because he loved her—because he wanted her to shackle her with a contract to work indefinitely as his children's governess. He'd manipulated her.

"I've done things I'm not proud of. I remember that much. A righteous man might call me a scoundrel. But my steward, Richard, a good, Christian man, stayed loyal to me until...until Sarah came."

"Sarah?"

"My children's governess."

"Oh, dear..."

"My children adored her, and I could see at once that she'd be a good influence on them. So I turned on my charm, hoping Sarah would succumb."

"You wanted to marry her?"

He laughed—and laughed hard. "Marry her? No. Sarah didn't come from money, and marriage is a business arrangement really."

"Not so."

"Well, that's all it's ever been for me." He recalled that much.

"In any case, I had only meant to persuade Sarah, pressure her to sign a contract and remain in my employ…*indefinitely.*"

"I see." The legs of his visitor's wooden chair scraped against the tile. "It seems you have, indeed, been something of a pirate, Mr. Blackeyes." Wendell patted his arm. "But God has delivered you out of that lifestyle. You are a new creation in Christ."

He didn't know what to say. The thought of Christ saving a wretch like him was an awesome one. Exhaustion fell over him like a thick drape, and he collapsed back into his pillows.

"Would you like it if I read some more of the Bible?"

"Yes, please." Perhaps it would soothe his troubled mind and spirit.

"All right."

After the whispering sound of delicate pages being turned, Wendell began to read from where he had left off last night.

~~eeexeee~~

"So you see, my little wren, the man has lived a life of lies and deception—and devoid of true love. His first marriage was more of a business arrangement that secured wealth and good social standing."

"How sad." Renna sat beside her father on the front porch swing. It seemed like a perfect night for it, although temperatures were falling as the sun set. Renna pulled her shawl tighter around her shoulders. "But Mr. Blackeyes can begin anew—now that he's a believer."

"Yes, and I told him the same thing."

Renna smiled. "Now if we could only find out who he belongs to."

"We will. I'm doing a bit of investigating, asking everyone I know who does business along Lake Michigan's shores. Surely there must be some news somewhere of a prominent man in a boating accident who is now presumed dead."

"Yes, of course. There must be news of him somewhere." She recalled the snippets of information she'd gathered when Mr. Black-eyes was admitted to the hospital. "The rescuing ship's captain said he and his crew found him floating near the Wisconsin-Illinois border."

"I'll do some digging."

"Good idea." Renna's mind drifted as she imagined her pirate's former lifestyle. A lady's man and prominent social figure, everything Renna abhorred in a man. He probably danced with only the most beautiful women, drank only the finest wine, and dined with only the rich and famous. He probably lived in the fanciest house in the best neighborhood and furnished it lavishly, from the paintings to the carpets. He was a man to be wary of, for sure.

"Renna, did you hear anything I just said?"

She pulled herself from her musings. "Sorry, Da, I must be tired. My mind wandered a bit."

"I said, after church tomorrow, since it is your day off, I thought we'd all go by the hospital and visit Mr. Blackeyes. Perhaps we'll even bring him back for a little supper, if he's up to it, that is."

"Bring him here?" Renna sat forward, disrupting the gentle sway of the porch swing. "To our home?"

"Why not?"

"For one, he's my patient. I can't bring home everyone I nurse back to health."

Da chuckled. "No, of course you can't. But Mr. Blackeyes is different, wouldn't you say? I mean, you were burdened for him right from the beginning. We all prayed for him, and God answered by sparing the man's life and saving his soul. That warrants a dinner invitation, I think."

"If you say so, Da."

"Well, I do."

Renna's heart began to pound. It would be better if she

distanced herself from her pirate, but instead he'd take part in a family outing tomorrow. Suddenly Renna couldn't seem to shake the feeling of impending doom.

# SEVEN

THE NEXT MORNING THE SUN SHONE BRIGHTLY THROUGH her bedroom windows. Despite her misgivings, Renna dressed with care. Mum assisted her with her corset and crinoline and didn't say a word about Renna's fussing with her appearance more so than any other day.

Gratitude mixed with relief filled Renna. She couldn't figure it out herself and didn't want to discuss the matter. Then, with her camisole and petticoat in place, she selected a lilac-colored poplin dress from her closet. Pulling it over her head, she chided herself for what might well be vanity. True, it was Sunday, and Renna wanted to look her best for church. But she also had to admit that she enjoyed dressing in something other than her gray nursing garb with its stiff white apron that she wore at the hospital. She wanted to look pretty today.

And, of course, it had nothing to do with the fact Mr. Blackeyes would spend the afternoon with her and her family. Far be it that she'd try to impress him, not that she'd be successful if he had his sight back.

*Goose!* She peered at her reflection in the looking glass. *You're acting as though you're sixteen years old and without an ugly birthmark on your face.*

Irritated with herself, she whirled from the mirror and finished dressing. Minutes later she left her room and ambled downstairs to meet her parents for breakfast. She wondered what on earth had happened to her common sense and when it took flight. Perhaps discovering that Mr. Blackeyes was a widower with four children had touched upon her female sensibilities. Or maybe finding out that, indeed, he was something of a pirate piqued her natural curiosity. Did he frighten her? Just a little. But why?

Seconds later the answer came to her. If her pirate could see, then he wouldn't likely be so friendly toward her. She, the nurse with the purple blemish on her face, would never compare to the pampered and powdered ladies of society with whom he probably associated.

"Not that it even matters!" she muttered, clearing the table after she and her parents had eaten.

"Did you say something, dear?" Mum removed her apron.

"Oh, no...nothing." An embarrassed heat crept into Renna's cheeks. She quickly strode to the hallway and pulled on her gloves. Next she donned her bonnet.

As she stepped out onto the front porch, a sweet, fresh scent filled her nostrils: Lake Michigan breezes. Renna inhaled deeply. A gentle wind tousled the treetops overhead, rustling faded leaves and dappling the walkway with sunlight.

Mum stepped in beside her. "My, what a lovely morning."

"Indeed." Renna smiled. An idea struck. "Let's take a picnic lunch to the lake today."

"A splendid idea, my dear. We'll come home after lunch and prepare it. Then we'll pick up Mr. Blackeyes."

With a sigh, Renna resigned herself to the idea. At least the man wouldn't be in her home, and the fresh air would do him good.

Da brought the carriage around. Arm in arm, Renna and her mother walked from the porch to the street and boarded the awaiting vehicle.

"How about a picnic today, Wendell?" Mum asked as she adjusted her skirts.

"I think it's a fine idea." Da flicked the reins, and the carriage jolted forward.

Renna sat quietly in the backseat and casually watched as they rolled by the shops, closed on Sunday, of course, and homes, built just a few feet from one another. When they reached the Illinois Street Church, she glanced around at the poverty-stricken area, and her heart swelled with gratitude for what she did have—and it was far more than just a roof over her head, food on the table, and clothes on her back. Pastor Moody had often spoken of charity, and he'd chosen this impoverished area in which to preach because of the great need here in the city. Mum often worked in the soup kitchen where she and other volunteers prepared meals for the hungry and penniless.

Da parked the carriage and climbed down. Next he helped Mum while Renna made her way to the ground. With the horse hitched to the post, they headed for the set of brick steps leading to the doorway. Da pulled one of the massive doors open and allowed Mum and Renna to enter first. Inside the dimly lit foyer the air felt cool on Renna's face.

The service began with song, followed by a guest speaker. About three quarters of the way through the sermon, Renna gave up trying to concentrate and begged her heavenly Father for forgiveness. The thought of picnicking with her pirate continually flashed through her mind. She both dreaded the idea and looked forward to it.

*Oh, Lord, I must be overtired…*

Once the service ended, Renna and her folks greeted several friends before riding home in the carriage. After shedding their reticules, gloves, and bonnets, Renna and Mum got right to work preparing a delicious picnic basket. Today's menu included zucchini bread, whipped butter, cold pork sandwiches cut into tiny squares, sliced tomatoes, and chocolate cake, which Mum had made for the dinner party yesterday that had thankfully been rescheduled.

Next, it was on to the hospital.

"Mr. Blackeyes?" Renna spoke softly, fearing she'd awaken him if he slept. It was hard to tell with the bandages around his head, covering his eyes.

He sat up straighter in his bed. "Nurse Fields?" He cocked his head, listening.

"Yes, it's me." She approached his bedside. "My parents are here too, and we wondered if you feel up to coming out with us for a picnic. Dr. Hamilton gave his consent."

"A picnic? I'd love to go. Anything to get me out of this hospital!"

"But are you feeling up to it?"

"I should say I am!"

Renna had her doubts. Mr. Blackeyes still looked pale, and she knew of his weakened state. However, he seemed more desperate than anything, so she sent her father an approving nod. "Will you help him dress?"

"Yes, of course." Da smiled. "Mr. Blackeyes, I brought along a suit for you since the clothing you wore when they brought you here was discarded due to disrepair. But these garments are well-tailored threads—my son-in-law's spares—and I think they'll make for a decent fit."

"I'm grateful. Thank you."

Renna and her mother stood outside the sick ward and waited while Mr. Blackeyes dressed. Finally, he appeared, his arm looped through Da's. He looked peaked, but he seemed steady on his feet. The borrowed clothes, however, didn't do the man justice. The pants were too big at the waist and too short at the hems. The crisp white shirt stretched tightly over Mr. Blackeyes's broad shoulders.

*I shouldn't even notice such things.* Renna pulled her gaze away.

They walked out to the carriage.

"I can feel the sun on my face." Mr. Blackeyes lifted his face to the sky.

"It's a beautiful day," Renna said. "Bright and fair with the smell of fall in the air."

"How poetic, Nurse Fields."

She smiled at his teasing. "For this outing you may call me Renna."

He inclined his head in reply before Da helped him into the carriage.

Renna noted his silence as they rode to the park. Once Da parked the carriage and they climbed down, Renna became concerned.

"Are you feeling all right?" She touched his forearm.

"I'm quite all right, I assure you." Mr. Blackeyes inhaled deeply. "The air is so fresh and clear. I feel like I can breathe again. I was beginning to suffocate in that sick room."

"Nonsense." Renna slipped her gloved hand around Mr. Blackeyes's elbow so she could steer him to their picnic spot. Mum led the way. "The window was open, so there was little chance of suffocation."

"An open window is not the same as the fresh air outside in the sunshine. It feels so good on my face. Thank you—thank you all for rescuing me today."

Da chuckled while carrying the picnic basket. "You're welcome, but I wouldn't say we exactly rescued you, Mr. Blackeyes."

"And I say you are!" He snorted in disgust. "Nurse Hatchet is on duty again today, and—"

"Now, now, let's not speak badly of Nurse Hatchet—I mean, Thatcher." Renna stomped her foot. "Now you've got me calling her Hatchet. You're incorrigible, Mr. Blackeyes."

Everyone laughed as Mum selected a grassy section of the park. She spread out the picnic blanket beneath a leafy elm tree. Ten feet away the lawn gave way to a steep cliff. Beneath it Lake Michigan's rocky shoreline stretched out for miles.

"I know this sound well. Hear it?" Mr. Blackeyes tilted his head from side to side and listened intently. "The sound of the waves coming ashore."

"That's it." A curious frown puckered Da's brow.

"Ah, yes, Lake Michigan. The very smell of her..." He inhaled deeply. "Like the scent of a familiar woman."

Mum cleared her throat uncomfortably. "I believe that smell belongs to the dead fish," she quipped, "so don't blame the lake or any of us women for that matter."

Mr. Blackeyes chuckled and Da grinned. Renna sent her mother an embarrassed smile.

Mum began to unpack their lunch. Renna assisted Mr. Blackeyes and then sat down. Once the food had been laid out, Renna made a plate for their guest. He gobbled the pork sandwiches and delighted in eating slices of zucchini bread. Renna exchanged amused grins with Mum.

"And chocolate cake...mmm...delicious." Mr. Blackeyes dabbed the corners of his mouth with the checkered napkin. "My compliments, Mrs. Fields."

Mum looked pleased.

After about an hour of lunching, Da stood and stretched. "I'm as stiff as a plank."

Mr. Blackeyes grinned.

"Should we go for a short stroll?" Mum asked. "Walk out the kinks, so to speak?" She stood as well.

"Are you suggesting that I'm growing too old for picnics, madam?"

"Oh, now, Wendell, you know I'd never suggest such a thing." She winked at Renna.

Da muttered something about being outnumbered then offered his arm.

Watching as her parents amble off, Renna smiled. "Even after thirty-two years of marriage," she told Mr. Blackeyes, "my mother and father still love each other very much."

"Yes, so I've sensed. Quite remarkable too, since I have always imagined that kind of love and dedication only occurring in storybooks."

Renna shifted uncomfortably, glad that Mr. Blackeyes couldn't see through his bandaged eyes. She didn't want to discuss the topic of love with him.

"At first I had hoped Louisa and I would have a strong love relationship, but after our marriage, it was soon apparent that she wanted a socialite's existence. She tolerated my affection, but in general the wife and mother roles were quite boring and often a nuisance for Louisa."

Renna picked a blade of grass, thinking he ought to be talking to Da about such things. Yet his honesty impressed her, and his mysterious past intrigued her.

"Even so, I had tried to give my children what I thought they needed by providing governesses. Those employed women, however, never lasted very long."

"Why is that?" She couldn't help asking.

"I wasn't ever sure, until Sarah told me." Mr. Blackeyes chuckled.

"Told you what?"

"About my sons' shenanigans. After a few grass snakes in their beds, the governesses packed their bags and left."

"Hmm, your boys sound like mischief makers." Renna shook her head, recalling her brother's pranks in his younger days.

Mr. Blackeyes still grinned broadly. "Yes, I suppose they are." He turned silent for a few minutes. "Sarah was the only one who could put up with them, and they loved her for it."

"Sarah? You've mentioned her before." Renna arched a brow. "Another wife?"

"No, no," Mr. Blackeyes said with a wider smile. "Another governess."

"You remember!"

"Yes, I remember..."

He grew pensive, so Renna prompted him. "Sarah was a governess who stayed on?"

"Yes. I hired her for the summer, but I don't know which

summer it was. This one, perhaps." He paused. "She fell in love with Richard. It was so obvious too. Even my mother commented on it."

"Richard, your bookkeeper?"

"Yes. Except Sarah couldn't make up her mind about him, even though Richard loved her right back. You see, Sarah enjoyed living in my large and, if I do say so myself, impressive home. She romanticized about the kind of lifestyle I led. She saw me rubbing elbows with the elite. She saw the parties, the dinners, the dancing—or at least she thought she did."

Renna nearly groaned aloud. So what she had suspected was true. Mr. Blackeyes was a man among the high-society echelons. "And Richard?"

"Richard wanted to farm."

Renna frowned. "But I thought he was a bookkeeper."

"He was…or is…I'm not sure. However, his ambition was to take over his father's farm. To work outdoors." Mr. Blackeyes chuckled. "He readily volunteered for any and every errand that involved leaving my store—"

"A store! You remember!" Renna sat up on her haunches.

Surprise shone on his face. "I own a store, yes."

Mum and Da came strolling back to the picnic site, and Renna stood.

"Mr. Blackeyes has just remembered that he owns a store. Isn't that wonderful?"

"I should say it is." Da eyed the man a little closer now. "What kind of a store did you own?"

Mr. Blackeyes's lips pressed together as he thought hard. "I don't know," he said at last. "I wish I remembered more."

"It'll come," Mum assured him. "It's coming already."

A man approached them. Da looked up and grinned. "Matthew! Matthew Benchley! What are you doing here?"

Renna stiffened and pushed to her feet. So she would have to meet Mr. Benchley after all.

"I was taking an afternoon stroll, and I spotted you here." He smiled at Mum. "This must be your beautiful wife."

"Yes." Da turned to her. "Johanna, dear, this is my newest associate, Matthew Benchley."

Mum dipped her head demurely. "Nice to meet you, Mr. Benchley."

His eyes slid to Renna, and she saw him assess her birthmark. A look of pity entered his gaze before it hardened like steel.

"And this is my daughter, Renna."

"Ah, yes, you've spoken of Renna to me before." Benchley reached for her hand and gave it a squeeze. "A pleasure."

Renna pulled free. She found it difficult to manage a smile. What was it about this man that gave her a sense of dislike?

But more importantly, why did Da think so favorably about him?

Curiosity alone caused Renna to peer boldly into Matthew Benchley's face. Icy gray eyes set into chiseled features stared back at her, reminding her of Lake Michigan during the winter months.

Despite the warm temperatures, a little chill passed through her.

"And this is the man I told you about," Da said. "We know him only as Mr. Blackeyes. He's recovering from a boating accident."

Mr. Blackeyes got to his feet.

Benchley stuck out his hand. "Pleased to meet you."

Renna frowned, confused. Didn't Benchley see the obvious?

"Likewise, I'm sure." Mr. Blackeyes reached out in the direction of Benchley's voice, but it was Benchley who made the contact.

"Injury to your eyes, I take it?"

Renna resisted the urge to cluck her tongue at the insipid question.

"Yes." Mr. Blackeyes fingered his bandages.

An uncomfortable silence ensued, and Renna found herself

wishing Matthew Benchley would continue on with his stroll. He had a disquieting presence, although it differed from the unnerving effect Mr. Blackeyes had on her. Renna had to admit, however, that Matthew Benchley was a handsome man in his own right. Little wonder Abigail Hoffmann found him so charming.

"Would you care to join us, Matt?" Da asked, much to Renna's dismay.

"Yes, thank you."

Everyone took a place on the picnic blanket. Benchley sat down beside Renna, so she moved closer to Mr. Blackeyes. It was either that or rub elbows with Benchley. Oddly, Renna much preferred her pirate to the likes of this newcomer.

"Our friend here," Da began with a nod toward Mr. Blackeyes, "was just remembering that he has a store."

"Is that so?" Benchley appeared interested. "And what is the name of your store?"

"I…I don't know. At least not yet."

"Mr. Blackeyes has amnesia as well as being blind," Mum informed him. "Both infirmities were incurred in that tragic boating accident Wendell just mentioned."

"What a shame." The tone of Benchley's drawl made Renna wonder over his sincerity.

"Yes, but his memory is returning, little by little," Mum added. "Soon our Mr. Blackeyes here will remember everything, I'm sure."

"You're a very fortunate man, Mr.—Mr. Blackeyes." Benchley glanced at Renna, and suddenly she felt like a cold, bitter wind had just blown off the lake.

She shivered.

# EIGHT

ACK IN THE HOSPITAL, THE DARKNESS, THE STONY DARK-ness, seemed to oppress him more than ever. Renna and her family had been like a soothing sun shower—like the one he'd felt on his face this afternoon in the park. It had been something of a holiday for him—at least until Matthew Benchley appeared. After that he sensed the atmosphere change.

Renna didn't like Benchley one bit. He could tell by her actions and the tone of her voice. Had it taken a sightless man to figure that much out? Her parents hadn't seemed to notice. But perhaps they had and he just didn't realize it.

His mind wandered back on the outing. Shortly after the man had joined their picnic, Renna moved away from Benchley and closer to him. He had felt her tense on more than one occasion, and a sudden urge to protect her rose up within him. That urge surprised him. From what he could recall, he'd never felt that way before. And what a helpless feeling to be blind and desire to protect a woman. Ridiculous, actually.

Benchley. He rolled the name around his mind some more. It sounded familiar, but he couldn't place it.

His fingers curled until he'd made tightly balled fists. *Why, God? Why can't I remember who I am? Is my blindness a punishment for things I've done in my past? You've allowed me to remember what a rake I've been...*

Something Wendell Fields said flitted across his mind. "Trials aren't meant to harm us but to make us more Christlike."

Could it really be that God wanted to do some sort of miracle with his infirmities and in his life? Or had he been correct presuming they were retribution for living a godless existence all these years?

*God, please…let me in on what You're planning to do in my life.*
A deafening silence replied. For now answers eluded him.

Making himself as comfortable as possible on this sorry excuse for a bed, he willed himself to fall asleep.

Another gorgeous day. Renna sighed happily as she walked to work. A warm breeze blew her skirts around her ankles, and leaves dusted the sides of the street. In a month treetops would turn shades of orange and yellow and a flaming red. Standing on a hill in front of the hospital now, Renna turned and looked toward Lake Michigan. Ships dotted the horizon. She thought of her pirate. Hopefully their outing yesterday hadn't been too much for him.

Entering the hospital, she found herself carried on a wave of business. In her ward, she fed those patients who weren't able to eat, changed bedding, and shaved men's beards.

Mr. Blackeyes was one of them.

"Are we alone, Renna?" He whispered the question.

"We're as alone as we can be in a room filled with sick people."

He grinned. "They're all unconscious, I hope."

Renna smiled, knowing he teased her. "Only three unconscious patients today. Two are asleep, and one is waiting for a bath."

"I just don't want to be overheard."

"Speak softly then."

"All right. Tell me about Matthew Benchley."

Renna looked at the water basin in her lap. "I don't know much."

"Then tell me what you know. I'm curious."

"He's a new associate at the Chamber of Commerce and works with my father. He's been there for about a month now."

"What does he look like?"

"He's got light brown hair and..."

Renna recalled his iceberg eyes and wondered if she should disclose her thoughts. No. Best to remain objective.

"He's got blue-gray eyes and a very straight nose." She continued with her shaving. "Fairly even teeth, though he doesn't smile much. When he does, it's rather lopsided." Cynical, is what she wanted to say, but she held her tongue. "And he reminds me of those men from the West—opportunity seekers. I met plenty of them during the war."

"Opportunity seekers, huh?" Mr. Blackeyes grinned.

"Hold still."

He kept talking anyway. "Do you mean to say that Matthew Benchley appears to be the sort who would take advantage of an unsuspecting young lady in order to seize an opportunity?"

"What is that supposed to mean?"

Mr. Blackeyes chuckled. "I sensed you didn't like him, Renna."

"Nurse Fields," she corrected. She sighed and sat back. "All right. I admit it. You're correct. There's just something about him that makes me wary."

"Even more than I do—a pirate?"

"Believe it or not, yes. Now, hold still."

She finished shaving and put the razor and wash bin away. Then she allowed Mr. Blackeyes to get out of bed and stretch so she could straighten the linens. The night nurse had taken pity on him and rummaged through a box of donations, producing tan-colored trousers and a wrinkled white shirt. But even wearing those rumpled castoffs, he was still a handsome man.

"What do you look like, Renna—I mean, Nurse Fields?"

"Me?" The question caught her off guard. Her hand flew to her cheek, the one marred by the birthmark. "I–I'm just regular-looking, I guess. Nothing special, and certainly not anything like the ladies with whom you're probably accustomed to socializing."

Mr. Blackeyes acted as though he hadn't heard her. "Could I...could I feel what you look like, Renna?"

Her mouth suddenly went dry at the thought of him touching her. "What on earth do you mean?"

"Please," he persisted. "I–I just want to have an image of you in my mind—that is, I do already, but I'm wondering if it's accurate."

"Mr. Blackeyes, I don't think—"

Before she could say another word, he stepped forward and touched her hair. Most of it was covered by her stiff white nurse's cap. "What color is it?" he asked, rubbing a few strands between his thumb and forefinger.

Renna could only stand statue still. She'd never had a man touch her hair like this before. "Reddish-brown."

"Curly?"

"Yes."

"I can tell by its texture." His hands moved to her face. "What color are your eyes?"

"Green," she squeaked.

"Like emeralds." His thumbs rubbed over her brows then down her cheeks. "Your skin is so soft...are you fair-skinned? With a smattering of freckles, perhaps?"

"Yes."

"Most redheads are—and I speak of both males and females."

Renna lifted a brow and immediately found her voice again. "Thank you for clarifying that, Mr. Pirate Blackeyes."

He laughed and touched her nose. "Pert, just like your personality."

Renna couldn't help but smile now. Her father liked to lovingly tease her that way too. *A pert little nose on a pert little girl...*

Mr. Blackeyes touched her mouth then, and one finger lingered on her bottom lip for a long moment. Renna thought he seemed wistful, and she wondered why. A heartbeat later she sensed he wanted to kiss her. Somewhat frightened by the thought, Renna brought her head back, and Mr. Blackeyes moved his hands down to her chin and neck.

"You're not very tall." Once more he'd accurately assessed her. His hands went to her shoulders. "And you're slight of build." He gripped her by her upper arms. "But strong for a woman."

"All right, that's quite enough." Renna stepped back out of his grasp. "There is nothing more for you to feel, so get back into bed."

He smiled and, much to her surprise, complied without a single complaint. He surprised her further by saying, "I knew you were beautiful."

Renna swallowed hard. She wasn't beautiful. Not at all. She had an ugly purple birthmark on her face that made men gawk and stare. Why, she'd even caught Matthew Benchley gazing at it with an expression of regret. He might as well have said aloud, "I might have been attracted to you if it weren't for that thing on your face. Doesn't it come off?"

Of course, Renna was actually glad that Mr. Benchley wasn't attracted to her. But that's what Mr. Blackeyes would say once he regained his sight. He would look at her face in horror, and his illusion of her would be shattered.

*I should tell him. I should tell him that I'm not the woman he imagines.* Renna's lips moved, but the words wouldn't come. Somehow, somewhere, she'd formed her own illusions—that of an old maid becoming a new bride and marrying a pirate.

*Oh, Lord*, Renna whispered in silent prayer, *this has never happened to me.*

During the course of her nursing career she had taken care of hundreds of men. But maybe she'd grown soft. Maybe Nurse Rutledge had been correct, and she'd become too emotionally involved with her patient.

She'd have to do something about that.

With a renewed respect for her position, she finished up her day. She was cool, yet kind; skilled, yet sensitive. But when the time came for her to go home, she couldn't help giving in to the urge to say good night to her pirate.

"You're leaving already?" He seemed disappointed.

"I've been here for twelve hours. I'm afraid I'm tuckered out."

He replied with a warm smile. "Go home and get some sleep, then. You deserve it."

"Thank you. And don't forget, my father is coming to visit you tonight. He's been doing a bit of investigating and has collected a list of the names of persons presumed drowned in Lake Michigan from here all the way north to Green Bay, Wisconsin."

"Good. Such a list may help jar my memory loose."

"And Dr. Hamilton may be by to see you too," Renna added. "He had a surgery to perform today, so he didn't make his rounds earlier."

Mr. Blackeyes's grin turned wry. "I had better get an appointment book."

Renna smiled at the quip. "Good night."

A pause.

She stepped closer to his bedside. "Mr. Blackeyes?"

"I wish you wouldn't go, Renna."

His admission melted her heart. However, she knew she wouldn't be any good to anyone if she didn't get some sleep. "I'll be back."

When he didn't reply, she forced herself to turn and leave the sick ward.

But all the way home her thoughts were crowded with him, the way he'd touched her hair, her face, her mouth. How could she tell him the truth about her appearance? She glanced upward at the darkening sky and sighed. When he regained his sight, he'd learn it for himself. Until that day came, she could imagine that he was a pirate and she was a beauty.

# NINE

THUNDERSTORMS AND PERSISTENT RAIN FILLED THE NEXT several days. Mr. Blackeyes grew continually stronger and less tolerant of his convalescing. Renna thought it a good sign, although he still couldn't see and remembered little else except for sketchy details, much to his frustration. Da continued to compile lists of names of men missing in the area, but they did little to help Mr. Blackeyes's memory.

By midweek the skies cleared, and Renna formed an idea. A stroll outdoors. It'd be the perfect way to lift Mr. Blackeyes's spirits. She quickly obtained Dr. Hamilton's permission, found a sturdy wooden cane, and soon a habit formed. She and her pirate strolled outside for an hour every day for the next few days. As long as Renna had his doctor's consent, Nurse Thatcher and Nurse Rutledge couldn't say a word about their daily walks.

Renna secretly enjoyed being out of the hospital in the middle of the day. The fresh air revitalized her so that she finished out her shift with more energy than she realized she possessed. And the company…

Renna found her pirate to be quite charming, amusing, and, when their conversations turned more serious, he was a confidant. Like this afternoon. He listened patiently while Renna fretted aloud about this evening's mandatory dinner party.

"Da rescheduled after Mr. Benchley canceled last week."

"You don't enjoy hosting dinner parties?"

"Oh, it's not that. It's just that my folks, bless their hearts, are quite the matchmakers."

Mr. Blackeyes chuckled. "Ah, the real reason finally comes out. I had been wondering why this dinner was such a big deal. Now I understand. You don't like Benchley."

She glanced at him, noting again that his ill-fitted clothing didn't conceal his good looks. "Well, to be fair to the man, I don't know him."

"But I remember our picnic last week. Benchley frightened you."

"No, he just made me feel uncomfortable." She tugged on Mr. Blackeyes's arm. "Watch your step." They crossed the street. When they were safely on the other side, Renna continued. "I don't want my parents forging a romance for me. When I fall in love, it'll be a man of my own choosing." She tried not to think that her heart might have already made its own decision.

"Ah, you're a capable woman with a mind of her own."

"Exactly. So why must I show up for dinner at home this evening? My parents and Mr. Benchley can have a fine time without me."

"Renna, I believe that you're putting undue pressure on yourself. I was in several matchmaking situations last summer. Men, as you know, aren't required by society to mourn for a year or more like women—especially if they have children, as I do. 'Get them remarried quickly' seems to be the general consensus, and soon after Louisa's death, my mother plotted and planned one romance after another for me. But even with her meddling, my attitude remained casual at best. I never felt forced into any relationship in spite of my circumstances. I never allowed myself to feel forced."

"Hmm..."

"My point is this: it's all in the mind, Renna." His cane scraped the boardwalk.

She mulled it over, wondering if Mr. Blackeyes was right. Perhaps she had been putting undue pressure on herself. After all, her father would hardly force her to marry. He simply tried to encourage her along those lines.

Moments later she smiled, realizing that Mr. Blackeyes had just recalled another little piece of his past.

"So you never fell in love with any of the beautiful women whom you were forced to escort or entertain?" Renna ventured, half teasing, half curious.

"Never, although I came close. A woman...we met at a spring fund-raiser for–for returning soldiers."

"You're remembering." Renna couldn't muster enthusiasm.

"I can't recall her name." He gave her hand a squeeze by a mere flex of his arm. "But it's no matter."

"I'm sure she's beautiful—whoever she is."

"Well, what man would pursue a homely female?"

"None, of course." The remark caused Renna to be reminded of her birthmark. Sometimes when she was with Mr. Blackeyes, she actually forgot it was there. He treated her like a woman— like a beautiful woman. But what would he think of her if he ever saw it?

"Besides," he continued, "love is as real as the fairy tales all those governesses used to read to my children. At least romantic love anyway. I am, however, convinced of another love. The kind a father has for his children."

"You're speaking of yourself?"

Mr. Blackeyes nodded. "And of God's love."

Renna smiled broadly. She delighted every time Mr. Blackeyes made a spiritual reference. He was growing in Christ, learning more of God's ways as her father continued to read to him from the Bible.

"You know, Mr. Blackeyes, you're not half the pirate you used to be," Renna remarked with a little laugh.

A wry grin pulled at his mouth. "Thank you...I think."

~~uellellee~~

Once at home that evening, Renna changed from her gray uniform into a fawn-colored dress with large white cuffs. She had decided that Mr. Blackeyes was right and resolved that she would not be "forced" into a relationship with Mr. Benchley. She would, however, try to look her best and be polite to him for her parents' sake.

Examining herself in the mirror, Renna smoothed down her skirts and surveyed her birthmark. She tried to imagine what she'd look like without it and decided she'd be beautiful if not for that purplish horseshoe. Then she found herself dreaming of looking differently, feeling differently. Why, she'd be an altogether different person if it weren't for the ugly thing.

"Stop it," she chided her reflection. "This is the way God made you. You'd think after thirty years you'd get used to living with yourself."

And maybe if Mr. Blackeyes hadn't happened along, she wouldn't care about her appearance.

Giving herself a mental shake, Renna left her bedroom for the parlor downstairs. Mr. Benchley had already been seated comfortably.

"Renna, I'm glad you finally made it." Da stood.

Mr. Benchley did the same.

"My daughter is a nurse at the hospital and works much too hard. She finally managed an evening off."

"I see." Benchley gave her a polite bow. "Miss Fields, I am honored by your presence."

"Thank you." The man seemed pretentious to her, although Da was a good judge of character. Why didn't he see through Matthew Benchley—unless, of course, there was nothing there to see?

Mum entered the room wearing her best green silk dress. Her amber gaze lit on Renna. "Would you care for tea, dear?"

"No, but thank you." Renna sat down in the armchair across from her father. Mum took the place beside him on the settee.

"How is Mr. Blackeyes today?" Mum inquired.

"He's feeling better. The daily walks have improved his spirits greatly. Dr. Hamilton says he's well enough to leave the hospital. He says Mr. Blackeyes is taking up time and care that should be spent on those sicker than he. Unfortunately, Mr. Blackeyes has no money and nowhere to stay."

"What about family?" Benchley interjected, as though such a trifling thing had been overlooked.

"I think I told you, Matt." Da's tone was patient. "Mr. Blackeyes can't remember who he is and to which family he belongs."

"Dr. Hamilton is looking into a temporary home for him."

Worry lines creased Da's brow.

"What's wrong?" Renna tipped her head.

"Oh, nothing."

However, he didn't fool Renna. Something troubled him. Concern weighed on his features until Mum announced that dinner was served.

Renna took her place across from Matthew Benchley, and her parents were seated at each end of the tastefully decorated dining room table. When all were at their places, Da prayed over the food and they began to eat. Roasted pheasant and all its trimmings were the sumptuous fare tonight, and passing dish after dish, Renna was reminded of a Thanksgiving Day feast, only one of smaller proportions. It wouldn't be long—just over two months— and the Thanksgiving holiday would be upon them. Renna smiled to herself, thinking of seeing the faces of her darling nieces and nephews.

"Renna, did you hear what I said?"

Da's question brought Renna to the present. "Forgive me. I must have been daydreaming. What did you say?"

"I said, I've figured out the situation with Mr. Blackeyes."

"Do tell, Wendell." Benchley cast him a curious glance.

"Why, Mr. Blackeyes can live with us."

"What?" Renna shook her head. "No, that's not possible. Mr. Blackeyes is my patient. I can't take home every patient—"

"But Mr. Blackeyes is a...a *special* patient. We prayed for him as a family, and now we're deeply involved in his rehabilitation, both physically and spiritually speaking."

"I wouldn't mind it," Mum said, "except what would I do with him while you and Renna are at work?"

A broad grin split Da's face. "I'll take Mr. Blackeyes with me to the Chamber of Commerce."

"Hmm, the idea does have possibilities," Benchley concurred. "But what on earth can a blind man do at the Chamber of Commerce, Wendell?"

"I don't know." Da drummed his fingers on the polished table-top. "I'll think of something. And I believe that if Mr. Blackeyes were in such an environment as the one we work in, he may get his memory back sooner. As I've said all along, I'm sure I've seen this man before."

"But you can't remember where?" Mr. Benchley dabbed the corners of his mouth with his napkin.

"No, and it's most frustrating too."

"Renna, dear..." Mum changed the subject. "Perhaps you and Mr. Benchley would like to go for a stroll after dinner."

Renna nearly choked on her buttered potatoes, while Bench-ley gave her mother a shrug. "Certainly. A stroll sounds pleasant enough."

Renna's feet ached at the very idea.

"What do you say?" Mum smiled.

Suddenly remembering her promise to herself, she spoke up. "Thank you, but I'm too tired for a stroll tonight, although it was good of Mr. Benchley to agree to take me."

He sent her a condescending grin. "I'm still more of a stranger than an acquaintance, aren't I? Well, I don't mind taking a few minutes now to introduce myself."

"Oh, that would be nice." Mum sent Renna a mild look of warning. "Where are you originally from?"

"Michigan, actually. I grew up in a small harbor town right on Lake Michigan. My parents died when I was a boy, and I was raised by my aunt and uncle." Benchley's ice gray eyes bore into Renna's, causing her to look down at her dinner plate. "My uncle Ralph, now deceased, sent me to West Point, and I held a commanding position during the war."

"Really?" Da sat back in his chair. "Did you see any action?"

Benchley nodded. "Served in the cavalry, Fifth Regiment. We assisted in battles and skirmishes along the Mississippi and Tennessee Rivers mostly, although we did some fighting in Georgia too." He sneered. "Those Rebs were no match for us."

"I'm glad the war is over." Da wagged his head sorrowfully. "So much fighting. So many lives lost."

"It's not over for everyone." Benchley's voice sounded strained.

"I suppose that's true enough." Mum's eyes grew misty. "My son served with an Illinois brigade but returned to us last Christmas unharmed. Many families aren't as blessed."

"He was blessed to have a family to return to, Mrs. Fields. I wasn't as fortunate. My aunt died while I was gone, then my uncle remarried, and soon after his marriage he passed away as well. I was to have inherited his shipping company, but it seems to be caught in a legal tangle."

"I'm sorry to hear that," Renna murmured politely.

Benchley continued on. "Wendell, didn't I tell you? The company is worth a fortune."

"You don't say?" Da's gaze met Renna's, and she saw that the news pleased him.

A sinking feeling pulled her insides. Had Da allowed his zealousness as a matchmaker to overtake his common sense? Did Mr. Benchley's wealth matter more to Da than his character?

She dismissed the thought. Of course her father wanted only

the best for her, and that included security of income with whom-ever she might marry.

Still, an intuitive nudge told her Benchley lied—or hid some-thing.

"Yes, I went to fighting in the cavalry to fighting in the court-room." Benchley grinned rather wickedly. "But Great Lakes Ship-ping will be mine soon enough. It's just that the devil is in the details."

"Yes, he usually is." Da took a sip from his water goblet.

"The trouble is my stepmother." Benchley sat back in his chair. "She recently sold the business against my wishes, then had the very bad fortune to die herself. I'm trying to prove that by the terms of my uncle's will, she had no right to sell the business in the first place."

Benchley parked on the subject of his inherited wealth for a good thirty minutes. Renna yawned quietly into her napkin, ignoring her mother's look of reproof.

Da managed to work a few words in edgewise and suggested they move to the parlor.

"I'll fix dessert. I made a lovely lemon cake with icing."

Renna pushed her chair back.

"No need to help me, dear." Mum set a hand on her shoulder. "I'd rather have you help your father keep our guest company."

Disappointment assailed her. Nevertheless she followed Da and Mr. Benchley from one room to the next.

"Like I said, I'm a wealthy man but for a tragic lapse of judg-ment on my stepmother's part." Taking a seat in an armchair, Benchley stared off in the distance.

Renna noticed the weighty scowl on his brow once more.

Da cleared his throat. "I gather you were not fond of your aunt."

He shook his head. "Never had a chance to be."

Another half hour passed, and Renna couldn't believe a man

could chatter away so much about himself. He was obviously his own favorite topic of conversation!

With Mum seated comfortably, Renna decided to make her escape. Pushing to her feet, she collected coffee cups and dessert plates and set them on a tray. "If you'll excuse me, I must retire for the night. We were busy at the hospital today, and I'm expected back there early in the morning."

"On a Sunday?" Benchley brought his chin back in surprise. His golden-brown eyebrows drew inward.

"All of us nurses have to take our turns working weekends. It's unfortunate but a reality."

"I think it's quite the sacrilege." He peered at Da.

"You wouldn't, Matt, if you were a sick patient." Da stood. "Go on, my little wren. Sleep well."

Mum took the tray from her. "I'll take care of the dishes."

"Thank you."

Da stepped forward and kissed her cheek. Then Renna bid Mr. Benchley a good night. Benchley replied with a small bow and a casual grin.

"I'm certain we'll see each other again soon," he added.

Renna pushed out a polite smile. Turing on her heel, she couldn't leave the parlor fast enough.

Upstairs in her bedroom, Renna undressed and pulled on her cotton nightgown. How glad she felt that Matthew Benchley had become so absorbed in himself that he forgot all about her. And tomorrow…

Tomorrow Renna would walk with her pirate and tell him all about Mr. Benchley and his shipping company. Mr. Blackeyes seemed to enjoy their conversations. And indeed, the more they talked, the more details he remembered of his own life.

But when his memory returned, he'd walk out of her life forever. She mustn't forget that; otherwise she'd nurse a lifetime of heartache.

Renna crawled into bed and pulled the colorful patchwork quilt that Elizabeth had sewn up to her chin. And if his vision came back, he wouldn't enjoy their talks nearly as much.

She closed her eyes, and it took every ounce of will to pray for Mr. Blackeyes's recovery.

# TEN

**H**OW DID THE DINNER GO LAST NIGHT, RENNA?"

"Not as badly as I anticipated." She sent her pirate a smile as she finished writing in a patient's chart. Dr. Hamilton would be making his Sunday evening rounds, and he'd expect the documentation to be in order. "Although I must admit, Matthew Benchley is not someone with whom I enjoyed conversing. I sense he's a bit narcissistic."

"Oh?"

"Yes, he talked solely about himself the entire time."

"And? What did you learn about the man?"

"Well, he's from Michigan and served in the cavalry during the war."

"Hmm…"

"He's embroiled in some legal battle involving an inheritance. I had to force myself to pay attention, but I must admit my mind wandered far and away at times."

Mr. Blackeyes chuckled.

Renna glanced his way. He sat in the wooden chair near his bedside. Despite his bandaged head and secondhand clothing, he looked rakishly handsome as the evening sun cast long shadows down the middle of the sick ward. Locks of his ebony hair hung over his forehead, and Renna could almost believe the man was truly a pirate.

"Aurora maintained that all men are narcissists," he said.

"Aurora?" Renna's heart did a dive. Another woman?

"My mother. I just remembered. Her name is Aurora."

"How wonderful!" *Thank God it's only his mother!* "See, you're remembering!

"I guess I am." He sounded both awed and pleased.

"Can you recall her last name?"

He gave the matter a few seconds of thought. "No. But I'll pray about it. Seems God answered and gave me my mother's first name."

Renna smiled and looked back at her charting. Her parents had taken Mr. Blackeyes to church this morning, where he met Pastor Moody, and then home, where he enjoyed one of Mum's delicious meals. Later Da returned him to the hospital and sat with him for a bit. The two men had an intensive discussion about prayer. Mr. Blackeyes wondered how God would speak to him. Da replied that God spoke through His Holy Spirit and His written Word. He might also use another believer to bear the truth.

"Tell me more about Benchley."

"There's not much more to say."

"Is he a religious man?"

"Apparently. But that doesn't necessarily mean he's a true believer in Christ. It could be that going to church only makes Mr. Benchley feel that much better about himself." Renna felt a sting of conscience. "But I shouldn't judge him. God knows I should try harder to get out of work to attend Sunday services."

"Maybe so, but I sensed your faith immediately. Do you sense Benchley's in that same way?"

"I don't know what you mean."

He gave an impatient sigh. "I'm trying to discreetly ask if you're attracted to him in any way, Renna."

"Heavens no!"

"I thought so, but I wanted to hear it from your lips." A slow grin stretched across his handsome face. "I'm glad."

Renna sent him a curious grin. "You are?" She held her breath, unsure if she wanted to know why, and yet she didn't think she could bear not to know.

But soon she realized Mr. Blackeyes, that savvy pirate, wasn't about to get sentimental here in the sick ward. "Why, Renna, whatever would I do if you set your sights on Benchley and ceased being so attentive to me? I'd be at the mercy of Nurses Ruthless and Hatchet."

She clicked her tongue. "Oh, stop it." Looking past the doorway, she hoped the women hadn't overhead the comment. "Mind your manners, or I might be ordered to scrub the floors before my shift ends."

"In that case"—he chuckled—"I'll behave myself."

However, he didn't elaborate. He didn't even try to explain himself, although Renna found herself wishing he would... sort of.

On one hand, she dreamed of hearing romantic words from this man's mouth, but on the other she realized that he didn't even know who he was, let alone understand any feelings from his heart. Besides, there was still part of Renna that held her own heart in check. Her lifelong insecurity haunted her—and with good reason. As soon as Mr. Blackeyes regained his memory and sight, he would, of course, want to go back to the life to which he was accustomed. He'd forget all about the lowly nurse with the purple birthmark on her cheek.

*And it's best he did too,* she decided. She certainly wouldn't want to share his pirate's lifestyle.

Renna let go a weary sigh. Such a myriad of emotions inside of her. They, coupled with her exhaustion from another twelve-hour day, seemed overwhelming.

"I've offended you, haven't I?" Mr. Blackeyes crossed his legs.

"Not at all."

"You're so quiet."

"Oh, I was just thinking."

"About what?"

"Why, Mr. Blackeyes"—she tried to inflect a teasing note in her reply—"do you really think I'd bare my soul to a pirate?"

"Aye, Captain." He grinned sardonically. "I feel like I'm back in the military." His expression suddenly changed to one of seriousness. "Captain," he repeated. "Captain...I believe that was my title. Captain."

Renna smiled. "Captain Pirate Blackeyes, huh?"

He didn't reply, so lost was he in his sudden reverie.

~~~⌇⌇⌇✕⌇⌇⌇~~~

*The wind whipped off the dark Mississippi River with the onset of a storm. He looked across the water for some of his men who had gone ahead in rafts to cut away the trees obstructing their ship's path. The gunner was headed toward Vicksburg to aid Grant in his mission to take the Confederate citadel on the Mississippi. He would see that they got there too, right after this new canal was completed. The shortcut would open into a system of bayous that would take his ship to a secret landing just below the Vicksburg batteries.*

*"Captain, do you think they'll get back before the storm?"*

*He turned and regarded the young officer standing beside him. "I'm sure they will."*

*"I heard there's snakes hanging from the branches of them trees they're cutting down—poisonous snakes, sir."*

*He smiled at the young man, thinking that snakes were the least of their worries. They were days away from facing Confederate gunfire. But if they could take Vicksburg, the Mississippi River would be completely open to Federal military. It was a battle they had to win.*

~~~⌇⌇⌇✕⌇⌇⌇~~~

"And we won," he murmured.

"What was that, Mr. Blackeyes?"

The past blended into the present at the sound of Renna's sweet voice. "We won the battle at Vicksburg. I was remembering..."

"Wonderful!"

He heard the genuine delight in her voice. It both comforted him and gave him courage.

"Little by little your past is coming back to you."

"I captained a Federal gunboat."

"On the Mississippi. Isn't that what you once told me?"

"Yes. But I wish I could remember my last name. It's right there, on the edge of my memory..."

"It'll come, Mr. Blackeyes—or should I say Captain Blackeyes?"

He grinned at the smile in Renna's voice. Then her hand gently touched his shoulder, generating warmth that spread through his whole body. He had always sensed her care, but lately he noticed that other male patients didn't get quite the same attention he did. For that, he was grateful. Even more than grateful. If he believed in falling in love with a woman, he felt certain he'd fallen in love with Renna—sight unseen. He didn't have to see her to know what a beautiful person she was. But, of course, he didn't believe in that sort of love, that fairy-tale love.

"Doctor Hamilton has arrived." Renna whispered the news close to his ear. He felt her breath on his cheek as she helped him sit up on the edge of the hospital bed. He resisted the urge to put his arm around her waist and pull her close. She was right there, innocently pressing against his arm as she worked to remove the protective bandages from his eyes.

He sighed.

"I'm almost done." She'd obviously misinterpreted his sigh of frustration for one of impatience. "There. Now I'll clean the salve from your eyes."

He nodded, trying to ignore the desire in his heart. Before his accident and his conversion to Christ, he wouldn't have hesitated to take advantage of a woman who stirred him the way Renna did. On the other hand, he couldn't ever recall meeting a woman like Renna Fields.

"Thank you," he said simply, unable to express the feelings he had for her…whatever they were, whatever their names.

"You're entirely welcome, Captain Blackeyes." Her tart reply made him smile again.

Moments later Dr. Hamilton joined them. "All right, man, look around. Tell me if you can see anything."

He blinked. Once. Twice. There was light. Everything was a blur, but he saw light. He turned his head and barely made out shapes and outlines, though not very clearly.

And then he glimpsed the shape of the woman who had to be Renna. He could make out her white cap, her dress, but the details of her face wouldn't come into focus.

"I can see." He aimed his vision at Renna, trying to force his eyes to focus. "But I can't make out details, I'm afraid." He turned to Dr. Hamilton and smiled. "You've got bushy whiskers and gray hair…but I can't see your face beyond them."

He heard Renna's tiny gasp. It sounded like one of dismay or skepticism. Confused, he turned her way, studying her and trying again to blink her into focus.

Dr. Hamilton chuckled merrily. "I had my doubts, but now I'm certain your sight will be returning soon. Good job, Nurse Fields. I might be inclined to believe in miracles after all."

"I'm happy to hear that, Doctor." However, something in Renna's voice didn't sound happy at all.

"Well, carry on, Nurse Fields. As for you, Mr. Blackeyes, I'm told you'll be leaving the hospital soon."

"I will?"

"Yes. Another stroke of luck for you—or a miracle, whichever way you choose to look at it. The Fields family has offered to take you in until you've completely recovered—or until you've at least recovered your memory. And what better family than one belonging to such a devoted nurse? You'll be in excellent care. Wendell Fields assured me of that, and knowing Nurse Fields, I'm convinced of it."

"I am indeed a fortunate man." He gazed in Renna's direction. But she was gone.

# ELEVEN

THE NEXT MORNING RENNA APPROACHED HER SUPERVISOR. She hoped to be alleviated of caring for Captain Blackeyes today. "Nurse Rutledge, may I speak with you?"

The nun turned her small eyes toward Renna. Her brows appeared like two dark, mad slashes across her face. "What is it, Nurse Fields?"

"Well..." Renna couldn't help fidgeting under the older woman's intense scrutiny. "I thought it might be best if I cared for Ward Nine on the third floor today while you assigned another nurse to my usual ward. It's bath day for the women upstairs, and I have a strong back."

"Hmm, I guess that can be arranged. Good of you to offer."

"Yes, ma'am." Renna lowered her gaze, praying the supervising nurse wouldn't glimpse the truth in her eyes. Was she a fool to think she could avoid the man today, come home late, leave early, and never see him again?

"Everyone in your ward is stable."

Renna looked up. "Yes, quite stable."

"Very good, then, you're assigned to Ward Nine today."

With a sigh of relief, Renna made her way upstairs. She'd known this day would come when her pirate's sight returned. He'd soon see her for what she was—a marred woman, unfit for his favor. It had happened before, so Renna reminded herself that she wasn't being overly insecure or indulging in self-pity.

Her mind took her back a few years ago when she lived and worked in Virginia. A special ball honoring medical personnel was to be held at General Lilley's stately home. Since Renna didn't have a beau to escort her, her roommate Gertrude set her up with a friend of her fiancé, a Lieutenant Frederick Dinsmore. But at tea the afternoon prior to the day of the party, Lieutenant Dinsmore took one look at Renna and promptly made his excuses, all the while staring at her purple birthmark. Disappointed, Renna returned to the army hospital and volunteered to work the night of the ball. The next morning a giddy young woman thanked her for her service, seeing it meant that she'd get the night off. She added, "I didn't think I'd be able to attend the ball, but then Lieutenant Dinsmore offered to take me."

Renna's heart shattered, even though the party meant more to her than Fred Dinsmore. Still, his shallowness hurt. And while Captain Blackeyes didn't seem anywhere near as inconsiderate and vain as that army lieutenant, he'd still been accustomed to beautiful women in his past. Renna knew she hardly qualified. Best to distance herself from her pirate. Soon he'd remember his identity, and, with his sight returned, there would be nothing keeping him in Chicago.

Yes, that plan was the best.

⁓ꬰꬰꬰꭓꬰꬰꬰⸯ

With his room now prepared at the Fieldses' house, the captain rode to their home on Wednesday with Wendell at the reins of the carriage. Upon finding out about his commanding position in the war, Renna's father had begun to refer to him as "Captain," as did Renna. The captain much preferred the title to the name Blackeyes.

"Beautiful day," Wendell remarked.

Looking through the dark spectacles he'd been given by Dr. Hamilton as a measure of protection, the captain nodded. "I can imagine how bright the sunshine is as I see glimmers of it and feel its rays on my face. But everything is still such a blur."

"Well, at least you can make out the shapes of things, people, horses, carriages, and such."

"I could make out the pointy nose on Nurse Hatchet this morning." He couldn't help the unkind remark. The woman had been plain old mean.

Wendell choked back a chuckle. "Now, now, Renna would have our hides if she caught us snickering over Nurse Thatcher's pointy nose. However, I will agree that the woman's brisk manner is often uncalled for."

"I agree. More's the reason I preferred to be in Renna's care." The captain grew pensive, wondering over the change in Renna the last few days. She had seemed to avoid him, even declining to take their usual walk. Finally he decided to ask about it. "Is Renna unhappy that I'm coming to stay with you?"

Wendell paused in thought. "Um, no, she's not *unhappy* about it."

"She's been distant lately."

"I'm sorry to hear that."

He waited for an explanation, and when none came, he pressed further. "I don't have to have my sight back to see there's something amiss between Renna and me. Did I offend her?"

"No, no, it's not you at all, Captain. It's Renna." Again he paused momentarily. "I'm going to be honest with you," he stated at last. "You deserve that much given Renna's recent behavior, and since you're coming to live in our home for a while, I think it best you know."

The captain's curiosity was sorely piqued.

"But please don't tell Renna I shared this matter with you. She would feel embarrassed. However, I believe that in telling you, you might prove part of the solution."

"You've got my word, and from what I can recall, it's honorable."

Wendell nodded. "Very good. The problem is, Renna is a very

self-conscious and insecure young woman when it comes to the birthmark on her cheek."

"Birthmark?"

"You haven't seen it?"

"No. Facial features are still a blur."

"Hmm, well, then she was right. Renna thought you hadn't seen it yet. But she's taking precautions for when you do. She's hardening that tough outer shell of hers. She's afraid to be hurt. You see, she has come to care about you—our entire family has—and Renna is certain that, because you've been accustomed to socializing with beautiful and affluent women, you will decide she's an ugly toad once you see it."

"A toad?" He hung his head back and laughed. "Wendell, your daughter would have to really be a toad before I thought she was ugly, and even at that, Renna would be beautiful in my eyes."

"I'm glad to hear it." An unmistakable note of pleasure edged Wendell's voice.

"But now I'm curious. What does her birthmark look like?"

"It looks like a violet horseshoe that goes from her jawline to her ear to her nose and back. But in all honesty a person doesn't even notice it after a while—after the initial surprise wears off. In fact, Matthew Benchley, my associate, thinks highly enough of Renna to want to court her."

"Really?" For some reason the idea troubled the captain greatly. The man's last name, Benchley, was still so familiar, and yet he still couldn't place it…

"Yes, Matt is looking for a wife," Wendell continued. "He feels being a bachelor holds something of a stigma in the business world. Matt says being unmarried makes him seem irresponsible, and he wants bankers to think his business ideas are worthwhile ventures."

"And have you given your permission—for the courtship?"

"I would if Renna wanted me to. Matt would be a good provider, and I know Renna would like to have children someday. But, unfortunately, she doesn't like Matt well enough for a courtship."

"Wendell, your daughter doesn't like Benchley. Period."

Wendell sighed. "I've told Renna that love might come later and that she could build a good life with Matthew Benchley. He's got money—"

"Money isn't everything, Wendell. I'm learning that the hard way."

"True, but wealth is worth something—"

"Not enough to enter into a loveless marriage. My first marriage was devoid of true love, and I've come to realize just how miserable it had been for Louisa and me."

Wendell grew quiet as the horses clip-clopped down the streets.

"I'm a candid pirate, aren't I?" A sarcastic chuckle rumbled in his chest. "I hope I haven't offended you with my straightforwardness."

"No, you haven't offended me. In fact, I'll consider what you've said about Renna and Matt."

The captain couldn't help a smile. "Wendell, your daughter seems very capable of falling in love with the right man."

The remark was left hanging between them until they reached the Fieldses' home, and suddenly Captain Pirate Blackeyes found himself wishing Renna would fall in love with him.

*Except I don't believe in falling in love.*

Wendell helped him up to the porch, where Johanna Fields greeted him.

"We're pleased to have you staying with us, Captain." He made out the gesture as she waved him into the house. "Dinner will be in about two hours, and Renna has promised me that she'll make it home in time. So if you'd like to rest, Wendell will show you to your room."

"Thank you."

"This way, my friend." Wendell clapped onto his right elbow. "Your quarters aren't much to speak of. We had a large pantry off the kitchen that I converted into a bedroom for you. I thought it would be better if you were downstairs since your sight is impaired. We wouldn't want you falling down the staircase, you know."

"I appreciate your thoughtfulness. Two weeks at that hospital were more than enough. I'm so happy to be discharged."

"I can imagine. I'd feel the same way."

They made their way through the wide kitchen, and tantalizing smells lingered in the air. Several feet later they made a right turn.

"Here we are. If you need anything, I'll be in my study, which is back through the kitchen and to the left before you reach the front door. Johanna will be about and can guide you if necessary."

"Many thanks, Wendell."

Alone in what reminded him of a whitewashed cabin, the captain found the bed and stretched out on top of it. He thanked God that he was no longer in that wretched sick ward. The only good thing about it had been Renna.

Thoughts of her gathered in his mind, her sweet voice, her gentle touch. The idea of another man courting her suddenly infuriated him. *If I don't believe in falling in love, then what are these emotions I'm feeling?*

He wanted to know—needed to know; however, one thing seemed sure. Without Renna, he would never find out. He would just have to do something—anything—to close the distance between them that she had created.

～ꙅꙅꙅꙅꙅꙅ～

Renna arrived home long after dinner had been served. The captain could hear her voice in the kitchen.

"Where's our new houseguest?"

He held his breath.

"The captain wants to speak with you." Wendell's reply sounded grave.

Brian nodded to himself. *Good! Good!*

"Apparently leaving the hospital was something of a strain and...well, he's totally blind again."

"Oh, no. He'd been doing so well."

"Why don't you go talk to him?"

"Yes. Perhaps I should."

The captain smirked then quickly wiped any traces of humor off his face.

A knock sounded on the thin wooden door.

"Come in." He sat on the edge of the bed, dressed in the ghastly charity garb he'd received from the hospital. How he'd enjoy a tailor and fine material right about now. But he had long ago forced himself to be grateful. Over his eyes he wore his dark glasses.

"I understand you've had a setback." Renna walked in and came to stand beside the bed, the door open behind her.

"Yes, and it's most discouraging."

"I'm so sorry."

The captain lifted his right hand, hoping he looked more helpless than ever.

It worked. She took his hand.

"Many times these things are only temporary," she told him, sitting on the bed beside him.

The captain had to force himself not to grin. He couldn't see her expression clearly, although he sensed her genuine concern. Best of all, the chasm between them had vanished.

Swallowing hard, he struggled with his next words. "I remembered something else—tonight as I waited for you to arrive home."

"What is it?"

He shivered at the memory. "My mother. She had been aboard the schooner with me." His voice broke. "On the day of the storm..."

93

"Drowned?"

"I'm afraid so."

"How tragic."

His heart crimped. "I saw her, waving her arms frantically in the waves. I couldn't reach her. I couldn't help her."

"There now..." Renna's grip tightened on his hand.

"And Elise too..."

"Elise?" Renna inched back slightly.

"Oh, Lord!" His head ached as he remembered it all. The screams. The thunder and lightning. The hard, driving rain. "I never felt so helpless in all my life."

"I'm sure you did what you could." She hesitated. "Who is Elise?"

"She was...my fiancée."

Renna slowly withdrew her hand.

He managed to recapture it. "It's not what you think."

"What a shame that you lost your love as well as your mother on that ill-fated day."

"No...I mean, yes, it's a shame that she and my mother perished. But Elise wasn't my love. I merely wanted her shipping company—and I obtained it too. I'd purchased it from her just days before the storm. I had been celebrating the acquisition out on the lake. Then ominous clouds began brewing to the north. I tried to sail the schooner to shore in time but couldn't."

Had poor navigating been a factor? Why hadn't he been able to steer the vessel to safety?

"Did you eat dinner?" Renna's soft voice intruded on his musing.

"No, I was waiting for you."

"How very thoughtful, but I suspect you're in need of some nourishment. I know Da came to get you after lunch, which means you probably didn't eat at the hospital."

"You're correct, Nurse Fields," he retorted. "The food at that institution is most atrocious."

"Oh, it's not so bad."

For the very first time, he saw her smile. Not clearly. But he'd glimpsed enough to see how it lit his dull existence. His heart beat a little faster.

"Allow me to escort you to the dinner table, Captain Pirate Blackeyes."

The smile in Renna's voice caused him to grin. This first victory tasted sweet.

# TWELVE

THE LAST WEEK OF SEPTEMBER THE WEATHER CHANGED dramatically, making the season feel more like fall with its chilly nights and warm days. Then rain came. The captain had sensed the barometer falling even before the first drizzle landed on the windowpane. He'd felt it in his bones. Not an ache, as some people have, but an inclination.

Like the one he'd experienced out on the lake that fateful day. What had happened? Had it been his fault?

He sat on the divan in the Fieldses' cozy parlor, grateful for the fire blazing in the hearth. He waited patiently for Wendell, his wife, and Renna to finish dressing for dinner. A week had gone by since he first arrived in their home, and he had regained much of his eyesight. Instead of rejoicing, however, he kept it a secret from Renna and her family. He felt certain that as long as he remained blind, Renna would continue her attentiveness, and he wanted that more than anything. Yet he had to admit it grew increasingly hard to continue his charade. Sometimes he had to close his eyes behind the dark spectacles he wore so he didn't see the step in front of him or know what food lay on the plate before him at the supper table.

But Renna affixed herself to his side, and he conceded to her coddling. He once needed it—even looked forward to it. Now, however, he bristled beneath it. But it couldn't be helped if he meant to continue with his plan of temporary deception. It appeared to be working better than he first thought.

And one thing was sure—Renna had feelings for him, feelings

that went far beyond what a nurse felt for her patient. He'd seen the way she looked up at him so adoringly, and it pulled at his heart in the most peculiar way. While he pretended he didn't observe it, the ardent expression on her lovely features was obvious—and, yes, hers were lovely features. True, Renna's birthmark was a curiosity—at first. But Wendell had been right. One hardly noticed it after a while. But now the captain wondered over Renna's insecurities. She had a kind, caring, devoted nature and a delightful sense of humor, and he found her petite and shapely figure physically attractive. What's more, he enjoyed matching wits with her.

The captain blew out a long breath. If falling in love were an illness, he'd have to say he'd succumbed. Completely. Hopelessly.

But, of course, falling in love was for fables and fairy tales.

Wasn't it?

"There you are." Renna entered the parlor. She wore a deep green corduroy dress with a fitted bodice and flaring skirt.

Standing to his feet, he thought the color of Renna's dress suited her features perfectly, especially her green eyes and wavy auburn hair. It was on the tip of his tongue to compliment her, but he quickly remembered to maintain his ruse. "I've been sitting here enjoying the warmth of the fire."

"Yes, it does feel nice on a cold, damp day, doesn't it?" She eyed him. "It appears you didn't have any trouble dressing for dinner tonight. Even your tie is perfectly straight. And your hair…" She smiled. "You must be getting accustomed to the feel of things, Captain."

He cleared his throat. "Yes, I suppose I am." Next time he would have to leave his tie a bit crooked. However, the cut of these clothes left something to be desired, and he longed for a visit to his tailor—

Whoever he was!

A knock sounded at the front door, and Renna bit her bottom

lip as an expression of apprehension washed over her face. "I suppose that's Mr. Benchley."

The captain smiled sympathetically. Wendell had taken his words to heart last week, but this dinner invitation had been in the works for some time, and he didn't feel right about abruptly canceling it.

"Excuse me while I answer the door."

"Of course." The captain gave her a gentle smile.

She left the parlor, and he heard her voice in the small front hallway. "Come in, Mr. Benchley. May I take your coat?"

"Yes, thank you. And may I say that you look especially lovely this evening."

The captain's shoulders tensed.

"Thank you, Mr. Benchley." Renna sounded less than enthused as she showed him into the parlor.

"Nice to see you, Captain... *Whoever-you-are.*" Benchley chuckled at his own facetiousness. He then extended his hand. But since he was supposed to be blind, the captain didn't acknowledge the greeting thrust at him. Eventually Benchley dropped his arm.

"Please sit down, Mr. Benchley." Renna claimed the seat beside the captain. The sweet scent of her subtle perfume wafted to his nostrils, and her elbow collided with his. "Oh, pardon me."

He inclined his head.

"So...Mr. Benchley, I trust you had a good day today."

"Quite good." He cast a slight frown in the captain's direction. But, at Renna, he smiled. "Any day is a good one when money is earned and invested wisely. A new shipment came in today from China—"

"Japan," the captain corrected him. He'd been with Wendell at the Chamber of Commerce when the shipment came in.

"Oh, right...Japan. Anyway, we were busy in our department. Working closely with the merchants made me long for the day when I'll be in charge of my own shipping company."

The captain had heard Benchley mention this shipping company several times now, and his interest continued to pique. However, until this moment, he hadn't had the chance to ask about it. "May I inquire about the name of your shipping company and where it's based?"

A steely look entered Benchley's gaze. "The name's Great Lakes Shipping, and it's based in Michigan—that is, it *had* been based there. The company belonged to my Uncle Ralph *Kingsley*," he said emphatically. "When he died, my aunt, his second wife, Elise Kingsley, nearly ran it into the ground, pardon the pun. Nevertheless, it supported her while she was alive. But she was killed earlier this month in a tragic boating accident. That's when I discovered she'd sold Great Lakes Shipping to some scoundrel. My uncle had meant for it to be mine. And what a coincidence, eh, Captain? You were injured in a boating accident too."

His heart drummed wildly in his chest as he realized Benchley was speaking of the woman he'd planned to marry in December—Elise Kingsley. Yes, of course, that was her last name. He had just purchased her shipping company—the very one to which Benchley referred.

Sitting back against the divan, he forced calm into his voice. "The names of your aunt's friends...do you know them?"

A soft gasp emanated from Renna, and he knew she suddenly understood why he'd posed the question. But he quickly placed his hand on hers, praying she'd keep her knowledge to herself. He didn't want Benchley informed. Not yet, although it was obvious that Benchley knew his identity.

"Their names? Hmm, let's see..." Benchley deliberately took his time searching his memory. "The only one I know who drowned was dear Aunt Elise's fiancé, Brian Sinclair—"

A jolt of recognition reverberated to his soul. He knew that instant he was Captain Brian Sinclair.

From out of the corner of his dark glasses, he could see Renna's face pale beneath the room's lamplight. He'd have to speak to her later.

"Ah, yes, Captain Sinclair…" Benchley sat back against the blue cushioned chair. "I never met the man, but he was a blackheart. He wooed and cooed Aunt Elise until she lost her senses. Then he convinced her to sell our shipping company…to him. She did because she was as smitten as a schoolgirl. I couldn't reason with her. I tried on many occasions. But she had set her sights on marrying the rake and told me she'd give him anything. It appeared Captain Sinclair not only took Great Lakes Shipping but my aunt's life too."

~~~~~~

Renna felt queasy, listening to Matthew Benchley. The individual he described certainly sounded like her pirate. And hadn't he said he'd been engaged to a woman named Elise? He'd all but admitted to everything Benchley said. But for some odd reason he wasn't revealing his identity. Renna didn't know why the captain would keep it a secret, unless he didn't realize he was that man—this Brian Sinclair. But he had to be. There was no mistaking the circumstances.

Da and Mum entered the parlor. The captain removed his hand from Renna's. She'd barely remembered he'd placed it on top of hers. It felt so natural. But Renna felt sure she was only an admission away from losing her pirate forever.

"Good evening, gentlemen," Mum said.

The captain and Benchley stood, and Mum smiled. "Please be seated." She gathered the skirt of her gold and black plaid dress and lowered herself into the armchair that matched the one in which Benchley sat. "Our dinner will be ready shortly."

Da ran his hands down the front of his waistcoat. "I'm anxious to eat. Lunch was meager today, eh, Captain Blackeyes?"

"Meager, but tastier than hospital food any day."

A grin lifted the corners of Da's mouth before he eyed the seating arrangement. Renna had a hunch her father would prefer if she sat beside Benchley, but she'd rather be parked next to a reptile.

"We were discussing our day at the Chamber of Commerce," Benchley informed him and Mum.

"Oh, well, seeing as the ladies are present now, I suppose we can talk about something more...um...sociable."

Mum gave him a grin before folding her hands in her lap. "Our Ladies for Christ group at church is organizing a picnic basket auction."

Renna caught the suggestive look in her mother's eye, and liquid dread ran through her.

"It's for all the unmarried men and women in our congregation. You see, a bachelor bids on the picnic basket that most appeals to him and then eats with the woman who made it." Mum leaned forward, smiling at Mr. Benchley. "Except he has no idea who that woman is until he's bought the basket."

"Sounds fun." Benchley sent a quick smile Renna's way. "I'm a gambling man, so I'd be willing to make a bet and eat with a nice lady."

Renna noticed he didn't use the word "pretty," and she lowered her gaze when his eyes lingered on her cheek.

"All the women at the Illinois Street Church are reportedly good cooks," Da said with a chuckle.

"But Renna outshines them."

"Oh, Mum." A blush heated her face.

"The best part, Mr. Benchley, is that the money made from the purchase of the picnic baskets will go to those families who lost husbands and fathers in the war."

"A noble cause," Captain Blackeyes—that is, Sinclair—said.

"Yes, those of us who served in the war certainly appreciate it."

Renna noticed a veil of tension hanging between her pirate and Benchley. But then Mum stood and announced she'd begin serving dinner. Not another word was spoken on the subjects of shipping companies and boating accidents, even though Matthew Benchley's cold stare seldom left the captain. Renna guessed that Benchley knew the truth too—that Captain Blackeyes was really Captain Sinclair, and he hated him.

Once they'd finished eating and everyone retired to the parlor, Mum excused herself to do dishes and refused Renna's help. But instead of returning to the parlor, Renna ambled to the back hallway, where she grabbed her knitted shawl. Then she made her way outside.

Da had constructed the wood, semi-covered porch that extended into the backyard. Renna liked to retreat out here to steal a quiet moment and think. She breathed in the cool, fresh air. The rain had stopped, only drizzles here and there when the treetops dried themselves in the night breeze.

Gazing up at the clearing sky, she saw a web of clouds waft across the moon. *Lord, why do Mum and Da want to match me with Mr. Benchley?* He had admitted to being a gambling man. Didn't that tell her parents all they needed to know about the man?

Suddenly a shadowy figure stepped onto the porch. A gasp escaped her.

"I'm sorry. I didn't mean to startle you."

It was her pirate. Renna relaxed.

"Benchley just left."

"I can't say as I'm disappointed to see him go." Hands on the railing, she turned to look out over the darkened yard.

Her pirate chuckled, a deep, rich sound. "Your sentiments are quite obvious—at least to me."

She groaned.

"But I believe your parents are beginning to see Benchley's true colors. In your father's defense, Renna, the man is quite professional at work."

"That may be. But I'll not be set up. When I fall in love, it'll be a man of my choosing."

"Yes, so you've mentioned in the past."

She heard the smile in his voice. Then he stepped in closer. Renna's heart thumped in her chest. Still she mustered the courage to turn and consider him beneath the dim glow from the dining room window and the half-concealed moon. He had removed his dark glasses and seemed to stare right through her. *Except he's blind. He can't see me—or my birthmark.* Oh, but he made for a handsome pirate all the same. No wonder Elise Kingsley took leave of her senses.

"Throughout dinner, I've been thinking…" He took another step toward her. The angles and planes of his swarthy features came into view, although a shadow of whiskers had darkened the lower half of his face. "I know who I am and where I've come from."

"You're Captain Brian Sinclair, aren't you?"

"Yes. I hail from Wisconsin, specifically Milwaukee. I remember everything."

Renna's heart crimped. Soon he'd be out of her life forever. "We should contact your family."

He gave a slight incline of his head. "Would you help me write a letter to them?"

She couldn't in good conscience refuse. "Of course."

He came to stand beside her, his large hands closing around the rail. "By now Richard and Sarah should have discovered they have joint custody of my children. I presume they've married or are close to it. I knew they belonged together the first week Sarah arrived in Milwaukee to be my children's governess. But I trifled with her, knowing Richard loved her, just because I"—he shrugged—"I could. It was like a game that I knew I succeeded in. I regret it all now."

Renna smiled. He'd been a black-hearted pirate, to be sure. But

God had given him a second chance. Would he take it? Turn his life around? Completely change his ways?

"In any case, Richard Navis is the man I must contact."

"All right. I'll see that the letter is sent to him." Sadness fell over her. Her pirate was getting ready to walk out of her life forever.

"Renna, please don't tell anyone who I am just yet. Not even your parents. When the time is right, I will tell them."

"What?" She blinked and turned to him. "Why?"

"I remember thinking that something was wrong with my schooner this summer—before the accident. You see, the boat drifted off course. I'd never meant to get so far out into the lake. When the storm approached, I couldn't maneuver the *Adventuress* and get her safely into harbor."

"You think someone tampered with it?" The implication horrified her. "Who would do such a thing?"

"I don't know for sure. And I don't want to falsely accuse anyone of–of murder. But I know my navigation skills aren't to blame." He inched his head closer. His voice was a mere whisper. "Days before the accident, Elise told me about her nephew, Matthew Benchley. She had argued with him. I never met him, but Elise said he threatened her with bodily harm if she sold the shipping company to me. Of course, she'd sold it already. However, she wouldn't tell him. She was too frightened of his reaction to the news." A rueful expression crossed his dark features. "I shrugged off the threat as typical female hysterics. I now know I should have taken it seriously."

Renna heard the remorse in his voice. She tipped her head. "You think he tampered with the boat?"

The captain lifted a dark brow. "Perhaps, although I have no proof. And until I can determine if there's any real danger surrounding my circumstances, I can only trust a few people with my identity."

"But Mr. Benchley obviously knows who you are."

"Yes, but he doesn't know that I know. Either that, or he's playing along with me."

Suddenly Captain Sinclair turned. His hands cupped her face, and Renna thought that surely he could see as his black eyes bore into hers. But of course she imagined it.

"Renna, is my secret safe with you?"

"Yes." She whispered the reply, her lips just inches from his.

He released her. "Good."

An odd feeling of disappointed coursed through her. She'd felt certain that this pirate-captain had been intent upon kissing her.

He grinned—she glimpsed it despite the darkness surrounding them, and it was a pirate's smile if she ever saw one.

"Renna, Renna," he said, "what shall I ever do with you?"

"W-what do you mean?"

He shook his head. "You were very close to getting yourself kissed just now—and quite thoroughly kissed too."

Her heart leapt into her throat.

"But don't worry," he assured her. "You have my word that I'll never be anything less than a gentleman."

Renna thought it over, and pirate or not, she believed him.

An awkward moment went by. She looked away. "Would you like a cup of tea?" A shiver passed through her.

"No tea, but I'll keep you company."

"All right. Thank you."

She moved to walk off the porch, and he stumbled loudly behind her. When she turned to assist him, they collided.

His hands went to her waist. "Sorry, it's this...blindness."

"Think nothing of it. I understand." She set her hands on top of his then stepped back. Dropping his one hand, she guided him into the house, holding his other.

"How did you manage to get out here on your own?"

"Well, um...it wasn't easy."

"I would guess not."

They arrived in the parlor, and she led him to one of the armchairs. He sat down.

"Da must have gone up to bed already. Mum is probably finishing the dishes. I'll see if she will accept my help while the water heats for my tea. Then I'll be back."

"I'll read while you're gone."

"You'll re—"

It took a few seconds, but then Renna realized he joked. Smiling, she made her way to the kitchen. Mum had all but a few pans to finish washing, so Renna dried the clean plates and put them in the hutch.

Mum lifted the basin and carried the water outside. Renna heard her dump it before she hung up the metal washbowl.

"Well, I think I'll call it a night." Mum removed her apron. "See you in the morning."

"Good night, Mum." Renna noted her mother's silent disappointment. Obviously she'd hoped Renna would take an interest in Mr. Benchley. But she didn't, and after Benchley's admission to enjoying the sport of gambling, Renna felt sure her parents wouldn't desire a match between them. Da probably shared Mum's discouragement.

*Good.* Renna made her tea. Maybe they'd stop husband hunting for her. She loved her parents, but their matchmaking had to cease.

Finding a wooden tray, Renna placed the teapot along with a cup and saucer on it. Next she carried it into the parlor.

"Are you sure you won't join me?" She set down the tray on the table in front of the divan, noticing Mr. Blackeyes—rather, Captain Sinclair, had stood. He wandered about the room, feeling his way around.

"No, thank you. I prefer coffee."

"Sometimes I drink a cup of coffee at the hospital. Here at home I prefer tea." She watched as he carefully picked his way back to the armchair and sat down. "You look troubled. Aren't you elated that you've remembered who you are and where you're from?"

"It's bittersweet, Renna. It's a relief to have that part of my memory return, but it bothers me that my name didn't appear on any list of dead or missing or in any obituary column."

"My father said a compilation of such lists takes time."

"But I considered myself an important man in Milwaukee."

Renna poured out her tea, unsure of what to say.

"I can only presume that I wasn't as important as I thought."

"No. Da had no name to look for. It was like searching for that proverbial needle in a haystack."

"I'm eternally grateful for his efforts. Please don't misunderstand me, Renna. I'm not feeling sorry for myself, exactly. I'm...humbled, really."

"I understand." Renna sipped her tea. "But it could be your family wasn't quick to declare you dead."

"I have no family, save for my children. Besides, my attorney would have had to make quick work of declaring me dead in order to see that my wishes for my children be carried out."

"I suppose that's how Mr. Benchley learned of his aunt's demise—through family."

"On the contrary. Elise had a household of staff. Her family resides in Michigan."

"Seems such an impersonal, even lonely existence."

He snorted a little laugh. "In some cases that makes life easier."

"Perhaps." Renna thought of her parents and their well-intentioned matchmaking. She didn't have to deal with meeting possible suitors during the war when she worked in Virginia. Then she thought of holidays and how this house seemed to come alive when her brother and sisters arrived with their spouses and children. Da often invited guests to join their celebration. Oftentimes they were people who had no one with whom to spend Thanksgiving or Christmas. "But that entity known as a family is so vital to one's being. Even if that family is made up of a close circle of friends. It's a part of you and influences your choices."

"Then my family was a detriment to me."

"Maybe so. However, you've said yourself that God has given you a second chance at this life. And your children…you must be eager to see them and let them know you are alive."

"Yes…" The captain paused momentarily before answering, "I can't wait to see them, but the sad truth is they may not be happy to see me." He stood and carefully picked his way to the divan.

She set down her teacup. "Here. Let me help you."

"I'll do this myself, Renna."

The warning in his voice held her in check. In seconds he found his way and sat down beside her. Next he reached for Renna's hand. His touch was warm as his palm folded around her fingers.

"I am not proud of the man I was before my accident. I've been thinking of all the wrongs I did, and I can't imagine how I'll ever make them right. My children may not want me back. I wasn't the best father in the world." He expelled a heavy sigh. "They needed so much more than I was capable of giving. Their guardian, Richard Navis, on the other hand, is a fine man and a devout Christian. Time and time again he tried to tell me about Christ and invited me to church. I didn't listen until the day of my accident. As I bobbed in the dark, stormy waters of Lake Michigan, fighting for my life, I prayed that if God gave me one more chance, I'd turn into a churchgoing man. I promised Him."

Renna smiled. "Looks like He took you up on your offer."

"Indeed." The captain nodded soberly as if realizing for the first time that a true miracle had occurred.

"But now what of Matthew Benchley and his aunt's shipping company, Great Lakes Shipping?"

Her pirate shrugged his broad shoulders and released her hand. "I purchased it legally. Nevertheless, it appears I have a fight on my hands."

"A fight—and your life may be in danger too?" Renna shook her head. "Then you must stay here in Chicago."

"But my children—"

"Think of their safety. If someone attempted to kill you once, he'll likely strike again. You may unwittingly put your children in harm's way by going home."

"I hadn't thought of that." He pressed his lips together.

"And if you stay here with us, your children can make visits. You can reintroduce yourself to them so there will be no shock or ill feelings."

"Another good point." Slowly the captain nodded as a little smile worked its way across his shadowy face. "A reintroduction to my children. I like the sound of it."

Renna liked the sound of it too, selfish as she may be. But it seemed too soon for good-byes.

Still, she knew they were coming just as sure as the dawn.

# THIRTEEN

TUESDAY MORNING BRIAN SINCLAIR SAT IN THE SMALL bedroom that the Fieldses had afforded him and secretly penned a second letter to Richard. He could trust his faithful steward.

Which meant he might question the letter written by Renna. However, Richard would recognize his employer's handwriting.

Brian scribbled on. In his note, he divulged everything—that he knew who he was and that he could see. He explained about Renna and his feelings for her, whatever they might be. Then he went on to tell of his deception, something of which he wasn't proud. *But you must not let on that I can see,* he wrote. *For Renna's sake...and mine.*

Brian wrote of his misgivings regarding Matthew Benchley and explained in detail what had happened on the lake that fateful day. He instructed Richard to notify the authorities.

With the more important information out of the way, Brian proceeded to ask Richard to bring him some funds. He designated a generous amount for Dr. Hamilton and the hospital and, of course, the Fields family for their hospitality. Finally, he ended with, *And please bring me some clothes. Not to sound ungrateful, but I feel like some poor slob off the docks in the charity rags I've been wearing!*

Signing his name, Brian sat back on the bed, his back against the cold wall. He wondered what he should do about the children. Move back to Milwaukee and insist upon becoming a family once more? Or should he take Renna's advice and stay here and allow the children visits until they adjusted to his presence and until they knew whether Matthew Benchley posed a threat?

*Renna.* At the very thought of her, the corners of Brian's lips moved upward in a slow smile. Who did she think she was fooling, anyway? She didn't want him to leave, and truthfully, he didn't want to go. Nonetheless, he had his children to think about—and he so desperately wanted to make things up to them. He had always loved them, always wanted the best for them. But he'd been selfish, wanting to satisfy the desires of his own heart and hiring others to fulfill his responsibilities to his children.

A knock sounded at his door. "Captain, are you up and dressed?"

"Yes." He recognized Wendell's voice.

"Food's on the table and getting cold."

"Be right there." Brian swung his long legs off the bed.

"Do you need any help?"

"Um, no, I believe I can manage." He slipped the letter into its envelope. The trick would be posting it today.

Donning his dark spectacles, he left his room. In the kitchen Johanna Fields had prepared a breakfast of fried eggs, toast, and jam.

"Smells good." He pulled out a chair, realizing his blunder. *Oh, blast!* He wasn't supposed to be able to see the chair in front of him. He glanced at his host and hostess. They hadn't seemed to notice.

"Renna had to leave early this morning." Johanna set a plate of ham in front of him. Brian had to force himself not to snatch a few slices.

"Another twenty-hour shift?" In his week with the Fields, Brian had seen firsthand how hard she worked.

"Unfortunately, yes." Johanna came over with her cast-iron frying pan and scooped two fried eggs onto his plate.

"There ought to be a law," Wendell said, "against working a

person the way that hospital does. But I suppose one can't put a price on ministry."

Johanna served her husband and then sat down. Wendell prayed over the food. Afterward he explained to Brian that there were ham slices in front of him and eggs on his plate.

"They ought to outlaw the food they serve in that hospital," Brian remarked. "It isn't fit for animals, let alone humans." He turned toward Johanna. "My gratitude, madam, for your expertly prepared dishes."

He saw Johanna's cheeks pink. "You're entirely welcome, Captain." With that she poured him a cup of very strong-smelling coffee—just exactly the kind he enjoyed in the morning. "Now don't burn yourself," she warned. "The coffee is to your left."

"Oh, indeed, don't go and burn yourself, Captain!" Facetiousness filled his tone before Wendell dabbed the corners of his mouth with a checkered napkin. Then he grinned. "Renna would have a conniption if she found out we harmed her patient."

Brian pushed out a polite smile, although it bothered him to be referred to as Renna's "patient." Is that how her parents saw him? Only her patient and not a possible suitor?

*Suitor?* He shook himself. He'd gone crazy. That's what happened. He sustained more of a whack to his head than he'd first thought. *I'm a pirate who recently found God. What father in his right mind would consider me a possible husband for his daughter?* Brian sent a glance in Wendell's direction. He seemed caring but not overprotective. And Renna was hardly a child. *But I'm a man with a past…and four children.*

And what about his children?

Brian felt certain that Richard took good care of them. Would they be glad to hear their father was alive? He hadn't been much of a father to them. But if he did as Renna suggested…would it be right to continue deceiving her and her parents?

Deception had been part of his past. It didn't belong in his future.

"Is everything all right, Captain?" Wendell asked later as they rode in his buggy to the Chamber of Commerce building. "You've been awfully quiet."

"I don't mean to be. I've just been thinking."

"Hmm…"

Then, suddenly, Brian could stand it no longer. His conscience pricked and couldn't be ignored. "Wendell, you were honest with me once—about Renna and her birthmark. Now I need to be honest with you."

Wendell turned. "You mean you've been dishonest?"

"Yes."

A frown settled on his brow. "All right. Go ahead."

"I remember who I am."

"Really?" He turned, and the leather seat creaked with his movement. "That's splendid!"

"My name is Captain Brian Sinclair. I'm from Milwaukee, Wisconsin. It all came back to me in a rush yesterday."

"Brian Sinclair. Captain Brian Sinclair." Wendell wore a look of awe. "My, my, but I thought I had heard of you. Your name has come up at the Chamber of Commerce because of your business ventures. Renna will be delighted that you remember."

"Renna already knows. But I asked her not to reveal my identity."

"Why ever not?"

"In short, my life may be in danger. You see, I remember the boating accident. Every bit of it. And…well, it may not have been an accident at all."

"Not an accident?" Shock fell over his features. "So now what?"

"Nothing's changed, other than you know my secret too." Brian drew in a deep breath and let it out. He wondered about sharing his suspicion of Benchley. Wendell thought the other man a friend. Whose side would Wendell take?

The steady clip of horse hooves and the jangling of harnesses on the busy street filled the sudden silence. People called to one another. A woman swept the walk in front of a store. Smells of freshly baked goods hung in the air.

"Is that what you've been dishonest about?" Wendell turned to him again. "Your identity?"

"That's part of it. The other part Renna isn't aware of either." Brian paused to collect his thoughts. "Wendell, I'm not blind anymore. I can see clearly. I've been...*pretending.*"

"Pretending?" Wendell's jaw dropped, and he nearly lost his grip on the reins. "But why?"

Brian wetted his lips, unsure of how to explain. Finally he just blurted out the truth. "Because of Renna."

"What? I don't understand." Wendell brought his chin back, giving him a curious look. But then an expression of understanding washed over his features. "It's her birthmark, isn't it?"

Brian inclined his head. "She became so distant when she thought I could see, and I longed for her friendship." He looked at Wendell. "You were right. One hardly notices the birthmark at all. Renna is a lovely woman."

The man smiled broadly, but then it slowly slipped away. "I've told my daughter that a hundred times. But do you think she'll believe me, her own father? No!"

"And I didn't think she'd believe a pirate either." Brian sported a grin, thankful his host understood.

Wendell chuckled. "I understand now. And maybe it'll teach Renna a lesson." He sobered. "Have you prayed about this, Captain? Are you sure that playing in the shadows, as it were, is what God wants?"

Brian shifted uncomfortably in his seat. No, he hadn't prayed about his trick on Renna. Maybe he hadn't wanted to pray about it because he was quite certain God would not approve of the deception. He met Wendell's stare. "I know I have to be honest with her. I just want to be sure I've won her..." He cleared his throat, feeling somewhat intimidated to be discussing the matter with Renna's father. Seconds later he shook it off as ridiculous. "Oh, for heaven's sake, Wendell, we're both adults. I'm romantically interested in Renna."

"Is that so?"

Their gazes met, and even behind the dark glasses, Brian could see humor and pleasure glimmering in Wendell's eyes.

Then all at once Wendell turned serious. "Many a male patient has thought himself in love with Renna. She's told me about them. Apparently it happens frequently, but Renna guards her heart. Usually when the patient recovers, his ardor wanes."

"My feelings for Renna have only intensified. I've become something of a confidant to her, and likewise, I trust her with my secrets."

"Except for one."

"And you understand why I haven't told her that my sight has returned."

"Yes."

They rode in amicable silence for several minutes, and then Wendell turned to him again, this time wearing a serious, very fatherly expression.

"As a father, I'm concerned. You've got a reputation, Captain Sinclair, and I'm not blind either. I can see my daughter has feelings for you and that they go beyond the call of her nursing duties."

Brian fought a grin.

"That's why I pushed Matthew Benchley on her. I thought that if Renna had an interested suitor, she'd turn her attentions from you to him. From the day that you were brought into that hospital, half-drowned, my daughter became obsessed with your care. She had Johanna and me praying for your life and salvation. Even when our prayers were answered, I felt concerned about Renna's involvement with you, so I continued to invite Matt over for dinner."

"I wondered what you were up to."

"Yes, well, Matt is interested, you know. He just behaves strangely around my daughter. Can't figure out why. Perhaps he's trying too hard to impress her."

"Perhaps. But he's hardly a match for Renna. She's smarter than he is. She'd grow tired of him."

"Oh? And are you saying that you're the right match for my daughter?"

Brian pursed his lips. Was he? "I would like the chance to find out."

"Hmm, well, I don't believe a man and a woman can be friends, as you say. If you want my daughter's friendship and affection, Captain, you're going to have to court her properly."

"*Courtship?*" Brian almost laughed out loud. He was hardly a young swain seeking a child-bride.

However, he soon remembered that Renna hadn't ever been with a man. She was a good, decent, pure, and Christian woman. He, on the other hand, had been married to Louisa and, later, engaged to Elise—and those were only two of the women he'd known in his lifetime.

"All right. I'll go along with the courtship. There's just one problem. Renna thinks of me as her patient. She dotes on me like a mother hen. Do you think she'll consent to it?"

"She thinks you're blind and in need of her nursing abilities."

"But if I tell her the truth, she won't want anything to do with me."

Wendell frowned. "Hmm…yes, I see your point."

"I represent everything she's loathed in a man—and probably with good cause." Brian clenched his jaw. "But my new faith has made me a different man. I need Renna to give me a chance. Ironic as it sounds, if I'm blind, she'll see."

Wendell sat by silently listening.

Brian glanced to his right as they passed a millinery shop. "On top of that, I must battle her insecurities. Why is Renna so preoccupied with that birthmark anyway?"

"Oh, I don't know. Somewhere along the line she got the idea that she's not as pretty as other women. And while it's true that her birthmark is unusual, it's not as unsightly as she thinks."

"It certainly doesn't bother me." Brian thought she was beautiful.

"It doesn't bother Matt Benchley either," Wendell said as if to goad him.

Lifting a brow, Brian shifted his gaze behind his spectacles. "Whose side are you on, anyway?"

Wendell cocked a brow. "My daughter and a…a *pirate*. Imagine it?"

"I do. And keep in mind that I'm a *reformed* pirate," Brian said in his own defense.

Wendell chuckled. "So it seems."

"Besides, I'm a very rich reformed pirate."

"As well I know. But so is Matt Benchley—rich, that is."

"So he says." All humor left him. Brian didn't trust the man. But he trusted Wendell Fields. Seemed now was as good a time as any to voice his concerns. "Do remember when I told you that I had been engaged to be married, but that my fiancée drowned the day of the accident?"

"Yes. Such a terrible shame."

"Horrible." Brian's heart ached at the way he'd used her. "That woman's name was Elise Kingsley, and she just happened to be Matthew Benchley's aunt."

"You don't say!" Wendell's eyes widened. "What a coincidence!"

"Is it?" Brian shook his head. "I'm not so sure."

"What do you mean?" The older man's brow puckered.

"Something happened that day out on the lake." Remorse filled him. "I saw the storm coming. I'm well seasoned. I knew enough to get my schooner and the souls aboard it into safe harbor. But I couldn't. Something was wrong with the vessel's rudder, making steering it impossible."

"Well, Matt would hardly have anything to do with malfunction of a rudder."

"Maybe. But maybe not." Brian wetted his bottom lip. "But Benchley had good cause to want his Aunt Elise dead. He stood to inherit her shipping company—except I had already purchased it."

Wendell gasped. "You!"

"That's right."

"You're the one!"

Brian nodded. "But I beg you not to reveal my secrets. Benchley must not know that I have regained my sight. I feel my life depends on it. And Renna has to believe I'm still blind."

Rubbing his hand over his jaw, Wendell nodded. "All right. I can keep your secrets. For a time, anyway. But if I'm asked outright, Captain, I can't lie."

Brian considered his new friend. Far be it for him to insist that Wendell violate his conscience. "Fair enough. Thank you."

They rode for another block in silence.

"Captain, do you really believe Matt is capable of...murder?"

"Obviously I do." Raising his chin, he gazed at the road ahead. "But we won't do anything just yet. It's business as usual. The truth will come to light. In other words, if we give Benchley enough rope, I believe he'll hang himself. In fact, Wendell"—he glanced his way—"I'm counting on it."

# FOURTEEN

"WHAT'S WRONG, MY LITTLE WREN? YOU'VE MOPED AROUND all weekend, and your disposition hasn't changed after a Sabbath and a good night's sleep. Something's troubling you. What is it?"

Spoon in hand, Renna made swirls in her porridge. "It's nothing. I–I'm just tired, I guess." She found it hard to eat breakfast when the sun hadn't yet risen. With the first of October came a later dawn. "It was nice of you both to get up with me this morning." She managed a smile for Da and then Mum. "But we'd best keep our voices hushed so we don't awaken the captain. Besides, I must be off to the hospital soon."

"You work too hard. I wish you'd take some time off for yourself." Beneath the dim light of the lantern, Renna saw Da frown. "Either that, or demand shorter hours."

"I've made that very request several times. But my request fell on deaf ears. Nurse Rutledge called me selfish and pointed out that it's not like I have a husband and children to care for." The remark broke Renna's heart. "My life's work needs to be the hospital."

"Why, that miserable old—"

"Da, please!" Renna quickly lowered her voice.

He pressed his lips together.

"No wonder you look discouraged, dear." Mum gave a slight wag of her head. Her hair was still tied in rags.

"Well, I'm strong. I'll persevere. I always do." Standing, Renna cleared her place. She now wished she wouldn't have shared so much of her heart. But since she had, she figured she might as well be completely honest. "Nurse Rutledge called me into her office Friday, and both she and Nurse Thatcher scolded me for getting too personally involved with my patients. They referred not only to the captain but also to a young woman who's been very sick—dying, in fact—who wanted me to write a letter for her. How could I refuse? I sat with her for quite a long while. That's why Nurses Rutledge and Thatcher were miffed."

"I'm sure I would have done the same thing." Mum sipped her coffee.

"I believe nursing goes beyond seeing to a patient's physical needs." Renna cleared her dishes. "It's seeing to their spiritual and emotional needs as well. However, my superiors don't agree, and they reprimanded me for taking care of my patients the way I believe is honoring to God."

"Would you like me to talk to them?" Da offered.

"No. It's best to leave it alone, I think. If you talk to them, they'll only get angrier and treat me worse than they already do."

"Oh, Renna, I'm so sorry you're facing such persecution."

Renna noted Mum's frustration, but it couldn't begin to match her own. Nevertheless, she had to remember that God was in control of every aspect of her life. "It'll all work together for the good, I'm sure."

She gathered her shawl and the colorful shoulder bag Elizabeth had sewn for a birthday gift. In it Renna carried a book, some peanuts, and a change of clothing should she be unable to leave the hospital tonight.

With a weary wave Renna bid her folks a good day and left the house. The sun had just peeked its head up over the horizon as she began her trek to work.

※※※

Brian hated the boredom at the Chamber of Commerce, although Wendell found small tasks for him to do—like counting the bottles of ink and the number of pens in the department. He felt his way around the three rows of desks, and if he came up short, he made note to order more. What more could a blind man do?

Except he wasn't really blind, and the charade grew tiresome.

Sitting down in a wing-backed chair in Wendell's office, he wondered for the umpteenth time if he'd made the right decision by staying here in Chicago. The question haunted him. The desire to see his children and get back to his own business wasn't easy to quell.

But then he spied Benchley through the glass window, and his hackles went up. For a clerk he wasn't often at his desk. Instead he lurked. Something definitely wasn't right about him, and God forbid Brian endanger his children as well as Richard and Sarah and maybe even their families. As it was, Brian feared for the Fieldses' safety. However, Wendell assured him God would protect them.

Brian believed it. However, he also felt a strong prompting to stay put. He wanted to keep an eye on Benchley without him knowing that he was watching. The man enjoyed pumping Brian for information, to see if *poor Captain Blackeyes's* memory had returned. Brian suspected that once Benchley learned the truth, he'd make an attempt on his life. If he did, Brian would be ready.

Yes, he'd made the right decision to remain in Chicago.

He sat back in the chair, resisting the urge to read the newspaper on the desk. Blind men didn't read, and if Benchley caught him, he'd know the truth. That couldn't happen. Not now. Not yet.

Allowing his eyelids to flutter closed behind his dark spectacles, he wondered what was happening in Milwaukee. Why hadn't Richard responded yet? Nearly two uneventful weeks had passed since he'd sent the letter. With the train service between Chicago and Milwaukee, mail delivery was swift. Surely he'd received the missive by now.

An hour tickled by, and finally Wendell entered the office. "Time to call it a day, Captain."

*At last!*

Brian stood and let his friend guide him down the marble floor of the hallway and down the stairs. *Lord, I despise this charade.* He said nothing as they descended the stairwell. Once outside, they boarded the carriage, which Wendell had summoned from the stables, where it had been parked since this morning.

People crowded the wooden walks, shoppers and street venders likely on their way home or storekeepers who had closed up for the night. Buggies filled the white pine-blocked street. The clop of horse hooves echoed between the tall wooden buildings.

"What time is Renna expected home tonight?" Brian glanced at Wendell as the carriage jolted to a halt amidst the traffic then lurched forward again.

"I'm not sure. It all depends on whether the hospital is busy and if she's required to stay an extra shift."

Brian shook his head. "Nurses shouldn't have to work so hard and for such long shifts—especially when the said shifts are against a nurse's will."

"I agree."

Settling back into the black leather seat, Brian grunted out a laugh. "It won't be easy to court your daughter if she's never at home."

"A problem, to be sure." Wendell sent him a sideways glance. "Are you ready to tell Renna of your intentions to court her?"

Brian shifted in his seat. He still felt awkward with the notion of this courtship business. "What, pray tell, is the difference between courtship and pursuance? I believe I pursued my first wife and my fiancée."

"Hmm…good question." His older friend paused to ponder a moment. "In my mind courtship is more refined and courteous. Less dogged determination."

"All right. I can step back and be nonchalant."

"Well, no…" Wendell cleared his throat. "Let me put it this way. Courtship is buggy rides on a Sunday afternoon as opposed to cocktail parties every night of the week."

"Ah." A wry grin tugged at half of Brian's mouth. "I believe I understand now."

They shared a laugh, and for the remainder of the ride home, they exchanged tidbits about their day at the Chamber of Commerce. Brian realized his mood had lightened considerably.

Arriving at the Fieldses' cozy home, he climbed from the buggy. Wendell came around and gripped his elbow in a dutiful manner.

"Now close your eyes, Captain, so you'll stumble up the stairs a bit in case someone might be watching."

"Wendell, I cannot stand this game of pretend a moment longer!"

"Now, there, Brian, we've discussed this and determined you must keep it up—at least for now."

"I know…"

They entered the house, and a tantalizing aroma wafted to Brian's nose. Seconds later, Johanna Fields met them. Brian noted, and not for the first time, how much Renna favored her mother in hair color and stature, although she'd inherited her father's keen green eyes.

"Dinner's ready. I made a beef stew." Mrs. Fields wiped her hands on her checked apron.

Brian's stomach rumbled with hunger as he shrugged out of his coat. How he wished Richard would answer his letter and wire funds. His clothes were a sorry fit, although he was grateful to have them.

Wendell took his arm and led him to the supper table. When Mrs. Fields disappeared through the doorway connecting the dining room and kitchen, he let go.

Brian pulled out the chair and sat down. "This is ludicrous," he whispered. "We should at least tell your wife that I can see."

"She'll tell Renna." Wendell took his place at the large round oak table covered with a tablecloth. He placed a linen napkin across his lap.

Minutes later Mrs. Fields reentered the dining room, carrying two plates on which bowls of steaming stew had been placed. "Here you go, gentlemen." She placed the food in front of them then left to serve herself. As always, they'd wait for her before praying over their meal and beginning to eat.

"If I beg her not to tell Renna and explain why—"

"I don't think that would be wise."

"Are you telling me she can't keep a secret?"

"Yes, she can. But—"

"Wendell, I need a safe place where I can be who I am. Someplace where I can sit and read the paper. Or the Bible. A place where I don't have to close my eyes while I'm eating so I appear blind and helpless."

His friend sighed.

"Nevertheless, I promise to take care while Renna is at home, which, may I remind you, isn't often."

"You needn't remind me of that." Wendell frowned at the circumstance. "Still, I don't know. I can't say that I like the idea."

"What idea, dear?" Mrs. Fields returned with her plate and bowl of stew along with a basket filled with freshly baked rolls. She set down her burdens before taking her place at the table. She peered at her husband askance.

A look of resignation fell over Wendell's countenance. "Let's pray. After we're finished eating, the captain can tell you his news, Johanna."

"But you don't think it's a good idea?" She looked wounded.

"Yes, but I will allow Brian to explain why." Wendell looked his way. "I don't like secrets."

"Nor do I." Brian shook out his napkin then laid it across his lap. "But keeping a few seems imperative." He managed a smile at Mrs. Fields.

"I assure you, Captain, I'll guard the news you share with me."

"Thank you." He removed his dark glasses.

With all heads bowed, Wendell gave thanks for their meal. Afterward, Brian lifted his knife and fork and began slicing a piece of beef. He forked it and a piece of potato into his mouth. Chewing, then swallowing, he looked directly at Mrs. Fields. She met his gaze.

"This is delicious," he told her.

"Why, thank you, Captain." A blush entered her cheeks.

He helped himself to a roll, split it, and added some butter. He noticed Mrs. Fields's jaw begin to slack.

"Why, you can see, Captain!"

"Yes, I can." He smiled.

"What wonderful news. When did it happen? Today at the commerce building?"

"Actually, it happened the day I came home from the hospital. But I've feigned blindness because..." He glanced across the table at Wendell, who appeared preoccupied with eating his meal. "Mrs. Fields," he began again, "the truth is, I'm interested in courting Renna. But I'm afraid to tell her I can see because I fear she'll reject me."

"Because you're not blind?"

"No. Because I've remembered who I am. My name is Brian Sinclair, and I hail from Milwaukee, Wisconsin, where I own a store and, most recently, a shipping company. I'm very wealthy, Mrs. Fields, and I've been accustomed to the best and finest of all things. Renna despises the kind of man I am—or rather who I was."

"Oh..." Her hand flitted to her throat. "Then my small home

and meals like this stew must seem so beneath what you're accustomed to. I apologize."

"On the contrary. I have never felt so at home as I do here, even in my own house in Milwaukee. Your meals are delicious. So are your baked desserts. In fact, I'm hoping you baked another apple pie."

She smiled. "Yes, I did."

Brian smiled. "Now, getting back to my secret, Renna is very insecure. She doesn't believe herself good enough to become my wife because of her birthmark and the differences in our social classes. Personally, I don't give a whit about either. And I think Renna is beautiful. I don't notice her birthmark anymore. But they matter to Renna. However, as long as she thinks I can't see and that I need her, she enjoys my company. I'm hoping to tell her the truth soon because I sense she has feelings for me that go beyond a good nurse and her patient."

"Captain, I would agree." Mrs. Fields nodded. "And, yes, Renna is insecure, as you said." She drew in a deep breath. "Her father and I have tried everything—"

"Please. There is no need to explain. It's nothing you did or didn't do. I have seen her insecurity play out with my own eyes. However, I believe with my help she'll overcome it. There's a reason God put me in Renna's care—and not just for my benefit."

Johanna Fields's frown of concern disappeared. "Do you really want to court Renna? Are you in love with her?"

"Johanna!" Wendell squared his shoulders.

Brian chuckled and covered Mrs. Fields's hand with her own. "I see where Renna gets her straightforwardness." His smile lingered. "And, yes, I think I just may be in love with your daughter." Removing his hand, he sat back. "But I must know for sure. I can't say I've ever been in love, even though I've been married and engaged to be married for a second time. I need to find out what these feelings are that I harbor for Renna. Courtship is what your husband has insisted upon." Brian caught Wendell's eye and arched a brow. "I think I'm beyond the years of courting a woman, but I will comply with his wishes."

"Oh, I think that's wonderful!" Mrs. Fields clapped her hands together in glee.

"But it's a secret for now, Johanna," Wendell reminded his wife. "You cannot tell Renna that the captain can see. Furthermore, Brian must ask Renna if he can court her."

"I won't say a word." She grinned like a satisfied mama feline.

Brian stifled his amusement. "But there's another, more pressing reason that I've hidden both my blindness and my identity, although Renna knows who I am. I asked her to keep it quiet for now. I've been a pirate in more ways than one. I can't say that puts Renna off. She's very forgiving. But she's averse to the fact I'm a wealthy widower who has known beautiful, rich women."

"Renna feels she can never compare."

"Oh, but she outrates them. I wish she would understand that."

"I do too, Captain, but it doesn't help that Renna was snubbed by a wealthy lieutenant in Virginia during the war."

"She was?" Wendell brought his chin back. "I didn't know about that."

"Renna felt too ashamed to tell you, dear. And the incident heightened her feelings of insecurity. Now, she not only believes a handsome man could never love her because of her birthmark, but she also thinks a wealthy man would never love her."

Brian heart crimped, and he wanted to punch that lieutenant right in the nose!

Again, he covered Mrs. Fields's hand. He smiled into the older woman's eyes. "With your permission, I'd like to dispel such a myth."

"Permission granted." A smile shone from her eyes.

"But for now, no one must know he's Captain Brian Sinclair from Milwaukee," Wendell said. "His life may be in danger. Brian suspects someone tampered with his ship and that's the reason he couldn't get to shore before the storm hit on that tragic day more than a month ago. If he's right, whoever did such a deed is a murderer."

"Oh, my!" Her brows drew inward, and her lips pressed tightly together.

"But please don't be afraid, Mrs. Fields." Brian couldn't bear to be the one to put fear into the older woman's heart.

"God will protect us, Johanna." Wendell took a bite of his stew.

"You're right. He will. He always has." Smiling, she lifted her fork. "Captain, your secrets are safe with me."

"Thank you.

She began eating her meal, and Brian took note of the Fieldses' calm and confidence. It seemed contagious, and moments later, Brian sensed that God would work everything out. His hosts were safe in God's hands—and so was he.

~~~

Richard Navis leafed through the missives on Captain Sinclair's large oak desk. The correspondence had piled up in his absence. He and Sarah had married on the twenty-ninth of September and taken a weeklong honeymoon at the Dells in Kilbourn City, a village on the Wisconsin River and a popular vacation spot. Richard was glad he'd selected it. He smiled to himself, recalling how the wild and romantic scenery had provided a much-needed respite for both himself and Sarah. Here at home, Sarah's parents had minded the Sinclair children, seen them off to school, and visited Richard's folks on the farm over the weekend. All had gone well.

But now, back from his brief honeymoon with his new bride, the burdens of his roles as business owner and guardian of four children fell on him anew.

As he sorted the mail, one envelope in particular caught his eye. It was addressed to him, although he didn't recognize the sender's name.

Breaking the seal, Richard suspected the news was business-related, but as he read on, a paralyzing sense of shock gripped him.

September 25, 1866

Dear Richard,

I'm writing to you via my nurse and friend, Miss Lorenna Fields. Since the accident, I've been in a Chicago hospital suffering from a head injury and the effects of amnesia. Only recently did my memory return. However, my vision remains impaired. Nevertheless, I am alive and I have God to thank for it!

"Sarah!" Richard didn't even glance up from the captain's post as he called for his wife. When no answer came, he realized she was upstairs with the children. Quickly reading the rest of the letter, he exited the captain's office, Reaching the banister, Richard called to his wife again. "Sarah!"

Moments later, she leaned over the top of the railing and smiled. "You bellowed, my beloved?"

Under normal circumstances, Richard would have grinned at the retort. "Come down here. Quickly. You've got to read this to believe it."

He heard Sarah's skirts rustle as she made her way down the stairs. "What is it?" Concern etched her lovely features.

Richard handed her the letter. "Read this."

She did, and the color drained from her face. "He's...*alive*?"

"Apparently so."

"It can't be." Her blonde head snapped up, and her blue eyes darkened with suspicion. "This is a horrible prank, meant to upset us. Look. The author of this missive asks for clothing and funds."

"Because his were lost in the lake during the storm."

"But it can't be possible. How could the captain have survived while the others didn't? Besides, the author of this note thanks God. Why, Captain Sinclair never thanked God for anything, let alone his existence."

"Sarah, you're right on all accounts, but I think the matter is worth investigating."

"But I...you...the children..."

Richard enfolded his wife into a snug embrace. "Don't worry, Sarah." It's all he could think to say. He shared her feelings of shock and disbelief.

For more than a month now, they had been mourning the captain's death, handling his business affairs, caring for his four children. The fact that the captain named both him and Sarah as guardians in his will had spurred them to marry quickly. And now to learn the captain wasn't dead...

Or was he? Maybe this letter was, as Sarah said, some twisted mind's idea of a joke.

"If he is alive..."

Pulling back, Richard stared into Sarah's upturned face. "Yes?"

"Will you be sorry you married me?"

He laughed. He couldn't help it. "You're kidding, right?"

"Well..."

"Sarah, how could I ever regret making you my wife?" He meant what he said too, even though he knew she had once held a flame for the captain, tiny flicker that it was. "And what about you? Will you have regrets?"

"None whatsoever. No one could ever love me as much as you do."

"And I do love you, Sarah."

Her eyes darkened with sincerity. "I know." As she gazed up at him, a pretty pink blush entered her cheeks. "I love you too."

Inhaling deeply, Richard wished they were alone right now so he could show her how much he loved her…again. But he had work to do. So did she.

Sarah's gaze moved to letter. "Should we tell the children about this news?"

Richard shook his head. "Not just yet. I'd like to do some checking first."

"You know…he'll want them back—the children. Except they won't want to go. They want to live on the farm. With us. Why, we're preparing to sell this house. We wanted to move before the holidays. It's all planned that the children will attend a new school at the first of the year." Sarah stepped back and glanced around the captain's mansion. "Gabe and Michael are just beginning to adjust—"

"Except those two boys never believed their father drowned in the first place."

Sarah's shoulders sagged forward. "Yes, you're right."

"Sweetheart, don't fret." He kept his arms around her waist, enjoying the feel of her so close to him. "God loves these children even more than we do. As with everything, we'll just have to trust that His ways are best."

Somewhat reluctantly, Sarah nodded. "It's a good thing we held off on selling the house and the captain's store and newly acquired shipping company. And you, Richard, are the one who has been marvelous at keeping up the books and running his businesses. I hope the captain finally appreciates you."

"He always has in his own way." In spite of the circumstances, Richard couldn't help but grin. "I wonder what the captain will have to say about my marrying his children's governess."

Sarah smiled at his teasing. "And don't forget you allowed his housekeeper, Mrs. Schlyterhaus, to go with my brothers Luke and Jake to the Arizona Territory."

He felt a twinge of insecurity. "Envious?"

"Not a whit." Sarah smiled. "But you're in trouble. Marrying me and letting Mrs. Schlyterhaus go."

"Hmm, but perhaps the captain won't remember that he had a governess and a housekeeper." He arched a brow. "The letter states he's suffered from amnesia and that only some of his memory has now returned."

"Amnesia...yes, I suppose that does explain why it's taken a month to hear from him." Sarah wore a concerned frown. "The poor man. He never did have a good memory."

"No, he never did." Richard sobered and reread the rest of the letter. "It also states that Captain Sinclair is blind. Another consequence of the head injury he suffered. It's unknown if the damage is permanent at this point."

"Oh, mercy! What are we going to do?" A frown furrowed her brow. Then she massaged her temples. "It's all so overwhelming. The captain...alive but physically and mentally impaired. What does that mean for our future?"

"I don't know." Richard couldn't help placing a kiss on her sweet lips. "But I plan to find out."

# FIFTEEN

THE MID-OCTOBER SATURDAY ARRIVED AS A PERFECT FALL day, blue skies, a light wind, and the treetops aflame with color. Renna enjoyed a reprieve from her nursing duties. She spent the morning at the market, purchasing fresh vegetables for their Sunday dinner, then helped her mother tidy the house. The men stayed occupied, and Renna was glad to see that her father and Captain Sinclair were getting along so well. In the last two weeks the captain had settled into a routine and become quite independent. Nevertheless, she still felt that he needed her too. He seemed to need this family, for he was making great strides in his recovery—except for his blindness. Renna had thought the temporary setback would have corrected itself by now. Even Dr. Hamilton was stumped by it.

Around midafternoon a hard knock sounded at the front door, and Renna answered it. A young man, blond and blue-eyed, stood before her.

"Is this the Fieldses' residence?" He politely removed his hat.

"Yes." Renna's first thought was that the hospital had sent a messenger to fetch her for duty. She tried to suppress the rising dread of going in today.

"I'm Richard Navis. I'm here to see Captain Sinclair."

Renna inhaled sharply. "Yes. Of course. The captain's mentioned you quite frequently."

"All in a good light, I hope."

"Of course." She beckoned him inside and took his overcoat. "You must have received the letter."

He nodded as his gaze quickly took in his surroundings. "A charming home."

"Thank you." She faced him. "I'm Renna Fields, and I'm pleased to meet you."

"Likewise." He gave her a friendly smile.

"Allow me to show you into the parlor." She led him a ways down the hallway. "Make yourself comfortable. I'll fetch Brian, um, I mean the captain, for you." She felt her face flush from the informality. "Please, make yourself comfortable."

Mr. Navis smiled again and took a seat.

Renna hurried out to the backyard and into the stables, where she found her father and Brian working on one of the horse's harnesses and having a lively political debate. However, they stopped when they saw her coming.

"What is it, Renna?" Da straightened. His light blue shirt was stained with perspiration.

"There's a visitor here for the captain." She stepped in beside Brian. "Mr. Richard Navis is here to see you. I'll guide you inside."

"Richard? That's wonderful!" Instead of taking her arm, he reached for Renna's hand and tucked it around his elbow. "I guess I need an escort. Blind men need escorts, don't they?"

Da snickered, but Renna didn't know why. "What's so funny? I'd planned to assist you into the house."

"Well, then, lead on."

As the walked to the house, Renna was sure he could feel her heart banging inside her rib cage. Would it soon be time to say good-bye to her pirate?

Inside, Mr. Navis's face split into a broad grin when he saw him. "Captain Sinclair! It's so good to see you! We thought you were dead!" Mr. Navis shook his hand heartily, but then embraced him in all his exuberance.

"It's good to see you too—" The captain paused. "Well, you know what I mean. I'm blind. It's good to hear your voice."

Pulling back, the younger man frowned slightly. "Sir, I'm sorry to hear about the loss of your sight."

Brian cleared his throat. "No need for sorrow, Richard. I've had excellent care."

Renna felt his hand go to the small of her back. Embarrassed, she glanced at the carpet. "I only did my job." That wasn't exactly true. It had been her pleasure to care for her pirate.

"Well, it was a fine job, Renna, and I'm indebted to you and your family."

*Is this good-bye?*

She glanced up in time to see Brian's warm smile. Then he turned his attention to Mr. Navis. "I hope you brought me some clothes, Richard."

"I did indeed. I brought you an outfit to wear home."

"*Home.* The word has a wonderful ring to it."

Renna's heart suddenly plummeted. Had Brian changed his mind? Would he leave with Mr. Navis and return to Milwaukee in a matter of hours? Minutes?

Suddenly it felt as though her whole world had come undone. "I'll leave you both to some privacy." With that she whirled around, tears blurring her vision, and hastened from the parlor.

"We thought you were dead, sir."

Brian bobbed his head a few times. "I'm sure my letters came as quite the surprise."

"Yes, particularly the second. I found it in the stack of mail on your desk just minutes after I found the first letter."

Brian removed his dark glasses. "Thank you for keeping my secret from Renna."

Richard rolled one broad shoulder. "You've always been able to trust me, sir. You still can."

"I know—and I'm grateful." Beneath one arched brow, Brian

peered at his steward, who hadn't changed a bit in the last month. With straw-colored hair, intelligent blue eyes, and a strong young body, Richard had been only sixteen years old when Brian hired him. A few years later Brian had paid Richard's way through business school. And then last August, before the accident, he'd shamefully coerced Richard to sign a contract binding him into an indefinite service, something he knew now that he needed to rectify. It hadn't been fair. He'd all but threatened Richard—with Sarah.

Brian settled into a chair, gesturing to Richard to do likewise. "How are my children?"

"Adjusting, but they are all well." Richard crossed his legs. "We've kept them in the same school as opposed to moving them to the farm, and the children have continued to live in the home they've always known. We decided that the less change for them, the better."

"We?" Brian regarded him askance. "You and Sarah?"

"Yes. She never returned to Missouri and has been loving and nurturing to the children. But I must say, I think she's disappointed."

"That I'm alive?" Remorse surged through him. He hadn't exactly endeared himself to many individuals, Sarah in particular. He'd trifled with her emotions solely because he could.

"She's disappointed because suddenly she was a mother and now suddenly she's not."

"Understandable." Brian gave the situation a moment's thought. "I imagine she's been a very good mother too. She's always loved my brood. That's why I wanted her to sign on as a permanent governess."

Richard rubbed his jaw. "Sir, Sarah and I married a couple of weeks ago. You see, your attorney had you declared dead. We read your will, and—"

"No need to explain." Brian grinned wryly. He'd known all

along that Richard and Sarah were perfect for each other, thus the reason he'd changed his will in August and named them both guardians.

Standing, he reached for Richard's right hand and gave it a firm shake. "Congratulations."

"Thank you, sir." Richard appeared rather chagrined. "I hope you don't mind, but we've been living in your home—for the children's sake."

"I don't mind—and you can stop calling me 'sir.'" Brian narrowed his gaze. "You're about the best friend I've ever known."

Richard blinked as if covering his emotion. "I've thought of you as my friend too, and I can tell you that I've been…mourning. I had a rough couple of weeks after the accident. I wasn't myself."

"I appreciate your sentiments, Richard." Brian folded his arms and leaned back against Wendell's oak desk. "Tell me, did anyone show up for my funeral?"

"We actually didn't give you a funeral, sir. I mean, Captain."

Brian tossed a glance upward and grinned.

"Gabriel and Michael refused to believe that you perished in Lake Michigan, mostly, we thought, because your body never washed ashore like the others."

Brian winced and thought of his mother, her friend, and Elise Kingsley.

"We held a beautiful service for Aurora, though, and it was well attended. However, Gabe threw a fit when we suggested even holding a memorial service for you. All this time your sons have maintained you were alive."

Pride and pleasure stole over Brian's being. "I'm speechless." He turned his head toward the bookcase.

"Gabe and Michael keep saying you just forgot to let us know your whereabouts." Richard chuckled. "It seems they're right."

"My amnesia." With a nod, Brian admired a few volumes on Wendell's tall bookcase before gazing back at Richard. "And what do they say now that they've been proved correct?"

"We haven't told them yet. I was skeptical about the letters. I guess I wanted to see you in the living flesh before I made the announcement."

"Very wise." Brian approved of the decision. It would have been senseless to upset the children all over again if the letters had been a hoax.

But they weren't. This wasn't a hoax. Brian was very much alive. What's more, he wanted his children with him.

"I'm sure it'll be a shock when I walk back into their lives."

"I'm afraid it will be, especially for the girls. They've become very attached to Sarah—and she to them. Nevertheless, I'm prepared to take you home today, if you'd like."

Brian pursed his lips, thinking. "I don't want my homecoming to be a traumatic event for my children. They've been through so much, what with Louisa dying just before last Christmas, all the governesses who've come and gone, and the death of their grandmother, not to mention my disappearance."

"I must admit, Captain, you're right. The children have been through their share of upheaval. Of particular concern is how unemotional and detached both Gabe and Michael have behaved since your boating accident."

"Unemotional? Detached?"

"Like they don't care, sir."

*Maybe they don't.*

Brian's heart twisted. He hadn't been a father. He realized then that he had much to prove to his sons. "I'm a different man, Richard, and I want my children to know it." He didn't care for the look of disbelief that briefly wafted across the younger man's face.

Brian figured he had a lot to prove to Richard also.

"I'm taking Renna's advice. I've decided to proceed slowly where my children are concerned and remain in Chicago for a time."

Richard gave a single nod. "As you wish."

"Now, let's discuss my business." Brian rubbed his palms together. "I'd like to begin by telling you about a man named Matthew Benchley and the reason everyone must continue to believe that I've lost my sight."

A mischievous glimmer shone in Richard's blue eyes. "I'd rather hear about you and Miss Fields. She seems like a lovely person. "

"A truly lovely person."

"Not your usual choice of women, if I may say so."

"You won't be the first, I'm sure."

"Do you see in her a mother for your children? Because if that's all you're after, then Sarah and I would like to—"

"Richard, I don't intend to use Renna like I've used people in the past. I really am a different man."

Richard said nothing.

Brian understood why. "Let me start at the beginning, from the morning of the day of the accident…"

~~uuoxleee~~

"I've set aside some food," Mum said, "even though our guests said to go ahead and begin our dinner."

"Good idea." Renna peered at the ivory face of her locket watch. "They've been talking for more than two and a half hours."

"They'll come out when they're ready." Da folded his hands and bowed his head. "Let's pray."

After he asked the blessing on their meal, Mum talked about the picnic basket auction coming up at church.

Renna hoped she was scheduled to work that day. She lifted her fork and pushed the buttered squash around on her plate. Normally she loved the vegetable, but tonight she couldn't seem to even choke down a single bite—not with her pirate soon to be walking out of her life forever.

Da buttered a warm, flaky biscuit. "Stop your fretting, my little wren. Brian will finish his meeting soon enough."

"I just can't figure out why the men are discussing matters here. There would be plenty of time for discussion on the train ride back to Milwaukee." Renna dared to hope Brian hadn't changed his plans.

"I'm sure much of the discussion surrounds his children," Mum said.

Of that, Renna had no doubt.

"Yes," Da agreed, "he's concerned about their welfare—like any good father."

Renna had to smile, recalling the time that her pirate admitted he wasn't a good father at all. But with God's help he could turn the matter around.

Da spoke her thoughts. "I often remind Brian that he's been given the chance to start all over. He can, as the apostle Paul said in his letter to the Ephesians, put off the old man and put on the new."

Renna wondered, *Would he?*

Minutes later, Brian and Mr. Navis entered the dining room.

Mum stood. "Can you stay for dinner? We just began."

"Yes, thank you." A grateful grin split Brian's face. "Wendell, Mrs. Fields, I'd like to introduce my steward and good friend, Richard Navis."

"A pleasure." Mum lifted a hand, indicating a chair. "Please be our guest at the table."

"Yes, have a seat. It's good to finally meet you." Da wore a smile. "Brian has told us many good things about you."

"Thank you." Richard inclined his head politely to Mum and then walked the short distance to grip Da's hand in a friendly shake.

Renna pushed to her feet and helped Brian to the table. Next she hurried into the kitchen to help Mum serve up two more plates. She carried them back into the dining room.

Mr. Navis bowed his head in a quick prayer and then forked

some veal and gravy into his mouth. "Mmm, delicious. My compliments, Mrs. Fields."

"Thank you, Mr. Navis, but Renna made dinner tonight."

He glanced her way and grinned. "Do you enjoy cooking?"

"Yes, actually."

Mr. Navis bobbed out a reply that seemed approving.

Renna smiled, although the question burned on her tongue. Would Brian walk out of her life tonight? Tomorrow?

Small talk ensued, but Renna paid little attention. After dinner they moved to the parlor, where a fire blazed in the hearth, lighting the room with glowing warmth. While the weather today had been mild, temperatures dropped as the sun set.

Mum and Renna put off serving dessert and coffee just yet at Brian's request. Once everyone was seated, he stood to his feet and adjusted his dark spectacles. "I'm sure you're all wondering over my intentions. First of all, I'd like to thank you all for your generous hospitality."

Renna steeled her heart for what was sure to come next.

"Words cannot express my gratitude, and neither can monetary means. However, I would like you to have this—"

He nodded at Mr. Navis, who pulled out an envelope, thick with national bank notes. He handed it to Wendell.

"Oh, no, I can't accept your money, Brian."

"You must, or I will be deeply offended."

"But…" Da counted the bills. "Brian, this is an outrageous sum!"

"Take it, Wendell. I always pay my debts, and I feel I owe this family a large one."

"Nonsense."

Mum suddenly stood and walked over to where Da sat. Taking the envelope from him, she tucked it into the folds of her full green and blue plaid skirt. "Thank you, Captain. This money will be put to good use." She glanced at Da. "There's a family at church, the Reeds, with eight needy children. We'll consider it a privilege to help them out."

"Oh…the Reeds…" Da gave a nod. He obviously hadn't thought of sharing the funds. "Yes, and I guess we have a few needs here too." He smiled, looking chagrined. "Forgive me, Johanna, for being so prideful."

Bending over, she kissed the little bald spot on top of his head. "All is forgiven, dear."

Renna smiled at her parents, then lowered her gaze to her hands, folded in her lap.

"Well, I'm glad that's settled." Brian grinned and squared his shoulders. "And I've decided to take Renna's advice and stay on a while. Due to the circumstances surrounding my boating accident and because of the situation with my children, I think it's best. Richard agrees. In addition, my life may still be in danger. Richard alerted authorities after hearing from me last week and will speak with them in depth when he returns home."

"Stay as long as you'd like, Brian." Da gave him an easy smile. "And, Mr. Navis, you're welcome to spend the night and attend church services with us in the morning. I believe there's an afternoon train back to Milwaukee."

"Yes, sir. That would be great. Thank you."

*And thank You, Lord,* Renna prayed. Brian wouldn't be leaving just yet!

He lowered himself into one of the armchairs. "Again, you have my thanks as well. And I'd like my children to visit next Saturday."

"That would be lovely," Mum said. "We'd enjoy meeting them." She snapped her fingers. "Next Saturday's the autumn festival at church—to raise money for the soup kitchen. I'll be selling apple pies at a booth, but there's lots of things for children, like the carousel and games galore." Mum regarded Brian with a little gleam in her eye. "Come and bring the children. Perhaps if they associate a fun outing with seeing their father again, you, Captain, will be a few steps ahead in reuniting yourself with them."

"The children love festivals." Richard grinned and glanced at Brian. "It's a good idea."

"They love festivals, eh?" Brian wagged his head. Remorse filled his being. "I never knew that."

"It's not too late to learn that and more about your kids, Captain."

"Thank you, Richard. You're right."

"And plan to spend the night here," Mum said. "It's all too much for one day."

"I'll plan on it. I'm sure Sarah will be delighted to meet you all."

Brian rubbed his jaw. "I hope she'll be able to forgive me."

"She will—and she does."

"Might I ask why forgiveness needs imparting?" Mum's brows knitted together in question.

Renna knew the answer, but it was for Brian to tell.

"Dear lady, I'm afraid I did a terrible thing this last summer. I sported with Sarah's emotions as a way to manipulate her into staying on as my children's governess. She'd only been hired for the summer. So I wrote a poor recommendation to the music school here in Chicago at which Sarah hoped to teach. I purposely dashed her dreams, for which I'm as sorry as I can possibly be."

A moment of silence passed in which Renna felt proud of Brian. It took a brave man to admit such a wrongdoing.

Mr. Navis cleared his throat. "The letter worked out well for me," he said with a wry grin.

The tension abated at once. Renna saw her folks and Brian smile.

"Renna, can you beg off of work next Saturday?" Da asked.

"I'll try. If nothing else, perhaps I can leave early." Oh, how she hoped Nurse Thatcher and Nurse Rutledge would give her the day off!

"I want you to meet my children, Renna."

"And I want to meet them. Here's hoping my supervisors will cooperate."

"We'll pray to that end," Mum said. "Now if you'll excuse me, I'll bring in our dessert and coffee."

"I'll help you, Mum."

Making her way to the kitchen, happiness rose up inside of her. Her pirate wasn't leaving. Not yet. She still had time...

But time for what? Time to hope a man like Brian Sinclair would fall in love with her? The very thought was ludicrous and virtually impossible. Brian was accustomed to having women around him who were ten times more beautiful and sophisticated than Renna could ever hope to be.

No. She must stop her fanciful ideas now while she could. Her pirate would leave sometime. How foolish to imagine such fairy-tale-like endings. Perhaps Nurse Rutledge and Nurse Thatcher had been correct, that she got herself too personally involved with her patients. She'd only get hurt—they both said so.

But too late. It seemed her heart had already made up its mind.

# SIXTEEN

RENNA WORKED THE NEXT EIGHT DAYS STRAIGHT AT THE hospital. Three of those days were comprised of eighteen-hour shifts. Her stern superiors knew her former patient's children planned to visit, and they not only denied her a day off but also lopped on extra work in order to teach her not to become too attached to her patients. Renna still fumed at Nurse Thatcher's antics. But by Sunday night, Renna could barely form a thought—which she'd decided was good thing. Thinking this past week not only caused her a good amount of frustration, but it also made her heart ache, because each time her pirate came to mind, so did her birthmark.

*If you continue in My Word,* that still small voice seemed to whisper in her ear now as she made her way home, *you shall know the truth and the truth shall make you free...*

"Well, good evening, Renna—or should I say good morning? It's midnight."

Renna started at the sound of the hushed male voice. She stood in the hallway between her father's study and the parlor, her wrap hanging loosely around her shoulders. "What are you doing awake? You should be sleeping."

"So should you." Brian stepped out of the shadows.

Renna leaned back against the wall. "We've been busy at the hospital...and shorthanded."

"Well, your excuse is better than mine. I just have insomnia tonight."

"I'm sorry to hear that. Would you like me to make you an herbal remedy?"

"No, thank you." He stepped toward her. "But I wouldn't mind company. Would you like to share the last of the firelight with me?"

"I don't think I'd be very good company. I was just trying to gather my strength to go upstairs to bed."

Brian moved forward and helped her off with her wrap. Just when she was about to ask how he knew to politely assist her, he stumbled loudly before hanging it on the wooden rack near the front door. It pleased her to see how well he'd been adapting to his disability while she'd been so busy this last week.

Brian turned back to her and held out his hand. "Why not gather your strength by a warm fire?"

Renna considered him. Even through her weary eyes, Captain Brian Sinclair made a handsome sight. He wore his own clothes, which fit him much better than the old charity garb. A crisp, white shirt was tucked into suspendered black pants.

"Renna?"

Mentally shaking herself, she accepted the offer she didn't have the energy to decline. His large palm felt warm as it covered her hand. Suddenly she realized how cold she was.

In the parlor darkness shrouded all but the golden hearth. An opened Bible sat on the coffee table in front of the settee. "Was my father reading to you tonight?"

"Um...well...about that, Renna..."

"Saint John, chapter eight." She viewed the page at which the Bible had been left open. "Was that the reading tonight?"

"Yes."

Renna studied the words, and the last part of verse 32 seemed to jump out at her: "...the truth shall make you free." With a heavy sigh, she sat down on the settee beside Brian. Her conscience pricked her. She should tell him about her birthmark and spare him—and her—further wasted time.

"You missed meeting my children."

Renna noted the disappointment in Brian's voice. It matched her own. "I know, and I'm so sorry."

"You've been so busy and gone so much." He sounded dismayed. "They work you too hard."

"I'm aware of that as well." Renna felt the physical effects taking their toll on her body, mind, and spirit. She smoothed back a lock of hair, more than glad that Brian couldn't see it. Under her cap for days, it needed a good scrubbing. "Tell me, how are your children faring?"

Brian blew out a weary-sounding sigh of his own. "My girls, Libby and Rachel, were frightened of me. They wouldn't stay here, so Richard and Sarah took them to the hotel to give them some space to…recover. They wouldn't warm up to me in spite of the fact that Richard and Sarah had tried to prepare them and we attended the autumn festival as planned. But it didn't help."

"I'm sure that had to be difficult."

"Yes, it was. The only bit of good I gleaned is that Richard and Sarah seem very happy together."

Renna noticed the lilt in his tone. "I'm glad." She smiled. "But you knew they would be." She wished she could have met the woman who married the quick-witted steward.

"Yes, well, I didn't anticipate my sons' reaction to me nearly as expertly. Michael, my ten-year-old, kept his distance, and Gabriel…" Brian left his son's name dangling.

"What about him?"

"He's my oldest son and he hates me. He said he hates me."

"No!" Renna drew herself back.

"It's true."

"I'm sure those words must have wounded you terribly. But he can't mean them."

"He does. I'm afraid he means every syllable." Brian picked up her hand and turned it in his much larger one in a way that made Renna believe he could actually see her rough, dry skin from giving so many baths and shaves, not to mention all her hand-washing. "Renna, I don't know what I would have done without you all these weeks."

"You were in God's control the entire time."

"But He set me in your care, and you were more than my nurse, Renna. You were—you are—my friend."

"I only did my job." Renna slowly pulled her hand free, wondering if things might have been different if she'd been here to meet his children. If they liked her and had seen that she was fond of their father, perhaps...

"You did more than your job, Renna." His voice sounded as rich and velvety as Mum's chocolate cake. "My children's disappointing reactions might have devastated me if I couldn't rely on our friendship."

His admission both pleased and frightened her. "I'm honored to be your friend, Mr. Pirate Blackeyes."

He chuckled, although the smile began to slip from his face. "I would like to be more than—"

"Don't say it." She stood.

"What's wrong? Have I misinterpreted your feelings somehow?"

Renna peered at him from over her shoulder. "You noticed?"

He grinned and lowered his gaze. "Renna, you're very transparent."

She worked her lower lip between her teeth, aghast that she hadn't sufficiently covered her emotions.

Brian only laughed. "Come back here and sit down."

She stood statue still.

"Come here. I'm not as much pirate as you think."

"I shouldn't..."

"I'm asking you. Please."

Renna swallowed hard as Brian moved to take hold of her elbow and bring her in beside him.

"Let's talk about our feelings once and for all. I've had to do some heavy soul-searching this weekend, what with my children here."

Feelings, Renna could handle. It was the admission about her birthmark that she struggled with. She knew she should tell him about her appearance. And, again, she heard her conscience say, *The truth will make you free...*

"First, I have a confession, Brian."

"You?"

"Yes." Her heart seemed to bang against her rib cage. "I'm not the woman you think I am."

Sitting back against the settee, he frowned slightly but appeared unconcerned. "Oh? How's that?"

"Well, you said that I was...beautiful. But I'm not." She paused then pushed the words out in a rush. "I'm blemished by a large purple birthmark. It's an unsightly thing—it even clashes with the color of my hair." She chanced a look at him, noting that he didn't seem appalled—yet. "People give me curious glances everywhere I go." Renna forced herself onward. "I doubt a man of your caliber should be seen with a woman like me. It could ruin your social standing and affect your influence with prominent people."

She held her breath, wondering at his reaction.

"Hmm..." Brian sat by, momentarily pensive, wondering how he should reply. Renna was both right and wrong. Wrong, because his influence had never been based on appearance but on money. The social standing part might have been a legitimate concern at one time. Now, however, Brian couldn't care less what others thought. "Renna, it's true that in the past I made friends according to how they might profit me. But I'm a changed man. God spared my life for a reason."

"I don't doubt it."

"Then believe me when I say that your birthmark makes no difference to me." He felt Renna stiffen beside him.

"It'll make a difference to others, and you'll be subject to ridicule if you're seen in public with me."

"What others might say or think will not intimidate me." Brian considered her for a long moment. He had to admit the fact that he was romantically interested in a woman at all was sure to make the society page of the newspaper in Milwaukee. He knew the local gossips could be vicious.

Oh, well, he'd just have to make sure he protected Renna from all that. And he could.

Suddenly he wondered if he ought to be honest with her too. Perhaps now was the perfect time to tell her that he wasn't blind and that he'd seen her every expression and that she was, most certainly, beautiful in his eyes.

Then, thinking better of it, he decided to use the situation to his advantage.

"Renna, are you ashamed to be seen with me?"

"What? Why would I be ashamed?"

"Because I'm blind. What will your friends think? What's more, my disability may burden you."

"Never. And no friend of mine could ever shame me for falling in love with a blind man." As she realized her admission, her cheeks flamed a deeper crimson than Brian had ever seen.

He chuckled softly under his breath. "Renna, the same is true for my friends. No true friend of mine is going to look on you and judge you to be any less of a person because of your birthmark."

"And you don't mind that it's there?"

"No."

"But you haven't seen it."

"I have a very good imagination."

"Oh." She lowered her gaze.

Brian grinned at her reaction before growing serious again. There was one thing he had to be boldly honest about with her.

"Renna, there is something I'm struggling with, and you should know."

"What is it?" She met his stare and expectancy shone from her green eyes.

"After being around your family, and then after hearing Richard and Sarah together—well, I want to believe that two people really can fall in love and live happily ever after. I guess I do believe it's possible now, whereas I didn't before. I've witnessed it. However, I've never experienced it for myself." He paused momentarily to collect his thoughts. "I guess what I'm trying to say is, will you be patient with a pirate like me who's trying to figure out if he's in love with you?"

Renna sucked in a breath, obviously taken aback by his candidness. But then her features softened, and that sweet, gentle expression of which he'd grown so fond replaced her surprise.

"You're a worthy pirate, all right." She smiled. "I'll have no problem being patient."

"But you can't treat me like one."

"Like one…what?"

"An invalid. I am not your patient, Renna, so don't treat me like one. I'm a man, and I don't want to be coddled."

"But you're blind."

"And I'll have to learn to deal with it like a man."

She peered down at her hands, folded in her lap. "I'm a nurse, and I only wanted to do my job."

"You've done a fine job. I doubt I'd be alive today if you hadn't taken pity on me from the beginning. But now I'm getting stronger, and if I need your help in the future, Renna, I shall ask for it."

She lifted her head, looking so hurt that Brian felt tempted to apologize. He wondered if she were going to cry. Oh, a woman's tears—Brian had seen a million of them. A sea of them! Was

Renna going to use tears as a form of manipulation to get her way? To make him feel guilty for his honesty?

Much to his relief, she was made of stiffer stuff. She turned back to him, appearing as tired as she said but no worse for wear. "Your request is not unreasonable," she stated at last, "and I'll try to refrain from…*coddling* you."

"Thank you." He smiled. "My children could use the coddling, though. I want your help, Renna, in winning them back."

~~ee9xeee~~

He needed her. No wonder her birthmark didn't make a difference to him. He probably didn't expect to be able to attract anyone worthwhile as a blind man. Or perhaps he thought someone would try to take advantage of him as he had done to others over the years. In any case, it wasn't love. He'd said as much. He didn't believe in romantic love. Could she stand a marriage based on need?

Renna stood. "I have to think about this."

"Think about it?" Brian slowly got to his feet.

"Yes. Now, if you'll excuse me, I must turn in. I'm nearly delirious with fatigue."

"Quite understandable." He cleared his throat. "I suppose the proper next step would be for me to speak with your father."

"Yes, do."

Brian walked with her to the stairs. "Good night, Renna." Taking her hand, he pressed a kiss onto her fingers.

Her heart skipped a beat, and Renna was glad her pirate couldn't see the tears that formed in her eyes. "Good night."

As she walked up the steps, a heavy veil of despair fell over her. What if they did marry and he gained back his sight? Would he want her then? Could any man, aside from Da, love her for who she was, birthmark and all?

## SEVENTEEN

Renna, I'm afraid I had to put my foot down this afternoon," Da said.

Darkness shrouded the small foyer as Renna shrugged off her coat and hung it up. She'd put in another eighteen hours at the hospital and felt numb from exhaustion. "What on earth are you doing still awake?" she asked her father.

"Waiting for you, of course."

"It's nearly one in the morning."

"I'm well aware of the fact." He inclined his head to Brian, who stood from the armchair in which he'd been sitting. "Brian was good enough to keep me company."

"Good evening, Renna, or more accurately, *good morning*."

She sent him a smile she knew he couldn't see. "Hello, Brian." She filled her gaze with the sight of him. Renna had thought her reason would have returned by now, but seeing him so close, darkly handsome beneath the dim lamplight, made her realize how much she missed him.

Renna forced her feet farther into the parlor. "Now what's this, Da? Putting your foot down...where?"

"You are working too much, my little wren. Things cannot go on as they are."

"It can't be helped. Nurses Rutledge and Thatcher—"

"Aren't human, I don't think." Brian sat back down.

"Oh, they're human. They're lazy and jealous of Renna."

She'd wondered that very thing, although she couldn't think of why the two women would be jealous. The laziness she'd seen.

"I'll say this—" The sternness in Da's voice matched the frown furrowing his brow. "I had made up my mind that if you weren't home in another hour I was going to fetch you myself!"

"Oh, Da, I was at the hospital and perfectly safe."

"You're overworking yourself, Renna, and you have been since you returned from the military hospital eighteen months ago. I'll not have it anymore. You have no time for church, your family, or your friends."

Renna leaned against the doorframe and exhaled audibly. "And what do you propose?"

"Well, I spoke to Dr. Hamilton about it this afternoon."

"You spoke to him?" She straightened. "What did he say?"

"Dr. Hamilton said you're free to take a sabbatical."

"I can't." She shook her head, thinking of her patients. They needed her, depended on her. Just like Mr. Blackeyes had.

"You must take some time off, or you'll burn out like an old candle, Renna. Why, just look at yourself. You've got dark circles under your puffy eyes."

"Da!" Renna's hands flew to her face. She was only too glad her pirate couldn't see.

"Someone had to step in. As your father, I felt it was my duty."

"I'm not a child, Da." Although Renna had to admit that, at the moment, she felt like an old, burnt-out candle. "But I suppose a few days off will do me good."

"More than a few days, my little wren. Dr. Hamilton agreed to allow you the rest of the year."

"What?"

"This way you can enjoy the upcoming holidays and not worry about being scheduled all the time."

Disbelief caused her head to spin. He'd never interfered in her life like this before. "But Da—"

"No arguments." He stood and came toward her. "Brian needs

our help. He's got a noble mission of winning his children back, and I've promised we'd do whatever we could to assist him."

Anger flashed inside of her. "I see." So he'd enlisted her parents' help in getting her to go? She sent him a glare that he couldn't see.

"Brian needs our help, so he's asked us to take a holiday and spend a month in Milwaukee with him. We'll celebrate Thanksgiving with him and the children. Won't that be a treat? Your mother is quite enthusiastic about it since we haven't been on a holiday in years."

"Seems it's already been decided." Renna could barely contain her anger. Her father had meddled not only in her personal life but also her professional one. She turned away and stared at the porcelain figurines on the sideboard. If only Brian believed in true love, then she might be willing. But it seemed so pointless.

Brian's voice broke in for the first time. "Renna, I shared our last conversation with your father. You might say I made my intentions known."

"You did?" Excitement and dread mixed with confusion filled her being. She kept her back to him and Da, recalling how Brian asked her to be patient while he determined whether he loved her. She agreed to it—before realizing his intentions were misguided.

Or were they?

Brian crossed the room. Standing behind her, he set his hands on her upper arms. "I pray you haven't changed your mind, Renna."

His voice, so low and husky near her ear, sent shivers down her neck and spine. This pirate had stolen her heart, all right. "No, I haven't changed my mind." *But I should*, she silently added. They couldn't be happy without love as a foundation.

She turned quickly and found herself practically in his arms. Her gaze went from the top button of his waistcoat to his shadowy jaw then finally his unseeing black eyes. They seemed to bore right into hers, keeping her transfixed.

"I'd be terribly disappointed if you had a change of heart."

Renna's lips moved, but no words came out as she stared up at him. She'd never stood this close to a man under nonmedical circumstances. And that she'd somewhere, somehow fallen in love with this particular man made his nearness a veritable thrill.

As if he'd divined her thoughts, an amused grin turned up the corners of his mouth. Next he lifted her hand and placed a kiss on her fingertips.

"So there, you see?" Da came around Brian. "This holiday is quite necessary."

Renna felt her face heat with an embarrassed blush. She'd forgotten her father was in the room. This pirate made her take leave of her senses!

Slowly she pulled her hand free.

Brian chuckled before turning to Da. "It gives you good reason for investigating my household, Wendell."

"Ah, yes, something like that." Da sent Renna a good-natured wink.

"Investigate all you want. Hopefully Richard will have rehired all the needed household staff. I'm grateful he is still so willing to help me after everything that happened this summer." Brian took Renna's elbow and led her to the place on the divan closest to the glowing hearth.

"What kind of household staff do you have?" Renna wanted to know, although she suspected she already did. How could she possibly fit into that world?

"In the past, I've employed only two live-in employees: a house-keeper and a governess. The others, like my cook Isabelle, go home to their own families at the end of the day. I never cared for an overabundance of live-in household staff. One tends to lose his privacy that way."

Renna nodded for lack of a better reply.

Then, suddenly, she remembered. Something extremely important. How could she have forgotten? "What about your life being in possible danger?"

"I am in as much danger here as I will be in Milwaukee. Besides, the authorities have been alerted. They're investigating the boating accident."

"I'm glad to hear it."

Still, Renna couldn't shake her frown. "I worry about you, Brian. If there truly is a person trying to take your life—someone who's responsible for the deaths of three other individuals, including your own mother—well, you're helpless to see him coming."

"I'm not as helpless as you may think."

"What do you mean? You're blind."

"Renna, a man either believes that God is in control of everything, or he believes God is in control of nothing. Under your father's tutelage, I've come to believe God is in control of the very next breath I take."

Renna believed that too.

"Besides, I manned a gunboat on the Mississippi River during the war. My crew and I saw plenty of battles." He was grinning straight at her now. "I can handle Matthew Benchley."

He'd made his case. Renna's confidence in him was restored.

"If the murderer is indeed Matt"—Da wore a pained expression—"I don't want to believe he's involved in anything illegal. He seems like such a fine man."

"By day I would agree with you, Wendell. And maybe I'm wrong. Time will tell. What does the Bible say—something about our sins finding us out?"

"The passage is in Numbers, I believe." Da appeared pleased. "Be sure your sin will find you out."

"Right," replied Brian, looking rather proud of himself for remembering.

However, no one could have been happier than Renna. Her pirate had just put his small bit of biblical knowledge to practical use.

"It won't be long before Benchley is found out—if he's guilty, as I suspect he is."

"So what do you say, Renna?" her father pressed, changing the subject now. "It's late and I'm tired. We need your answer now. A holiday in Milwaukee? How about it?"

"Sounds nice." She felt mesmerized by Brian's close proximity as he sat beside her on the divan, so it was easy to push aside all apprehensions. She knew what sort of man Captain Brian Sinclair was—a very rich, high-society man and one who could charm the thorns off a rose. He'd soon discover that she didn't belong in his world.

It was a shame that he couldn't stay in hers forever.

∼ellXlee∼

After a second day of shopping, Renna looked around her bedroom, shaking her head in amazement. Store-bought dresses lay everywhere, ten of them. Da had been so proud to buy them for her, and he'd purchased nearly as many for Mum. However, Renna thought such extravagance could be better spent on medical supplies—although Brian did make a generous donation to the hospital. She smiled inwardly. What would Nurse Rutledge and Nurse Thatcher have to say about him now? The obstinate blind man in Renna's ward turned out to be a very wealthy shipping magnate from Wisconsin.

Renna glanced at the list Brian had given her earlier. "This is practically indecent," she muttered.

"A dress?" Her sister Elizabeth stroked the pile of silk, velvet, and satin. "Which one?"

"No, no. Not the gowns. This list! Imagine having to own all these dresses just because of receptions and balls."

"You do own them. What's to imagine?"

Mum laughed softly at Elizabeth's quip. Her mother's and sister's exuberance actually pained Renna. She knew they both hoped this holiday would end with a marriage proposal and the spinster nurse would marry the rich, handsome captain. However, it was quite common for men, suffering with serious trauma, to fall in love with their caregivers. As soon as they healed, their ardor waned. It would be no different with Brian when he regained his eyesight.

"Oh, Renna," Elizabeth said, "this is a blessing, not a curse. I mean, I wish I could afford store-bought dresses like these, not that I don't get one occasionally. It's just more economical for our family that I sew all our clothes."

"Most everyone does, these days," Mum said. "Only wealthy people can afford an entire wardrobe from Palmer's."

Renna blushed. "I'm not wealthy."

"Well, your father's not a pauper either."

Pressing her lips together she realized she'd insulted her parents. Da had spent almost all the funds Brian gave him on clothes for himself, Mum, and Renna so they'd look every bit as respectable as the dignitaries in Milwaukee. But more than that, Da wanted to show Brian that he wouldn't be marrying beneath him if he wedded Renna.

Her breath caught. But if Brian regained his sight, this holiday could end in sheer humiliation for all of them.

"Oh, Mum, I don't want a holiday in Milwaukee with Brian." She tossed his list aside. "I've changed my mind."

"He needs us, Renna."

With a sigh, she supposed he did. She recalled how he'd asked for her assistance. Matt Benchley could be a threat to Brian's existence. Renna would have to be his eyes and keep a lookout. What's more, Brian longed to win his children back. And what of his sons? At ages ten and eleven they could pose a great threat to their blind father. Why, they might even try to injure him if, indeed, they resented him as Brian feared.

"Well, I suppose…if he needs us…I'll go."

"That's the spirit." Mum smiled.

Renna hated feeling so indecisive.

"Oh, it'll be fun. Just think of all the interesting people we'll meet." Mum sent a merry glance toward Renna and Elizabeth.

But dread overcame Renna. Brian would require her presence at all the social functions. She couldn't compare to the beautiful women who'd likely be in attendance.

Picking up a dress from the bed, she began to pack her trunk. *Lord, Your Word says You see me. You formed me in my mother's womb.* With her back to Mum and Elizabeth, she blinked away sudden tears. Surely the Lord wouldn't allow her to suffer more ridicule. She'd battled it her entire life—except at the hospital. When she nursed men and women back to health, her appearance didn't matter.

Perhaps, then, that's the mind-set she should have. Focus on others and care for them. Brian and his children. Marry Brian if he proposed, and become a mother for his children. That's what he had asked her.

Every part of her being cried out in protest. When Renna married, she wanted to be a wife. She wanted love and happiness.

"I really don't want to go." She plunked down on the edge of the bed.

"It's not like you to be so wishy-washy, Renna." Elizabeth sent her a quizzical look.

Renna touched her cheek with her birthmark.

"So that's it!" Elizabeth put her hands on her curvy hips. "Your birthmark. You feel inferior."

"Oh, now, Elizabeth, don't start scolding me."

"Well, I will. Why not just let go and be yourself. Show the captain and his friends that certain pluck you have. Show them the Renna we, your family, know and love. And if they can't accept you in Milwaukee, you still have us. You'll always have us."

Suddenly touched by her sister's words, Renna fingered one of the lacy flounces they'd purchased. "Thank you, Elizabeth. I love all of you too."

Mum peered at Renna and smiled tenderly. "You see, dear? What have you got to lose?"

*My heart!* Renna wanted to scream as she let the lace slip from her fingertips. *My very heart!*

# EIGHTEEN

THE SHOPPING AND PACKING LASTED THROUGH THE WEEKend. Finally Monday came, and Renna and her parents, along with Mr. Pirate Blackeyes, boarded the train to Milwaukee. Renna couldn't help using her pet name for Brian. Certainly he'd become a new creature in Christ. His thoughts reflected the change, and Renna marveled whenever Brian shared them with her. Nevertheless, his pirate name seemed to suit him at those times when he appeared so darkly handsome that it made her pulse race.

"So you still think I'm a pirate, eh?" The train rocked them back and forth as it chugged north toward the Wisconsin border. Autumn colors still flamed the treetops, looking like a patchwork quilt made of orange, burgundy, and gold pieces.

"Well, you're reformed for the most part." She couldn't help teasing him. "But I'm sure you've got a speck of pirate in you." Renna glanced ahead. Her parents sat a few seats away. Looking back at Brian, she smiled.

A grin tugged at the corners of his mouth, and his eyes seemed to behold her behind his dark eyeglasses. But of course he couldn't see her. "Then I'll be sure to show you a pirate's good time in Milwaukee."

Renna feigned a gasp and covered her mouth with one gloved hand. "You'd better not."

He laughed in a rakish way, and the woman sitting across the aisle turned and gave them both a curious stare.

Renna nudged him with her elbow. "Now you did it." She

leaned closer to him. "There's a woman across the aisle with a large golden feather in her green felt hat. She's overheard us, and now she knows you're a pirate too."

"I stand corrected, Nurse Fields." Brian changed his tone. "From now on, I shall keep my voice down—especially when we're speaking of my identity as a…a *pirate*."

"Good." She returned her gaze to the book in her hand. She hadn't read a single word since opening it. How could she with Brian so near—and pestering her the entire trip?

The easy banter continued for the rest of the way. Finally, after four hours of travel time, the conductor made his way down the aisle. "Milwaukee!" he called. "All for Milwaukee!"

Renna's stomach fluttered with nervousness. "Brian, do you think your children will like me?" Oddly, she hadn't felt overly concerned with his children until now that the time to meet them was at hand. But Renna had always loved children. She appreciated their honesty and innocence, and she took it for granted that she and Brian's children would become fast friends. However, a small seed of doubt still plagued her. "I do want your children to like me."

Brian gave her a sad smile. "I have a feeling they'll like you a lot more than they like me—especially the boys. The girls I think I will win in time. But my sons…"

"Your relationship with them is important to you, isn't it?"

"Extremely important." The downward angle of his mouth conveyed his remorse. "I have an entire decade to make up to them."

Renna put her hand on top of his. "We'll fix it, Brian. I'll help you." She could win his children—to herself, to Christ, and to their father. "By the grace of God, I'm going to help your children discover what a wonderful man their father really is."

His smile grew as he captured her gloved hand in his. "By the grace of God, Renna, I hope you succeed."

Adjusting her bonnet so it hid much of her cheek, Renna looked up in wonder. The Sinclair mansion stood three stories high against the backdrop of a crisp October sky. Renna thought it made an ominous sight if she'd ever seen one. The home had been constructed in red brick, its porch encased entirely in terra-cotta, and the massive oak front doors had lead glass panels covered with wrought iron grillwork.

Renna breathed an awestruck sigh.

"Do you like it?" Brian tucked her hand around his elbow.

"I…well…it's very…um…"

He chuckled and correctly guessed her thoughts—as usual. "It's not as imposing as it looks. Trust me."

"Captain, this is the most impressive home I've ever seen," Mum said, while Da stood by, nodding.

"Thank you."

"And the view of Lake Michigan is quite beautiful, Brian." Da looked out over the gray-blue water. Whitecaps rolled to shore on gusts of wind.

"I agree. That's why I chose this very location on which to build this home." He turned and inhaled deeply. "The fresh lake air is exhilarating, and yet I'm close to downtown and my store and shipping company."

"I'm looking forward to the tour." Da rocked on his heels.

"Of which? My home or my business?"

Da appeared momentarily chagrined. "Your home, of course, sir."

Brian laughed again. "Let's go in, shall we? Our luggage will be delivered shortly."

They walked up the steps. When they arrived on the front porch, the large doors of the manse swung open, and Mr. Navis greeted them.

"Welcome home, sir!" He smiled at the Fieldses. "Welcome to Milwaukee and the captain's humble abode."

"Humble, indeed," Da quipped.

"Thank you, Richard," Mum said.

They moved into the grand foyer, and Brian held out his hand. "You've done over, above, and beyond the call of duty here—as always—and I appreciate it immensely." He turned to explain. "I may have mentioned this in bits and pieces. For the children's sake, my attorney petitioned the courts to declare me dead so their guardians could be named. I'd chosen Richard and Sarah."

"The captain is a wise man." Richard grinned and puffed out his chest.

"Or a crazy one."

It seemed incredible that Brian could sense Mr. Navis's reactions.

"I also appointed Richard to oversee my affairs, along with my trusted attorney, of course. They deemed it in the children's best interest to remain here in the house until next year, when they planned to move to Richard's parents' farm. My children have always loved it in the country."

"And they're there right now, sir. Sarah and I left them in my folks' capable hands until tomorrow. This way you and the Fieldses will be able to get settled."

Brian's shoulders sagged as if in relief. "A good decision. I'm grateful."

As the men talked, Renna's gaze wandered around the magnificent vestibule with its terrazzo floor. Oil paintings hung on the papered walls. Renna smiled, thinking Mum looked speechless.

Brian suddenly shrugged out of his overcoat.

"Here, allow me hang up your wraps." Richard held out his arms.

"This is the kind of house I've only walked by and marveled at from a distance," Mum said. "Even some of the more elegant functions I've attended because of your business endeavors, Wendell, were never held in a home of this magnitude."

"I'm glad you like it, and I hope you'll soon feel right at home here."

Renna caught Richard's wry grin. Why did he appear so amused?

At the sound of light footfalls, Renna turned to see a lovely fair-headed woman coming down the front staircase. Her smile seemed tentative. "Hello, Captain Sinclair."

"Sarah." Warmth entered Brian's tone. "I've told Richard that I'm indebted to both of you."

"We're just…glad that you're alive, sir." Sarah turned to Renna. Her bright blue eyes silently appraised her but didn't linger on her birthmark. Sarah held out her hand. "I'm Sarah McCabe—"

Richard cleared his voice loudly.

"—Navis." She fought back a laugh. "I've been married less than a month, and I'm still adjusting to my new name, although I'm proud to have it." Her gaze sailed to her husband, and the pair exchanged adoring smiles.

Renna decided she liked Sarah already. "I'm Renna Fields, and these are my parents, Wendell and Johanna."

Sarah gave a polite curtsy. "Pleased to make your acquaintance."

"Renna and her family have been instrumental in my recovery," Brian added.

"It's a blessed relief, Captain, that you didn't turn up like the others." A pained shadow fell across Sarah's pale features.

Richard was at her side in a flash. "This is a happy day." He hugged Sarah around the shoulders, and she seemed to muster a smile.

"Well"—the captain brought his palms together and turned the subject away from himself—"I understand I no longer have a housekeeper."

"Partially so, Captain," Richard said. "Mrs. Schlyterhaus's last letter stated that she's enjoying her visit in Missouri. She and Sarah's brothers, along with others, will journey west come next spring."

"Hmm…" Brian straightened his russet-colored waistcoat.

"She, um, doesn't want to return, sir."

"Then I won't insist upon it. Gretchen deserves happiness like everyone else."

Richard and Sarah glanced at each other. Renna thought they seemed surprised by Brian's reply.

"But not to worry, Captain," Sarah said.

"Right," Richard announced briskly. "I managed to hire another housekeeper. Her name is—"

"What's goin' on in here?" A wiry little woman entered the vestibule at a breakneck pace. "I may not know much about la-de-da livin', but I know you don't leave company in the front hall, grand front hall as it may be. Guests are to wait in the main reception hall—and shouldn't I be the one to answer the door?"

Brian drew in a slow breath. "What have you done, Richard?" His voice was just above a dark whisper.

"Well, um…" Richard smiled, looking a tad less confident than Renna had ever seen him. "This is Hester, Captain. Your new housekeeper."

"Captain? Captain?" Hester moved toward him so quickly that she threatened the chignon sitting precariously on top of her graying, light brown head. "Welcome home, sir." She took hold of Brian's hand and shook it vigorously.

Renna swallowed a giggle and noticed that Sarah was hard-pressed to contain her smiles too.

"I'm pleased as punch to meet you, Captain Sinclair," Hester prattled on. "Why, this job is the biggest blessing I've had all year. I lost my beloved husband eighteen months ago, and I was in sore need of a job and a place to live. Had to sell the farm, and my kids are all grown and gone." Hester wiped a sudden tear off her cheek. "I just don't know what I would have done if Mr. Navis here hadn't approached me after the morning service a few weeks ago." The woman managed a tiny smile. "But he did, and here I am!"

"A pleasure to meet you...Hester." Brian gave her a slight bow, and Renna was proud to see him act so gallantly toward the less-than-sophisticated housekeeper. Nonetheless, his disappointment showed. No doubt Brian had wanted his housekeeper to be high-bred, at least in the way of household staff.

"Now, come out of this front hallway at once!" Hester smiled at Renna, then her parents. "Lemme show ya to your rooms. Why, put 'em together, and they're bigger than my farmhouse was!" Her light laughter echoed through the foyer as she beckoned the Fieldses up the front stairs.

Renna moved to follow her parents, but Brian caught her hand and pulled her up beside him. "What do you think?" he whispered. "About Hester? Do I need to interview other candidates for a housekeeping position?"

Renna momentarily fretted over her lower lip. Brian was asking her opinion on the housekeeper? What should she tell him? She had no experience in these matters.

"Renna," Brian insisted, "I want your heartfelt opinion, that's all."

"All right. I think you ought to let her stay. Give her a chance." Renna smiled up into his dark glasses. "There's something about Hester that's unpretentious and endearing. I like her."

Brian straightened to his full height of more than six feet, looking suddenly as imposing as his home.

"She's very quick, Captain," Richard added. "Hester had this whole house clean in a matter of hours."

"And she loves the children," Sarah said. "She plays games with them and teaches them funny tricks. They like Hester too. They call her 'Granny Hester.'" Sarah shook her blonde head. "For some odd reason, the boys think the word 'Granny' is hilarious, and Hester wears the title proudly."

"My sons never had a granny before." Brian turned to Renna. "I believe I told you that my mother insisted upon being called her by her first name. She was incensed by the idea of grandmother-hood."

"Yes, you said your mother was very unconventional." Renna had a feeling he missed his mother regardless of her eccentricities.

"Well, in Hester you've got a granny, a governess, and a house-keeper all in one." Richard wore an enterprising grin.

Renna raised her brows. Sounded good to her—but what did she know?

"You really want her to stay, Renna?"

"It's not up to me, Brian."

"Cast your vote."

"All right, then. Hester stays."

"Then, that's my decision too. Hester may stay on as my…housekeeper. I'm uncertain about the granny and govern-ess roles as of yet."

If Brian hired a nanny, he'd have no need for Renna, really. Meanwhile, she sensed his reservation regarding Hester. Renna could only imagine what all Brian's elite friends might have to say about the lowbrow servant on his staff.

And what about her? Renna wondered if they'd take one look at her, with her birthmark, and then at Hester, with her flash-fire efficiency, and they'd think Brian's head injury damaged more than his sight. His friends would think he'd lost his very mind!

Sarah managed to pry Renna out of Brian's grip. "Come with me, Miss Fields. I'll show you to your room. You must be tired from traveling."

"Thank you." She glanced at her pirate. "Would you mind, Brian?"

"Go ahead. Richard and I have business to discuss anyway."

Glancing back at Sarah, Renna gave her a grateful nod and followed her up the front stairs. They traipsed down a long hallway and then turned to the left. Sarah opened the door to a bedroom with sunny-yellow walls. The curtains on the windows were made of thick ivory lace, as was the wide canopy covering the bed. They complemented the thick Lost Ship quilt, which looked so soft and inviting that Renna longed to curl up on it and go to sleep.

"This house has seven bedrooms," Sarah explained. "One suite-like room is on the third floor. It serves as Hester's quarters. The remaining six are here on the second floor. Those are the captain's chambers," she told Renna, pointing down another hallway. "The captain has a bedroom and a dressing room. Then, here, there is a guest bedroom, across from yours, and that's where your parents will stay. The remaining bedrooms are reserved for a governess and, of course, the captain's children." Sarah smiled, although her expression looked uncertain. "I hope you'll be comfortable here."

"Thank you. I'm sure I will." Renna walked farther into the room and began to remove her bonnet. "Where do you and Mr. Navis stay?"

"We had taken over the captain's suite down the hall, but since he's not really dead...I mean..." Her cheeks turned crimson.

Renna smiled. "I know what you mean."

"We've since moved our things back to the farm, where Richard's folks reside. However, we'll probably stay a couple of nights here—in the governess room several doors down—until the children have adequately adjusted."

"Sounds like a wise plan."

Sarah replied with a tentative grin and toyed with the lamp on the nightstand. "Do you like children, Miss Fields?"

"I love children." She watched, then, as Sarah took note of the purplish mark on her left cheek. Renna touched the side of her face. "It's a birthmark."

"Oh..." Sarah seemed to dismiss the matter. "I'm so thankful to hear you love children." An expression of relief spread across her face. "Poor Gabriel thinks you'll be the kind of stepmother who'll send him off to boarding school, just as Mrs. Kingsley planned to do."

Renna stood totally speechless for several long moments. "Brian and I haven't talked about marriage."

"Oh, well, then, please pardon me for being presumptuous. It's just that my husband said... Well, you both seem to be..." Sarah's lips parted, but she couldn't finish her thought.

"Your husband said what?" Renna tipped her head, curious.

"Um... well, Richard made mention of the fact that you're much kinder than Mrs. Kingsley."

"Thank him for what I deem a compliment." Judging from Brian's description of his former fiancée, the woman wasn't the kind of person Renna aspired to be.

Sarah took a step toward her. "Miss Fields, I must admit to being something of a dreamer, and I assumed or imagined—whatever you'd like to term it—that you and the captain had fallen in love."

Heat surged into Renna's face. She'd dreamed the same dream. "I think Brian and I are taking things one step at a time." *There.* She'd sounded pragmatic enough to convince even Nurse Rutledge.

"Very wise, I'm sure."

Renna smiled.

"For the record, I love the children very much, and I"—Sarah swallowed hard—"I could very easily call them my own—and I have."

"I think I understand, and it makes perfect sense, particularly since you were named as a guardian and Brian was presumed drowned." Renna reached out and touched the sleeve of Sarah's printed dress. "I can tell you that Brian hopes to repair his relationship with his children. He wants to be a good father."

"He always has. In fact, when he hired me to be the children's governess, he said he wanted to be a–a family. But I'm afraid he has no idea what being a family member entails. In the past the captain's business and social life have taken precedence over the children."

"I believe he's aware of the mistakes he's made."

Sarah folded her arms and lowered her gaze. "I wouldn't mind signing legal documents if the captain decided he didn't want to be a father. Richard feels the same way."

Renna inhaled sharply. The children needed to be with their father. Still, it wasn't her place to say so. "That's something you'll have to speak with Brian about, but—" Renna gave her a pleading look—"couldn't you at least give him another chance?"

Sarah seemed both wounded and contrite all at once. "God extends grace to us all the time. I suppose it's my duty as a Christian to extend grace to others when I can. It's just that I love the children very much. It'll be hard to part with them."

Renna folded her into a sisterly hug. "It's not as though Brian will rip the children away from you. I suspect you and Richard will always have a major part in their lives."

"Do you really think so?" Sarah pulled back.

"Of course I do." Renna smiled. "I haven't known Brian for long, but he seems like a reasonable man."

"Sometimes. And at other times he's connived and meddled in people's lives in order to get what he wants."

Thoughts of Elise Kingsley and her shipping company came to mind, and she turned from Sarah so she wouldn't reflect her doubt. "Brian hopes to change all that."

"I pray he's successful."

Renna did too.

Sarah sidestepped toward the door. "Would you like a tour of the house?"

"Oh, yes, I'd like that very much."

Sarah led Renna around the first floor, showing her first the reception parlor.

"There's a sunroom, also called the solarium," Sarah said as they moved on. "One can access it through both the reception parlor and the dining room. It's glass encased and filled with plants and flowers. So peaceful…sometimes I have my morning devotions in that room."

"Sounds lovely."

"It is, but you can investigate it for yourself after I give you the overall tour."

"All right." Renna looked forward to it.

The ladies' parlor came next. Renna peeked inside, admiring the décor, the dainty furniture, and floral paintings on the walls. Next was the gentlemen's parlor. In contrast it had large, heavy furniture covered in dark-brown leather. Books lined the wall of shelves, and everything smelled of cigar smoke, which made Renna's nose tickle. Nonetheless, she felt awestruck by the home's magnificence thus far.

*Three parlors. Three!*

Sarah slid the doors closed, and they moved on to the music room.

"This is another of my favorite rooms." She sat down at the piano and played a quick melody. "I still hope to keep up the children's music lessons."

Renna couldn't see why Brian would object, although it wasn't her place to say one way or another.

Brian's office came next. They'd actually made a circle of the grand foyer and now stood near to where they'd begun—near the front door and the stairwell and across from the reception parlor.

"Are you ready to go upstairs?"

"Yes."

At Renna's reply, Sarah led the way up to the third floor and showed her Hester's suite. Next she led Renna across the hallway, through a double set of doors, and into a magnificent ballroom. Plaster sculpture work adorned the ceiling, from which hung two crystal chandeliers. The walls were lined with matching crystal sconces.

"This is the most beautiful room I've ever seen," Renna breathed, stepping across the shiny hardwood parquet floor.

"That was my reaction exactly!" Sarah exclaimed with a smile. "I was quite taken with this room—with the whole house, in fact." She shook her head as if remembering. "Why, I can still see Captain Sinclair and Elise Kingsley gliding across this floor. The children and I had to make an appearance at one of the captain's parties last summer, and the music and dancing, and the way the captain was holding Mrs. Kingsley—"

Sarah stopped in mid-sentence and blushed right up to her blonde hairline. "Oh, Miss Fields, please forgive me! I...I didn't mean to run on like that."

"It's all right, Sarah. I know Brian has been something of a—" She stopped before uttering the word *pirate*. "That is, I know his past hasn't been very God pleasing."

"I should say not." Sarah tipped her head. "But he did seem sort of different downstairs in the foyer minutes ago."

"I believe he is different, Sarah. The accident caused him to realize many things. But I'll let him tell you the details." Renna's gaze roamed around once again. "In any event, here's hoping Brian's ballroom days are over. Perhaps this could be a...a tearoom instead."

"It'd make a lovely tearoom." Sarah locked arms with her. "Allow me to finish giving you the grand tour."

"Of course." Renna smiled. In that second, she liked Sarah Navis for her esprit and candidness and easy acceptance of Renna. "Please, lead on."

~~⦵⦵⦵⦵~~

Brian stood in his richly paneled study with Richard. He shuffled through his mail. "How many parties can people in this city attend over the holiday season?"

"When news got around that you were still alive, sir," Richard informed him, "the invitations started pouring in."

"I'm flattered. There are several here I'll reply to immediately."

"I imagine you'll want to take Miss Fields along with you."

"Of course. I can't wait to introduce her to Milwaukee's society." He slapped the mail down on the desktop. Turning, Brian considered the young man standing in front of him. Blond and blue-eyed, broad-shouldered and faithful, Richard Navis had always been a very, very faithful steward, a fact that would not go unrewarded. "And I suppose I should have some kind of reception."

"A good idea, sir. Half of the city of Milwaukee will most likely pound your door down from curiosity if you don't." Richard laughed. "In fact, Lillian LaMonde has already been to your store, here at your house, and at my folks' farm."

"What?" Irritation coursed through him. "I'm sorry, Richard."

He waved off the apology and chuckled. "Actually, my mother was thrilled. Lillian LaMonde of the *Milwaukee Sentinel* at our home, searching for tidbits for her society page—Mama has stories to tell her friends for weeks now."

"Society page, my foot! That woman writes a vicious gossip column."

"I agree. And you've been the star of her column numerous times in the past. Have you warned Miss Fields?"

"No. But I will," he promised at Richard's look of warning. "I have no intention of subjecting Renna to the likes of Lillian LaMonde."

"Good luck, sir." Sarcasm rimmed his reply as Richard stood by, grinning. "And what about your sight? Does Miss Fields know you can see yet?"

"Not yet." Brian walked to the windows of his mahogany-paneled study and gazed out over the front terrace.

"Well, don't."

"What?" Furrowing his brow, he turned and peered at Richard.

"Authorities have advised me to persuade you to continue under this pretense. They think it will be easier for an assailant to strike if you seem like more of a victim."

"Hmm...interesting." Brian hadn't considered that angle. "But I hate lying to Renna. I have wanted to tell her that my sight has returned so many times. However, the authorities' victim strategy might lead to the killer's apprehension. Perhaps the more Renna knows, the more it could hurt her."

"You make a good point." Richard's expression turned grave. "You really think someone may be trying to kill you?"

Brian nodded. "I've thought it over, and I don't think I'm being overly anxious or paranoid. I know something was wrong with my schooner on that fateful day. That's why we were on the water when the storm hit. And then there's Matt Benchley, who is infuriated with me for buying Great Lakes Shipping. Elise told me he threatened her. I think he might try again to harm me."

"Benchley?" Richard squinted in thought. "There's a man named Benchley who is insisting that your attorney, Mr. Norton, look into the sale of Great Lakes Shipping. He claims the sale wasn't legal because his aunt, Elise Kingsley, wasn't sane at the time of the sale."

"Elise was as sane as she'd ever been." Brian shook his head before massaging his jaw. "Part of me wouldn't mind selling the company to Benchley and washing my hands of the whole deal. But I can't do that. Three lives were lost on the lake, one of them being my own mother, and all because of someone's contemptible actions. I owe it to their memories, Richard, to see that whoever is responsible is apprehended."

"And you think it was Mr. Benchley?"

"I do."

"But how will you prove it? The schooner was completely destroyed."

Brian grinned, feeling a measure of confidence. "The day before the accident, Toby Barton, the best dockhand a sailing man ever had, checked the schooner over and found it to be in excellent condition. Toby can testify to that."

Richard paled. "Toby Barton is dead, Captain—an accident down at the docks. It happened last week. I'm sorry I didn't tell you. I didn't remember that you even knew him."

"I knew him." Brian clenched his jaw. His heart ached for Toby, and anger over the senseless tragedy filled his being. Toby Barton had been a young man in his early twenties, not much older than Richard. "I wonder," Brian muttered, unable to keep the cynicism out of his voice, "just who might have been responsible for *that* accident."

"Captain Sinclair, you don't really think Mr. Benchley—"

"To the contrary, Richard. *I know.*"

And Brian vowed right then and there to see the man brought to justice.

# NINETEEN

THE NEXT MORNING RENNA GAVE HER REFLECTION ONE last glance. She smoothed the waist of her pale green and cream gown. She'd never owned a dress so fine. Despite her birth-mark, she actually felt pretty beneath all the frills. It made her wonder how she'd tolerated her black garb and pinned-on white smock for the last decade.

But, perhaps, until she'd met her pirate, she simply hadn't any interest in dressing up.

Renna re-pinned several locks. She'd neatly plaited her auburn hair then braided it from one side to the other, although several curls still refused to be confined. Having done all she could with her appearance for now, she left her enormous bedroom.

Walking through the long, impressive hallway, she wondered if she could ever be comfortable residing in a house as large as this one. Brian was proud of his home, to be sure, but she thought it felt rather impersonal.

In the dining room Mum and Da were sitting with Brian, who headed the long, linen-covered table. The men stood as Renna entered.

"Well, now, don't you look pretty!" Da beamed.

Brian wore his dark spectacles, which shielded his unseeing eyes. His lips parted as if to reply but closed again. Finally, he said, "I'm sure Renna looks as beautiful as always."

"Thank you." Feeling embarrassed, she glanced at Mum, who sent her a pleased smile.

Minutes later a plump and jovial-looking woman named

Isabelle served up a generous fare that rivaled Mum's meals, except Renna knew her mother enjoyed the break from cooking and dishwashing.

"I think you all should be aware that Richard and Sarah will soon be moving to the farm on which Richard's parents reside." Brian took a quick sip of his coffee. "That's where the children stayed last night, and they love it on the farm. I'm grateful to the Navises—Richard's parents included. I'm sure you'll meet them at some point during your stay."

"And will your children arrive back home soon?" Renna cut off a small piece of a flapjack covered with syrup and ate it. Thick and sweet, the maple flavor awakened her senses.

"Yes, although they've all made it perfectly clear they'd rather live with Richard and Sarah than with me."

Renna swallowed. Her heart went out to Brian. He looked so downcast. "You'll win them back quick enough."

"That's right, Captain." Mum wore a determined expression. "Children are amazingly resilient."

"Thank you. I'll need all the help I can get, I'm sure. But as much as I hope to win my children's affections, I want to reinforce the fact that Richard and Sarah will always remain a part of their lives."

"How good of you." Da gave an approving nod.

"Well, it's only right. Richard and Sarah stepped into parental roles after I was presumed drowned. They love my children, and I'm indebted to them."

Renna wondered if there was room in Brian's children's lives for her. She'd seen the portrait of their beautiful mother hanging above the mantel in the reception parlor. Would they compare Renna to her? Renna wouldn't come out on top. The artist had captured the essence of Louisa Sinclair's loveliness with his brush. Likewise, Sarah Navis possessed an outward, innocent sort of beauty all her own.

*First they lost their mother, and now Sarah would be relieved of the role.* Renna cringed at the vacancy in those poor, dear kids' lives. They'd been through so much already.

And what about Brian? Renna slid a glance his way. His hair was neatly combed, his face shaven. He'd managed extremely well for an unseeing man. What's more, dressed in his dark suit and crisp white shirt he made an impressive sight.

He smiled, looking amused, and Renna lowered her gaze. But before she had a chance to blush, she remembered that Brian couldn't have intercepted her admiring glance. He couldn't see!

"How are you feeling today, Brian?" Renna gently lay down her fork.

"I'm feeling fine, although..."

He fingered the open top button of his shirt. "I seem to have forgotten my cravat."

"I'll help you with it later, Brian," Da said. "Not to worry."

Renna breathed a sigh of relief. He'd merely laughed at himself for forgetting. Even so, what kind of monster was she that she could wish for Brian's sight to return and for him to remain blind at the same time?

Perhaps the sort of monster that his children wouldn't want around. Had she been guilty of wanting people to need her because that's all she expected out of life?

~~~~~~~

Hours later, the children arrived in the Rockaway, a multi-passenger carriage. Richard was in the covered driver's seat, while Sarah and the children sat all bundled up inside.

As Richard drove the carriage around to the side of the house, Renna watched from the windows of the enormous solarium. Her limbs tingled with nervousness as the four kids alighted and ran for the house. What would they think of her? Would they like her?

Renna was only too glad that Brian planned to ask both Richard and Sarah Navis to stay for a few days. To ease the transition,

Brian had decided to keep the children out of school for the week, and Renna hoped Sarah would help her get to know the children quicker.

Now if she could only help Renna find her way around this manse!

Turning from the windows, she had to laugh at herself. She'd gotten so mixed up minutes ago just trying to find her mother in the ladies' parlor. Her own home could fit in just the foyer of Brian's house.

Leaving the solarium, Renna heard voices wafting in from the kitchen as Brian welcomed his children back home. But she didn't hear responses. She stopped in the foyer, unsure what to do.

Finally Mr. Navis ambled into the foyer with the kids in tow.

"And here's Miss Fields." He shrugged out of his wool coat. Hester appeared from nowhere and hurried to hang it up. "She's the lady we told you about."

Murmurs of hello echoed through the vestibule.

"Don't be shy now," Richard coaxed them. "Introduce yourselves."

"I'm Libby." The taller of the two girls stepped forward. Her straight, ebony hair hung in two braids on either side of her impish face. "I'm six years old, and Miss Sarah is teaching me to read."

"She's not Miss Sarah anymore," one of the boys groused. "She's Mrs. Navis now...and she's supposed to be our new mom." He sent Renna a challenging glance.

Renna ignored it. She wasn't about to try to compete with Sarah, their beloved former governess. "Hello, Libby. I'm pleased to meet you."

The girl smiled. She resembled her father. Why, she even had his ebony eyes and thick lashes. The only thing Libby possessed that Brian didn't was a pretty pink rosebud mouth.

"I read too." The smallest of the Sinclair bunch stared up at her siblings. Her physical traits were opposite her sister's. Where Libby had black hair and eyes, Rachel was fair-headed with hazel eyes.

The little one whirled toward Renna. "I'm six too."

"No, you're not. You just turned four—and you don't know how to read, either!"

Richard set a hand on the boy's shoulder. "Easy, Gabe."

"But she's lying."

"She's *pretending*." He grinned and looked at Renna. "May I present Gabriel Sinclair, Captain Sinclair's eldest. He's almost twelve years old."

"Nice to meet you, Gabriel." Renna gave him a smile.

"And this little one..." Richard scooped the smallest girl into his arms. "...is Rachel. She just had a birthday last weekend."

"A birthday?" Renna brought her hands together, smiling all the while.

The little one nodded.

"We had an early celebration in Chicago," Richard explained, "but unfortunately you were working at the hospital."

"Brian didn't tell me that." Perhaps he hadn't wanted her to feel any guiltier than she already had. "I'm sorry I missed it."

"We could have another one." Brows raised, hope filling her gaze, Rachel obviously thought she'd made a grand suggestion.

"You've had two," Sarah said on a laugh. "I think that's all the birthday parties you need until next year."

"I can't wait for my birthday. I love parties!" Libby twirled around.

Richard chuckled. "Let's move on with introductions, shall we? Over here next to Gabe is Michael. He's ten years old."

The boy leaned his brunet head in closer to Richard. "She doesn't look like some of Dad's other ladies," he whispered loud enough for Renna to hear.

"A very good sign, I'd say." Grinning, Richard set Rachel onto her feet.

Sarah walked in and wrapped her hand around her husband's arm. They exchanged adoring looks while Gabe neared Renna.

"What's that thing on your face?" Curiosity coupled with cynicism edged his tone.

Renna's fingers flew to the purplish mark. "It's a birthmark, which means I was born with it." She couldn't blame the boy for wanting to know. At least he was honest and forthright instead of sneaking pitying glances her way and whispering behind her back the way many of her peers did.

"Will it ever go away?"

"Gabe!" Richard shook his head. "It's rude to be so personal with an adult."

"It's all right." Renna smiled, looking directly at the boy. "No, it doesn't come off, which, I'm sure, makes me less pretty than all the other ladies who've visited your father."

Gabriel's expression softened as he took several steps forward. He shrugged off Richard's hand on his shoulder and came up to Renna, boldly appraising her tarnished cheek.

The small veil of confidence she possessed unraveled quickly.

"Gabe." Richard's voice was thick with warning.

"I find your birthmark interesting, Miss Fields."

Richard's sigh was audible.

Sarah spoke up then. "Gabe, I must insist—"

"I don't mean any harm." With a frown he glanced over his shoulder at Richard then turned back to Renna. "You were fortunate enough to be born with something different about your looks."

A laugh burst out of her. "Fortunate?"

"Well, yes. Otherwise one lady is just the same as any other, really."

"I've never considered that perspective. Thank you."

Richard said, "Gabe is our resident artist. He likes to draw and paint. He tends to see things that we simpletons overlook."

In that moment Renna decided she liked Gabe Sinclair. "You're a fine young man," she told him just as Brian entered the foyer. He used a polished and carved wooden cane and continued to wear his dark protective lenses.

"I hope my children aren't making pests of themselves."

"Why, no." Renna felt a bit taken aback by the remark. She took a look at the girls, clinging to Richard and Sarah, then the boys' scowling countenances. Clearly the girls were afraid of their father, and the boys resented him. "We were just getting acquainted."

"Good."

Renna saw Libby tug on Richard's arm. "Are you and Miss Sarah going to keep living here with us?"

"No, sweetheart." Sarah's voice sounded constrained. "But your father invited us to stay for a few days, and we said we would."

"But why can't you stay forever?" A heavy frown settled on her brow.

Richard hunkered down. "Libby, things have changed. Your father is alive. Aren't you happy about that?"

"Yes, but—"

"It's only right that things go back to the way they were before that big storm hit with your father and Aurora in the middle of it." Richard cupped the back of the little girl's head and hugged her to him. "We talked about this before. Remember?"

Libby pouted.

Rachel eyed her father speculatively.

"Gabe said that if we can't live on the farm with the Navises," Michael began, "then me and him'll run away and be stowaways."

Gabe nudged Michael. "Why'd you have to tell, stupid?"

"Oops." Chagrin spread crimson across the younger boy's freckled face.

"Stowaways, eh?" Brian tipped his head.

Renna glanced at him, noting the grim lines around his mouth.

"That's a serious offense, boys. If you're caught, you could be beaten—or worse. And if you live, you'll be sentenced to a life of hard labor."

Gabriel was stone-faced, but Michael looked downright scared. His dark brown eyes widened with horror.

"They'd beat kids?"

"Well, Michael, it depends on who 'they' are. But, yes, I've heard of it happening, so I don't want to hear another word about stowing away. Is that clear?"

"Yessir." Michael muttered the reply.

Gabe said nothing.

"Now get your bags from the carriage, go upstairs to your rooms, and unpack."

Michael turned and ran up the stairs, but Gabriel paused in front of his father.

"Are you really blind?" A challenge loomed.

Brian hesitated. "Yes." He'd softened his tone.

Then Gabriel stuck out his tongue.

Renna brought her hand to her lips in shock. Such a bold display of rebellion! Sarah gasped, and Richard narrowed his gaze.

Gabe grinned and followed his brother upstairs.

"Daddy!" Libby walked over and tugged on his hand. "Gabe did a bad thing. The worst thing I ever saw him do. He sticked his tongue out at you."

Rachel copied her sister. "He sticked it right out."

"Are you going to whip him now?" Libby asked. "He should get a belt-whipping, don't you think so, Daddy?"

Renna bit the side of her cheek in an effort not to smile. She couldn't help it. She recalled numerous times in her childhood that she'd wished her brother would get a whipping.

Saying nothing of the sort, however, she glanced at Sarah, who peered at her husband. But no help there. Richard stood staring up at the ceiling.

"Libby, darling, I appreciate your concern. It was good of you to tell me. Gabriel probably deserves a whipping, but I think I'll settle for a good talking-to."

"All right." Libby's slender shoulders sagged with disappointment.

Just then the housekeeper reappeared, and both little girls ran to hug her. "Granny Hester! Granny Hester!"

"Well, now, look who's here." The older woman embraced the girls with a quick hug. "My two little chickens!" She placed kisses on the tops of their heads. "Isabelle's making cake in the kitchen, and if you hurry, she'll let you lick the spoon. Mrs. Fields is in there too. That's Miss Fields's mother, you know," Hester explained to the girls before setting them in the right direction. "Go see what's happening in the kitchen."

Libby turned to Richard. "Can we, Mr. Navis?"

"Best to ask your father."

Two small heads turned his way. "Can we?"

Brian smiled. "Yes, you may."

The girls skipped off down the hallway.

"Isn't the kitchen that way?" Renna said, pointing down the other hallway.

Sarah nodded. "You can go that way too."

Renna blew out a breath. "Oh, dear." She looked at Brian. "I think I need a map."

Brian chuckled. "Renna, in a few days you'll know this place like the back of your hand. I promise. Now then, turn me toward the front staircase. I need to deal with my eldest."

"Shall I guide you up the stairs?"

Brian shook his head. "I know my way very well."

"All right, then." Renna took his hand and walked him to the first step.

"Thirty-six steps in a curving staircase." Brian smiled. "Don't be surprised, Renna, if you see a couple of boys sliding down this banister from time to time." He paused. "And maybe a governess too."

"Captain Sinclair!" Sarah marched forward. "I never did such an undignified thing."

Richard cleared his throat. "That would have been the governess *before* Sarah, sir."

"Ah, yes…"

Confusion engulfed Renna. "How many governesses were there?"

"Too many to count, I'm afraid," Richard replied.

The children must have felt a measure of confusion over so many people walking in and out of their lives. Did Brian understand what he had put them through?

His next words allayed her fears

"Pray for me, Renna," he said softly. "My relationship with my son is already strained. I can't imagine what I might say to change his mind about me."

"I will." She watched him ascend the staircase. "I'll pray."

⁓ʊʊᘒ)(ᘖʊʊ⁓

Brian made his way to Gabriel's bedroom. He knocked once and then, without waiting for a reply, walked in. A large satchel sat in the middle of the room, still unpacked, while Gabe lay on his bed, staring at the ceiling, his jaw clenched.

"Gabriel, we need to talk."

No reply.

Brian walked farther into the bedroom. He glanced around at all the unframed artwork tacked to the walls. Why hadn't he seen it before? The watercolors, ink sketches, and chalk drawings were all very well done.

"What?" He blinked as he stepped closer to examine one of the pictures. "Are you the artist of all these pictures, Gabe?" Immediately he realized his blunder. He was supposed to be blind.

Turning slowly toward his son, Brian saw that Gabriel scrutinized him with a puzzled frown.

Brian removed his dark glasses. "I'd best be honest with you, son, although I pray I'm not endangering your life by doing so." He took in a deep breath. "I'm not blind, Gabe, although I was for a long time after the boating accident. But I've agreed to pretend that I'm still blind so the authorities can discover if someone tampered with my schooner the day of the killer storm on the lake. That same person—or persons—may still be trying to kill me."

Gabriel sat up and swung his legs off the bed. "You mean you can see?"

Brian nodded and watched the color drain slowly from his son's face. "And, yes, I saw you stick out your tongue at me minutes ago."

Gabriel swallowed hard, obviously expecting impending doom.

"You deserve a good thrashing for that one, but I think you're old enough now that we can…discuss the matter. Will you agree to that? A discussion?"

"I suppose so."

Brian moved to the round table at the far side of the room. Four chairs surrounded it, and pens, ink, paints, and brushes covered the top. Brian sat down and gently moved the art supplies toward the middle of the table. Gabe took a chair across from him.

"You're a very talented young man."

Gabe shrugged in reply, and Brian noted the wary look in his eyes. No doubt his son feared that after their discussion he might still get his thrashing.

Brian tried in vain to stifle a grin. "You know, I remember when I was your age. Aurora didn't know what to do with me, so she did nothing. I was very bored one summer and spent my free time down at the docks. I met a man down there whom every-one referred to as Corky. Captain Corky." Brian chuckled at the remembrance. "Corky was an old man with a sharp tongue, but he took pity on me that summer and taught me many things about ships. Once he even took me on a two-day journey across Lake Michigan. Aurora never even knew I was gone. But then the fall came, and I was talking of seafaring men and using bad language. Aurora was so aghast, she packed me off to boarding school.

I never got to say good-bye to Corky and his crew. I hated my mother for that."

"Aurora never liked kids much." Again, Gabe rolled his shoulders. His hazel-eyed gaze was fastened to the tabletop. "Maybe she liked the girls more cuz they could shop for dresses and hair ribbons."

"Hmm…well, I must agree with you there." Brian sat back. "I resented my mother for a long time. Then, after a couple of years at boarding school, I realized that, even though Aurora had no mothering skills to speak of, she wanted the best for me, and soon I wanted the best for me too. I married your mother, and we had four beautiful children, but I didn't know how to be a father because—well, except for Corky that summer, I had no father figure in my life. Even so, I wanted the best for my children…just like Aurora had wanted the best for me. Do you understand what I'm trying to say, Gabriel?"

"I don't know."

"Well, what I mean to say is I know I haven't been a good father, but I want to be. And now I have faith in God, and He will help me. But you're going to have to be patient, son."

Gabriel looked him squarely in the eyes. "Are you going to marry that lady and then send me off to boarding school like Aurora did to you—and like Mrs. Kingsley wanted to do to Mike and me?"

"No, not if you don't want to go."

"I don't."

"Then you won't go to boarding school."

Gabriel narrowed his gaze suspiciously. "How do I know that you'll keep your promise? You never did before. Or maybe you'll just forget."

Brian dipped his head. He hated the fact his son spoke the truth. "Before my accident, Gabriel, I had no use for God. But lately I've been studying His Word. I'm learning. I'm different. Everything is new now. I'm a changed man. Give me a chance to prove it."

"I guess I can do that. I'll give you one more chance."

"Only one more?" Brian sent the boy a patient smile. "What if I need fifty more chances? If I remember correctly, Jesus said we're to forgive 'seventy times seven.' That's four hundred and ninety chances, Gabe—for the same transgression." Brian leaned toward his son. "What about you? Do you have faith in God?"

Gabriel nodded. "Mr. Navis talked to me about Jesus. Miss Sarah did too."

The admission caused Brian to smile. "I'm glad. Richard and Sarah have been good to step in and take care of you while I've been gone. But now that I'm back and—well, a changed man for the experience—I'd like us all to be a family. A *real* family."

Gabriel studied him earnestly now. "You seem different."

"I really am, but I'm still learning. As I said before, I'm going to need your patience." He chuckled. "Miss Fields even said that I'm not half the pirate I used to be."

"Pirate?" Gabriel's young face split into a grin. "I remember all those pirate stories you used to tell Mike and me."

"I remember them too." How could he have neglected his son so long? Gabe was a fine boy.

He leaned his elbows on the table, looking more at ease now. "How long do you have to pretend that you're blind?"

Brian sobered. "I hope it's not much longer. But, please, Gabriel, keep this a secret from Miss Fields. She still thinks I'm blind, and I have to be the one to tell her the truth. I hate deceiving her this way." Brian chose not to disclose the entirety of the situation. "However, I don't want to put her life in danger too."

"So are you going to marry her now that Mrs. Kingsley is dead?"

Remorse filled Brian. He'd used Elise like a bar of soap. "Gabe, the next time I get married, it will be because the woman blends into our family and loves you and your brother and sisters."

"Like Miss Sarah?"

"Well—"

"She's married to Mr. Navis now."

"I know that." Brian also knew he needed to apologize to Sarah for his despicable ways.

"Maybe Miss Fields will be nice enough for you to marry."

"Time will tell. At least Renna is aware that my first priority is my children. I have a lot of years to make up for."

"You never cared about us before."

"It may not have seemed like it, but I did—and do." He gave his son a heartfelt glance. "I just hope I haven't endangered your life by telling you the truth about my eyesight. Oh, God, may it not be so!"

"Don't worry." Gabriel squared his shoulders. "I'm brave and strong. Old Mr. Navis even said so. Besides, people don't pay much attention to children, but we listen a lot." A gleam entered his eyes. "I'll bet I can find out a whole ton of stuff."

"Now, Gabriel, I don't want you to involve yourself. Leave this to the authorities. They know what they're doing. Another man has already lost his life because he knew too much."

"Really? Who?"

More regret assailed him. "Someone I had dealings with down at the docks. He repaired ships and had worked on my schooner just days before the accident." Brian paused and gave his son an earnest look. "Gabe, you mustn't repeat any of what I've told you to anyone. Understood?"

"Don't you trust me?" Gabe lifted his chin in silent challenge. "You never did before. Maybe you don't trust me now."

Brian lifted a brow. "Are you a trustworthy man?"

"Yessir, I am." The boy squared his shoulders.

"Well, then, I trust you, Gabriel." Brian got to his feet. "I trust you with my life!"

# TWENTY

AFTER A TASTY FARE OF ROASTED PHEASANT, RICE, AND Isabelle's famous canned green beans, followed by frosted carrot cake for dessert, the children were dismissed from the dinner table. Renna smiled as the boys bolted from their places like wild ponies. They raced each other and thundered up the staircase. The girls, on the other hand, walked sleepily away. Little Rachel yawned as she left the room.

"The children are used to eating earlier, I'm afraid." Sarah added a smile to her apologetic tone. "And the girls are usually in bed by now."

Renna brought the goblet to her lips and took a sip of water. Across the table, Sarah Navis toyed with the last bite of her cake. Clearly she was troubled. Renna guessed she wanted to follow the girls and prepare them for bed, but her governess and mother roles had been removed.

So who would care for Libby and Rachel tonight?

Renna eyed Brian. He seemed pensive. He'd indulged in a glass of white wine with his dinner, as did Da, and now twirled the stemmed glass between his fingers.

Hester strode into the room. "May I take your plate, Captain?"

Brian sat back with a quick glance at her. The woman wore a black dress with a white apron tired around her waist. "Yes, please."

Hester snatched the porcelain plate out from in front of him then proceeded to collect the rest with fast efficiency.

Renna looked at Sarah, who caught her eye. "How about you

and I help the girls get ready for bed?" She turned her gaze on Brian. "With your consent, of course." She stopped before adding, *Captain Pirate Blackeyes.*

"I normally don't allow my guests to put my children to bed."

"We're more than guests, Captain," Richard said. He sat at the other end of the table. "We're like family now. All of us."

"Thank you, and, in that case"—his eyes met Renna's, and she saw gratitude shining in their depths—"I'd appreciate your help with my children."

Sarah wore a similar expression of gratefulness as Richard helped her stand from the table. Brian did the same for Renna, and she followed the younger woman upstairs.

"The girls have a hard time undoing the buttons on the backs of their dresses," Sarah commented.

"I imagine so. Grown women even have trouble removing their own gowns," Renna agreed.

They strode to the girls' room, and inside they found Libby struggling to unlace Rachel's leather ankle boots. When she saw Renna and Sarah, relief spread across her features.

"I tried and tried…"

"It's all right, Libby." Sarah set to task and quickly removed the younger girl's shoes.

"Can I help you undress, Libby?" Renna asked.

Libby considered Renna for several seconds before nodding her dark head.

Renna removed the dark blue printed dress with its floppy white collar then helped Libby off with her petticoat. Libby knew how to do the rest. Renna collected the garments to be hung in the wardrobe.

"I think your dress is pretty, Miss Fields."

"Thank you, Libby."

"Maybe Miss Fields will read to you tonight," Sarah suggested.

Renna thought she detected a note of wistfulness. "I'm happy to read, but you may do the honors tonight, Sarah."

"Will you, Miss Sarah?" Hopefulness shone from Rachel's hazel eyes.

"Well, all right." A smile played across Sarah's mouth. "This will probably be the last time, though."

"Oh, hardly." Renna wouldn't allow this woman to feel sorry for herself, and yet she could imagine the sense of loss Sarah felt. "You heard your husband. We're all like family. The boating accident has somehow bound us together because of your love for the children and my lo—"

Renna felt hot crimson spread across her face. What had she been about to admit?

"Your love for the captain?" Sarah tipped her head and grinned.

"Do you love my daddy?" Libby smiled.

"Well, of course I care for the captain very much. I took care of him in the hospital and prayed for his salvation. My parents did too, and then he stayed with us until his memory returned."

"I think the captain could use the love of a good woman." Sarah slipped Rachel's plain white cotton nightgown over the girl's head.

"Our mom died last year." Libby's tone was informative more than sad.

Nonetheless Renna's heart melted. "I'm so sorry to hear that, dear heart." The little girls were so young to lose their mother. The idea caused Renna to appreciate her demure, caring mother all the more.

Libby gave a few shakes of her head. "Except we didn't like Mrs. Kingsley, and we're glad she's not going to be our mom. But it's sad that she died too."

"Yes, quite regrettable," Renna agreed.

"Let's get to our story time." Sarah reached for a book on the table between the girls' two beds.

Renna tucked Libby and Rachel into bed, placing a kiss on the tops of their heads.

Sarah read the book despite the interruption of an occasional yawn from the girls. Afterward she kissed each one and followed Renna out of the room.

"Now, to see what those boys are up to…" Sarah checked on Michael. "He's quite the bookworm," she told Renna. "He's reading." Next she poked her head into Gabe's room. "Gabe?" She opened the door wider. "Gabe, where are you?"

Renna detected the note of panic and strode into the bedroom after Sarah. They checked under bedcovers and the bed itself. Sarah even checked the wardrobe to see if he was hiding. No sign of him.

Then suddenly the boy came traipsing through the bedroom door.

"Where were you?" Sarah placed her hands on her hips.

Gabe shrugged like he didn't want to say. Next he eyed Renna. "Gabriel?"

"I just went down to say good night to my dad and Mr. Navis. That's all."

Renna knew the boy's actions had to make Brian feel good. "I'm glad you did that."

"It's nothing." The lad sounded a tad irritated.

Sarah laughed at his behavior. "Gabe doesn't like us to see that he's really a very fine young man, right?" She gave him a sisterly sort of shove.

A grin curved Gabe's mouth. "Could you please leave so I can go to bed now?" Laughter edged his tone.

"Miss Fields and I are happy to go." Sarah chuckled again. "Come on, Renna."

Outside the kids' bedrooms, they stood in the dimly lit hallway. "He's really a good boy. He and Michael both are. And they desperately want their father's love."

"I believe Brian wants to give it…he's just not sure how."

Sarah took Renna's hand. "Let's you and I pray…right now."

Renna closed her eyes and bowed her head.

"Lord, we come before Thee with humble hearts," Sarah began, "and bring Captain Sinclair before you. His children need him. His quiver is full, Lord, and he ought to be a happy man to be blessed with such wonderful children." Her voice crumbled with emotion.

Renna picked up the petition. "Lend Brian Your grace and wisdom to deal with his children. Meanwhile, heal Sarah and Richard Navis's hearts and bless them for their sacrificial service to this family. In Jesus's name, amen."

Sarah gave her fingers a squeeze.

Mum came upstairs just then and announced she'd retire for the evening. "Your father and the captain are smoking those dreadful cigars in the men's parlor."

Renna noted the disgust in her mother's voice, although the practice wasn't uncommon. Even preachers were known to enjoy a good cigar after a meal.

Sarah asked, "Is Richard with them?"

"Yes, but he's got the good sense not to smoke." Mum shook her head. "The very smell of those things gives me a headache." She massaged her temples.

"Then you're doing the right thing by coming up to your room, Mum."

"I thought so too." She kissed Renna's cheek and gave Sarah a nod and a smile. "Good night."

"Good night, Mum."

"Good night, Mrs. Fields." After she went inside her room, Sarah added, "I think I'll turn in for the night as well."

"Oh?" Disappointment fell over Renna. She hoped the two of them could be better acquainted while the men smoked. "Then I'll see you tomorrow at breakfast."

"Yes," Sarah gave her a quick hug. "Good night."

Alone in the hallway, Renna decided she didn't feel sleepy. Gathering her skirts, she made her way down the stairwell. She heard Da's voice coming from the men's parlor but couldn't discern his words. Next she heard Brian's chuckle, a rich sound, which made Renna recall his smiling handsome face.

She strode to the solarium. Opening the paned French doors, she stepped out and wished she'd brought her shawl. The cold air made her shiver, but the sight of the brilliance of the night sky through the windows caused her to forget her discomfort for the moment. Moonlight dripped over the potted foliage in the room. Stars studded the ebony heavens above.

A passage from the Book of Psalms came to mind, and Renna recited it aloud. "When I consider the heavens, the work of thy fingers, the moon and the stars, which thou has ordained...what is man that thou art mindful of him?"

"Indeed!"

She whirled around at the sound of the familiar male voice. "Brian..."

"I hope I didn't startle you." He stepped forward, and Renna noticed he'd removed his black dinner jacket to, no doubt, don a quilted smoking jacket while he enjoyed his cigar. Now, however, he looked more casual in his white dress shirt and gold brocade vest. "I felt the need to stretch my legs."

"And I wasn't ready to retire to the ladies' parlor or my room with needlework or a book." Renna's breath caught as Brian came to stand just inches away.

"Do you like my home, Renna?"

"It's very impressive." After only one day she couldn't exactly call it home.

"What about my children?" Brian faced her. "What do you think of them?"

"I think they are all intelligent, sensitive beings who long for attention from their father, seeing as he didn't perish out on the lake."

"Hmm, yes, and I have a lot of work to do, making up for the many years of neglect."

"What a miracle that you've been given a second chance."

"In more ways than one."

"Oh?" Renna sensed he tried to charm her. She raised her chin even though she knew he couldn't see her challenging gesture. "Whatever do you mean, Captain?"

"You know what I mean." His tone was low and husky.

"Yes, I believe I do. However, your bewitchery won't work on me." She couldn't contain a small laugh. "Do you know how many men have tried to charm me? Plenty." Crossing her arms, she thought back on the days she'd spent at various military camps, tending to the sick and dying.

"So why couldn't they win your heart, Renna?"

She had to wonder. "I think it's because I knew their words were empty. I was their nurse. They needed me. They thought if they told me I was pretty or that my touch as I bandaged their wounds felt soft and warm, I wouldn't neglect them."

"Is that why you think I asked you and your parents to come here to Milwaukee?"

"Yes. And we're happy to be of service for as long as we're... needed."

"I see." Beneath the moonlight she glimpsed his amused grin. "So I shouldn't tell you how beautiful you look tonight, how the color of your dress complements your green eyes, or comment on your sweet fragrance." He reached for her, and within seconds she found herself in his expert embrace. "I shouldn't say that you feel even more beautiful than you look. Nor should I do this..." His lips touched hers, and Renna felt herself melt into him as their kiss deepened.

But at last her senses returned. She pushed him away. "No, you shouldn't do such things." The chastisement lacked conviction.

Brian chuckled. "My dear Renna, you are very easily charmed."

"That's because I never met a pirate like you before." Guilt laced with longing assailed her. A slice of her being wished he'd kiss her again. She ran her fingertips over her lips. She'd never experienced such a kiss before, or the tumult of emotions that came with it.

"Renna, may I?" The softness of his voice plucked some wistful chord in her heart. He took her hand. "Forgive my boldness, but I meant every word."

"Except you can't *see* if I'm *really* beautiful or not."

He suddenly adjusted the frame of his dark lenses. "Well, um…"

"I could be covered in warts and wearing rags for all you know."

"Oh, Renna…it wouldn't matter." His hand caressed her cheek marred by her birthmark before getting lost in her hair. Then he kissed the area so tenderly it brought tears to her eyes. It almost seemed as though he could see which side of her face the birthmark stained, although she'd never told him. "Brian, please!" She forced herself to move away. She hugged herself, feeling utterly confused. From out of the corner of her eye, she saw Brian turn toward the window.

"I'm a man who has always had ulterior motives when it comes to romancing a woman. With Louisa, my goal was to marry into a wealthy family. After she died last year and I met Elise, I wanted to own Great Lakes Shipping without having to pay for it. That is, I did purchase it fair and square, but my thinking was that if I married Elise, her fortune would be mine, and ultimately I'd have my money back and then some."

"Yes, you've told me this before."

"Well, my point is, Renna, I don't believe I've ever fallen in love."

"And what do you want from me?" *A mother for your children? A nurse to care for you while you're blind?* she asked silently, unable to actually speak the questions aloud.

"What I want is the camaraderie that I get from true friends like you, your folks, and the Navises. I want your emotional support as I go through this pivotal time in my life."

"Of course." Renna nearly choked on the reply. She'd had loftier expectations.

"Renna…" Once more Brian reached for her hand and held it tightly. His voice was just a whisper as he continued. "I want you to help me figure out if I'm falling in love…with you."

She swallowed. Her throat went dry. *Could he be serious?*

"Please. Be patient with this pirate—er, *former* pirate." A smile entered his voice. "I have a lot to learn about love and relationships. I never learned the give and take—only the take."

Renna stood by speechless for an indeterminate amount of time. Brian had spoken her very heart, his words realizing her dream.

"Promise me again that you'll be patient."

"I promise," she managed to eke out.

He brought her fingertips to his lips. "Thank you." He guided her hand around his arm and led her toward the doorway. "Allow me to escort you into the music room. Richard went off to find Sarah and ask her to play the piano for us. She's gifted in the way of music. Perhaps she'll grace us with an impromptu concert."

"I'd like that very much."

But as they walked together from the solarium, shadows of doubt still haunted Renna. She couldn't hold a candle to the beautiful women in Brian's past. If he regained his sight, would he truly change his pirate ways—and want her?

Inhaling deeply, Renna decided this morning's autumn air had a rebellious feel to it. The day promised to be an exceedingly warm one. Yet today marked the last day of October. Funny how it seemed like God's creation didn't want to let the summer season go. She smiled wistfully. Who did, what with winter looming on the horizon?

The carriage jerked from side to side as it rolled through the streets of Milwaukee. Renna thought this road seemed particularly rough, although she didn't make mention of it. Brian and Da sat across from her and Mum and chatted about business and the various associates with whom they had contact. As it happened, Brian and Da knew a number of the same people.

"It's your third day in Milwaukee, Wendell. What do you think of our fair city?"

"Not much different than Chicago, although I see many more cream-colored brick structures here than I do wood ones. In Chicago, most of our buildings have wooden frames—even the streets are paved with wood."

"A veritable tinderbox, if you ask me." Brian adjusted the dark-lensed spectacles protecting his unseeing eyes.

"You aren't the first to say so."

Renna had heard similar complaints about Chicago and many of its hastily constructed buildings. She was only too thankful the hospital had been constructed with brick and mortar.

"Boatloads of immigrants arrive at our port daily," Da said.

"Same here in Milwaukee."

"Housing becomes scarce very quickly. That's why many of our neighborhoods are comprised entirely of wooden structures."

"Like our home," Mum said.

"You have a fine home, Mrs. Fields." Brian smiled. "I was very comfortable there during my stay."

"I'm rather embarrassed." Da's round face reddened slightly. "I made you stay in a converted pantry off of our kitchen. I just thought it'd be easier if you didn't have to maneuver the stairs—and, of course, I had to consider the appropriateness of the situation."

"Please, Wendell, stop with your explanations." Brian shook his head. "You took me in during my time of need. I shall never be able to repay you for your care and kindness. And Mrs. Fields, your delicious meals brought me back to health."

"Glad to do it, Captain."

"And don't forget, Brian, you met my lovely daughter, Renna." A gleam entered Da's eyes.

"That I did." Brian seemed to look right at her.

Renna narrowed her gaze at her father.

"She's very good with children," Mum said, "and she'd keep your house in order."

"Mum!" Renna gave her mother an indignant nudge. "Brian already has Hester for a housekeeper, and Mr. Navis is his steward." She glanced out the rattling window. "I'm sure he already has plans to hire a governess. He has no need for a nurse." She pressed her lips together, angry with her parents. They'd love nothing better than to see Renna marry. They'd been humiliated for years by her unwed status, but the more they pushed, the more Renna felt the need to push back.

"Actually, Richard is no longer my steward. I released him from his contract. It had been signed under duress last summer. In good conscience I couldn't hold him to it."

Renna glanced across the way at Brian.

"I do indeed need a governess, Renna. I hoped you would help me write an ad for the newspaper and then interview candidates as they apply for the job."

"I'd be happy to." She settled back against the leather-upholstered seat, feeling a tad more at ease now. Except if Brian ever said he loved her and proposed marriage, Renna wasn't sure she'd need a governess—or a housekeeper and cook. And she wouldn't want to live in such a rambling manse either.

Once again she noted that she and her pirate were worlds apart.

They passed the Bank of Commerce, located on the first floor of a large four-story building, and then rode over one of the city's many bridges.

Earlier this morning Sarah and Richard headed off for the farm and took the children along, as they'd insisted upon riding along with the newlyweds. No doubt they'd arrive before this carriage did.

"How much farther until we reach the Navises' farm?" Renna removed her hankie from her reticule and dabbed the moisture on her brow.

"Another half hour or so," Brian said.

Renna felt the weight of his scrutiny, and yet how could that be? The man couldn't see. She sent him a smile nonetheless.

"It was good of Richard to invite us out for the day," Da said. "I'm looking forward to meeting his folks."

"They're good people."

Renna heard the emphatic note in Brian's voice.

"Richard's father, Marty Navis, took a bullet at Vicksburg. He's confined to a wheelchair now. But that doesn't stop the man from milking his cows and tending to his other livestock. It's good that he'll have Richard around to help with all the chores. For as long as I've known Richard, his intent was to farm." Brian's mouth turned slightly downward. "God knows I'll miss him."

Leaning forward, Renna reached for Brian's hand and gave it an encouraging squeeze.

He smiled in reply. "Thank you, Renna. Whatever would I do without you?"

She laughed to cover her discomfort. "I'm sure you'd manage just fine."

"Don't argue with the captain, dear," Mum said with a nudge.

When Renna sat back again, she caught her parents' grins. Why, she could practically *hear* Mum planning the wedding.

She let go of a long sigh.

They left the city behind. The brick-paved road became dirt and gravel. Fields of drying feed corn suddenly spread out all around them.

Reaching the Navises' farm, the carriage proceeded around the circular front drive. Surprise engulfed them when they saw the unique farmhouse. With an apple orchard to its left, a pond, and a flowing fountain near the front doorway, the brick home looked large enough to house several families.

Brian helped both Renna and her mother alight from the carriage. Da climbed out on his own. Minutes later they were all greeted with a warm welcome by Marty and Bea Navis.

"Captain Sinclair, what a miracle that you're alive!" Mrs. Navis hugged him in a motherly fashion that had Brian covertly dabbing the corners of his eyes. "We, of course, feared the worst since the others' bodies washed ashore."

"I feel blessed to be here—and to be given a second chance."

Renna's heart went out to the families of the other drowning victims. In just a few weeks it would be Thanksgiving Day. The holidays seemed to make mourning that much more difficult.

Did Brian still mourn his mother, friend, and fiancée? Renna had to wonder. She felt sure he mourned the loss of life. But what about those specific individuals?

As the day progressed, Renna noticed how amazingly well Brian managed his blindness. He rarely tripped or bumped into furniture. She'd also noticed Gabriel's behavior. The boy seemed to have done a turnaround for the better. In fact, Gabriel acted as though he and his father were the best of friends. And Michael...he'd become his father's little shadow, quietly standing behind him, listening. What's more, Brian had been correct about his ability to charm his girls. Renna stood at the parlor doors watching him. Brian had perched Libby on his one knee and Rachel on the other as he conversed with the two Navis men and Da.

"I think the children are going to be just fine."

Renna turned to find Sarah beside her.

She wetted her lips. "As you know, I felt concerned. But in a short twenty-four hours it seems the captain has won his children's hearts. Of course, I always thought they adored him from afar."

"You and your husband did an excellent job in preparing the children for Brian's return. I know he'll always be grateful."

"Oh, I've no doubt about that."

"But you're sad to lose the children." Renna placed a hand on the younger woman's slender shoulder. She glimpsed the moisture glistening in Sarah's gaze. "I pray the Lord will soon give you children of your own, and they'll fill the emptiness you're experiencing right now."

"Thank you." Sarah glanced down and fidgeted with the white cuffs of her slate-gray gown. "Richard suggested we go to Missouri and visit my family and stay for Christmas. He's hired an overseer for the farm so his parents can come with us. I have brothers and sisters, nieces and nephews—and one nephew whom I haven't even met yet. He was born just last month to my brother Ben and his wife, Valerie. Now they have three beautiful children."

"It sounds like a fun holiday." Renna felt a twinge of envy. She always enjoyed it when Elizabeth brought the children to visit or when her brother and his family came to stay a few days. But at the end of the day, Renna still found herself alone. All she'd ever wanted was to meet the man of her dreams, marry, and have children of her own.

Sarah smiled. "I think getting away will lift my spirits."

"I'm sure it will." Renna took her hand. "When you talk about your family, your entire countenance brightened just now."

"My parents were the only ones from my family present when Richard and I got married last month, so I look forward to introducing him to the entire McCabe clan. And my two older brothers…" Sarah nearly giggled. "They met Richard last summer, and the three of them get along famously. I'm sure they'll pull a few pranks and get many laughs in return."

"You're a blessed woman, Sarah."

She leaned close and grinned. "Perhaps you'll be a bride soon, hmm?"

"All things are possible with God. Possible, but not always probable." Her gaze flew to Brian, and she fleetingly wondered what it would be like to be his wife. Would he cherish her?

Or would he find that he'd made a horrible mistake?

Renna's fingertips touched her birthmark. What if she and Brian married and one day he regained his sight? Would he be repulsed by what he saw? Renna knew some men might.

Wrestling with the onslaught of insecurity, she managed to fight it off—

This time.

~~~~~⚜~~~~~

The entourage of Sinclairs and Fieldses made it back from the farm before ten o'clock. Mum offered to ready the girls for bed. They'd fallen asleep in the carriage on the way home. The boys too seemed tired and stumbled up to their rooms without complaint.

Renna removed her wrap, then donned her ivory crocheted shawl before following Da and Brian through the expanse of the foyer and into the main reception parlor. Hester had stoked the fire so a soft glow from the hearth filled the room.

"Brian, whatever did you ever say to Gabriel to make him have a change of heart toward you?" Da lowered himself onto the dark-brown, velvet settee.

"I'm not sure, exactly." Brian hiked his elbow up onto the walnut mantel, leaning against it. "I merely had a conversation with him and…"

His black-eyed gaze, hidden behind those dark lenses, seemed to land on Renna, although she knew that'd be impossible.

"…and I shared something of myself with him."

"No doubt that's just what the boy needed," Da said. "Children like to be regarded as human beings too. Very few people understand that concept these days."

"True enough." Brian drew in a deep breath. "But around here, things are different now. In fact, I want my children at the reception Friday night."

"Reception?" Renna paused in smoothing out her fawn-colored skirt. "What reception?"

"Richard helped to coordinate the event and circulated the news of the party. It'll be held here, Friday night. It was either hold a reception or entertain curious, drop-in visitors from now until the New Year."

"I see." Renna tried to conceal her dread.

"It's just a simple open house," Brian said, as if sensing her displeasure. "However, I will warn you, we're all going to have to attend a ball or two for propriety's sake."

"Johanna's looking forward to it." Da chuckled. "It'll be something to tell her friends back home."

Brian grinned.

But Renna cringed inwardly. Soon, however, logic made its way to her senses. The sooner she met all of Brian's friends, the better. Why prolong the agony and humiliation? She'd dress carefully, and Mum would help her curl and pin up her auburn tresses, and yet Renna knew she'd never look beautiful. Not really. Not with her birthmark. And snide comments would surely be murmured. Brian would hear them, and he might even decide he was embarrassed to have her on his arm.

The same hurtful scenario had been played out before in the past. Renna knew it all too well.

She stood to her feet and glanced at Brian then Da. "If you gentlemen will excuse me, I think I'll retire for the evening."

"Is everything all right, Renna?" Brian moved away from the hearth. "I sense you're unhappy."

She forced a little smile. "I'm just tired. I'll see you both at breakfast tomorrow."

On that farewell she turned and left the parlor. But her sense of dread followed her up the stairs.

## TWENTY-TWO

RIAN SIPPED HIS MORNING COFFEE AND LISTENED TO HIS children playing in the backyard with Renna. The boys hollered, the girls giggled, and the sound filled Brian's being with happiness.

However, one obvious thing was amiss.

Sitting back in his chair at the dining room table, Brian glanced at Johanna then peered at Wendell. "She's not happy, is she?"

"Definitely not." Wendell took a drink from his coffee cup.

"Holding the reception tomorrow night is imperative." Brian wished he could get through to Renna. "Richard told me that the gossip has been circulating for weeks. Some say I'm an impostor, after the Sinclair wealth. Others have said I'm a specter since I've not yet been seen in public. And the recent talk is that I'm a blind invalid." Brian stood and walked to the sideboard and poured hot coffee into the lukewarm brew already in his cup.

"Do they think Renna's your nurse and...and nothing more?"

At Johanna Fields's question, Brian swung around. "No one knows Renna. Another reason to hold a reception here. As for my intentions regarding your daughter"—Brian reclaimed his seat and looked across the table at Johanna—"I've stated them before. Nothing has changed—except I hate the pretense." He glared at the spectacles on the table before peering at the wooden cane leaning against the wall in the corner. "Renna and three of my children believe I'm blind, and I feel despicable lying to them."

"Soon, Brian." Wendell's note of confidence gave him hope. "Soon this will all be over, and you can go public with the truth."

"The day can't come soon enough for me." He suddenly recalled his conversation with Richard at the farm yesterday. "Wendell, how about you and I tour my store, Sinclair & Company, and afterward inspect Great Lakes Shipping? Richard has had his hands full as of late."

"I'd like that." The older man smiled and straightened his brown, pinstriped waistcoat. "I'd like that very much."

"Good. We'll take my sons with us. Johanna?" He looked her way. "Might you and Renna be up for a bit of shopping with my daughters?"

"We love to shop, and the more the merrier."

"Thank you." Brian pulled his pocket watch from his black brocade vest. "We'll leave in an hour." Pocketing the gold watch, he took another drink of coffee. "Richard said that Matthew Benchley showed up at Great Lakes Shipping the other day and threatened a lawsuit."

"Matt? He followed us here to Milwaukee?" Wendell wagged his head. "And to think I tried to pair Matt with Renna. I thought he had such a promising future at the Chamber of Commerce."

Brian grinned wryly. "Yes, and I'd appreciate it if you'd forever banish that idea."

"Oh, I have, Brian." Wendell pulled himself up. "Of course I have! I just mean to say…well, you think you know a man, and then he turns out to be nothing but a–*a scoundrel*."

Regret pierced Brian's soul. He felt like a hypocrite. Denouncing Benchley while at the same time deceiving Renna and three of his precious children. If the authorities hadn't intimated that their lives could be in peril, he'd tell them all the truth this minute.

But for now he'd have to go on living the lie.

⁓⁓⁓⁓

As Renna brushed out her reddish-brown hair in front of the looking glass the following morning, she thought of how nice of a holiday it had been thus far. She hadn't taken a break from nursing since the war began, and she had to admit it felt good.

Yesterday after Brian and Da left, Renna took a walk along the lakeshore. The fresh air must have tired her out, for then she napped most of the afternoon away.

"You lazy creature," she told her reflection, but smiling all the while. She recalled playing with the children when they arrived home from school yesterday. If she wasn't mistaken, the boys had taken a liking to her, perhaps because she hadn't even gasped when they presented their "pet" grass snake to her. She'd even held the thing, much to Gabriel and Michael's wide-eyed amazement.

The truth was, after bandaging up severely wounded soldiers and oftentimes seeing them die after battle, a harmless grass snake didn't make her squeamish in the least.

Renna pinned up her hair and then gave her fawn-colored dress one last glance before leaving the room. She met her mother in the upstairs hallway. "G'morning, Mum. Sleep well?"

"Oh, yes." Mum stretched her arms before they descended the front stairway.

In the foyer, they found poor Hester running hither and yon. "The captain is having a reception here tonight, and he didn't even forewarn me," she complained. "Told me just this morning. He invites the entire city of Milwaukee, and he forgets to mention it." Hester threw her hands in the air. "Hallelujah!"

Mum replied with one of her demure grins. "What can Renna and I do to help you?"

Hester paused, looking surprised by the offer. But then she flung a list at them. "Here. The captain gave me these duties this morning. I've got to plan the hors d'oeuvres, hire some more staff—where will I get more people at this late hour? The captain is insisting on a butler and wants several maids too..." Hester shook her head. "Impossible!"

"And he forgot to tell you until now?" Renna didn't think that sounded like Brian.

Hester nodded.

Mum frowned and glanced from the list back to the harried housekeeper. "Where's the captain now?"

"Oh, he and Mr. Fields went to his store on the riverfront. They're meeting Mr. Navis there."

"And the children?" Renna asked. "Where are they?" She hadn't heard them awaken this morning, and neither she nor Mum had helped the girls dress. Apparently they hadn't required any help today—

Or their father had assisted them with buttons, buckles, and laces.

"Oh, the captain and Mr. Fields took the children with them," Hester replied. "It was the captain's idea, actually. He told Gabriel and Michael that he'd like them to get involved in his business affairs, little by little if they wanted it." Hester smiled for the first time since Renna had seen her this morning. "You should have seen those boys' faces too. Beaming, they were! Even Gabriel, who's not so easily impressed. Why, the captain made his sons feel real important." But then her expression fell. "But the man's going to be the death of me with his lists and last-minute receptions!"

"Now, Hester, we'll help you," Renna promised. "Here, give me that list. We'll divide up the tasks and ask Isabelle about how to go about hiring more hands."

"Oh, me," Hester sighed. "I didn't even think to ask Isabelle for guidance. But that would only make sense. Isabelle has been employed with the captain for quite some time."

Renna smiled. "Sometimes two heads are better than one, as the old adage goes."

~~~~~~~~

By three o'clock the food was arriving with Isabelle, the cook, manning the kitchen. With a bit of monetary persuasion, Isabelle agreed to stay until after the reception and clean up. Then she incorporated the help of her thirteen-year-old daughter. Together they polished silver and prepared the hors d'oeuvre trays.

A while later, the children came home and the little girls took a short rest. Brian insisted his children be in attendance tonight. Just as she and Mum finished settling Libby and Rachel upstairs, a flurry of activity ensued as everyone began to dress for the evening.

"Who's helping Brian dress?" Renna asked when Mum came in to assist her.

"Your father went to see after him just now. But you know men don't require the attention women do when we dress for the evening."

"But Brian's blind."

"He'll be fine."

Mum swept up Renna's hair and pinned it in an elegant style. Next came the evening gown of golden taffetas with an overskirt of ivory tulle. Mum helped her into it, then Renna adjusted the V-necked bodice. She didn't care for its revealing cut.

"You're used to your high-necked hospital dresses." Mom smiled. "Even though this gown is worn off the shoulders, it's quite modest, really. I've seen much worse, and I'm sure you have too. Just take care when you bend forward."

"Yes, I should say I will." Renna rolled her eyes and picked at the shimmering gold shoulder knots, which helped puff the tulle sleeves.

Mum sighed and covered her heart with her hands. "You look stunning!"

"Oh, Mum…" Renna's cheeks pinked with the compliment, although she had to admit she'd never worn such finery, and its colors did complement her green eyes and auburn hair.

And if she turned her face just so…

"No one is going to notice your birthmark." Mum clucked

her tongue. "Not when there's so much other beauty to notice about you."

"Perhaps too much." Renna tugged her bodice up a bit higher.

Wearing a frown, Mum stepped between Renna and the looking glass. "Your hair is so thick and rich, and those crystal-studded pins we found yesterday at the department store sparkle each time you move your head. Your skin is like alabaster, and your dress brings it all together in the most amazing way. I wouldn't lie to you, Renna. I'm your mother. So think about my words tonight as you stand beside Captain Sinclair. God has blessed you, my dear. Now behave like you're grateful—because you should be."

Renna opened her mouth to argue—her parents didn't understand what it felt like to have a purple mark on her cheek. Except her heart convicted her. Why couldn't she simply accept the fact her dreams were coming true?

"It just doesn't seem real, Mum."

"Shall I pinch you?"

"Mum." Renna narrowed her eyes and wagged her head.

"Honestly, Renna, the captain thinks you're beautiful, and that's all that matters. He's positively smitten. He's rich, handsome..."

"But he can't *see*, Mum. He's blind."

"Oh, he can see quite well. Why, he said just yesterday that he's only going along with this charade because the authorities suggested it."

"What? What charade?"

Mum blinked then suddenly paled.

Renna stood statue still. "Are you saying Brian *isn't* blind?"

In reply Mum began to wring her hands. "I've never been good at keeping secrets—especially from you."

"Secrets?" Renna hiked a brow. "Charades? What's this all about?" She came forward quickly and clutched her mother's shoulders. "Tell me, Mum. Tell me everything right now!"

# Twenty-Three

"HESTER, I AM IMPRESSED." FROM BEHIND HIS DARK glasses, Brian surveyed the foyer with Renna at his side. "Isabelle said everything is perfect. I gave you some tall orders, but you were able to follow them to the letter." He bowed graciously. "Thank you."

"You're welcome, Captain," Hester replied with a bit of a curtsey. She had donned a black dress and white apron that matched the serving maids' uniforms. "I must tell you, though, sir, I had help from—"

Hester paused, and from out of the side of his dark glasses, Brian saw Renna shaking her auburn head vigorously. He tried not to grin. "Yes, Hester? You had help from whom?"

"Ah, well, I had to offer Isabelle a slight bonus for staying late tonight and helping me out."

"That's to be expected, and it's not a problem."

"Thank you, sir. Now I'll be running along and making sure those hired maids aren't slacking off."

"Yes, see that you do." Brian quelled a chuckle as Hester hurried off. Then he leaned over to Renna and whispered, "You did a wonderful job with the preparations for tonight." He couldn't help placing a kiss on her temple then. "Thank you."

She pulled away from him.

He frowned. "What's wrong?"

After a deep breath she squared her shoulders. "Not a thing."

He pursed his lips. Judging from the hard set of her delicate jaw and the smoldering look in her emerald eyes, Brian sensed more than nothing was amiss. "Has it anything to do with Hester?"

"No."

"All right." He tamped down his impatience. What was it about women that they couldn't just speak their minds? Would she make him have to guess all night?

"Renna, this is a very important evening."

"Yes, I know."

Hearing her softer tone, Brian relaxed. "I must say, you look so beautiful tonight, Renna, that I—"

She looked up at him. "Why, thank you, *Captain*."

A chill fell over him. His blunder followed by her clipped reply let him know the problem. She'd somehow learned the truth. "Renna, we'll talk later, all right? I'll tell you everything, I swear. For now you must keep my secret. Please. It could be a matter of life and death."

"You lied to me." She whispered the accusation.

"For your own good." He pulled her arm more tightly around his. "For all our safety!"

Her wide emerald eyes and tight lips made him think she'd like to scream at him. She'd have the right to—perhaps she'd even come to hate him. *Oh, God, why did I think deception was the answer?*

Guests started a queue at the front door. The well-trained butler announced the invitees as they headed into the foyer.

"Mrs. Lillian LaMonde."

The wiry little woman stepped right up. Her thick dark hair had been swept up and piled on her head. Brian wondered if it weighed more than she did.

He forced a polite smile. She wasn't exactly his favorite of guests. However, her presence had been required if he intended to dispel rumors.

He held out his hand.

She took it.

"Lillian. How nice that you came tonight."

"How nice that you're not dead, Brian," she quipped, sliding her hand from his. Her perceptive gaze slid to Renna. "And who's this sweet-looking thing at your side?"

Brian made the appropriate introductions, praying Renna would withstand the scrutiny tonight and wouldn't hate him all the more for it. "Allow me to present Miss Renna Fields, from Chicago."

"Chicago? The Windy City. Are you a widow?"

Renna shook her head. "No, ma'am."

"Never been married?"

"No" Renna looked puzzled by the queries hurled at her. "I'm a nurse."

Lillian seemed amused. "A nurse? How interesting. You and I will have to talk soon." Looking back at Brian, she added, "And you and I, Brian, will have to talk soon as well."

"I'll look forward to it." He couldn't keep the cynicism from his tone, but he gave her a bow nonetheless.

Lillian LaMonde waltzed away, heading for the punch table.

Brian leaned over to Renna. "Watch every word you say to that woman. She writes the society page in the *Milwaukee Sentinel*. Everything you say can and will appear in her gossip column."

"Thank you for the advance warning," Renna said dryly.

A lead ball of guilt dropped in Brian's insides.

"Mr. and Mrs. Marcus Norton," the butler announced.

"Thank you for coming." Brian blindly held out his hand. Marcus took it and gave it a firm shake. Next Brian introduced Renna. He had a hunch she'd like the Nortons. They were thoughtful, decent, and devout people, although Brian hadn't ever appreciated those qualities in them until now. And tonight he viewed them as valuable assets in his trusted banker and his wife.

The Nortons walked off, and the butler announced the next set of guests. "Miss Fayre Waterford and Mr. Matthew Benchley."

"What is he doing here...and with Fayre?" Closing his eyes, Brian prayed Fayre would behave herself. But it didn't look as though she would if she'd paired up with Benchley. "He wasn't invited." Brian pulled Renna close until his lips touched her ear. "Be very careful around Benchley. He's a dangerous man, Renna. I'm still convinced he tampered with my schooner."

Apprehension drifted across her features. She nodded.

And then the pair stood before them.

"Captain Sinclair..." Benchley gave him a rap on the arm, and it was all Brian could do to keep his clenched fist at his side. "We meet again. How wonderful that you have regained your identity. And Renna..." Benchley sidestepped him and lifted Renna's hand to his lips. "What a pleasure to see you again."

After a prim little smile, she pulled her hand free and tossed a worried glance at Brian.

His arm at her waist, he hugged her to let her know she did fine. Just fine.

Meanwhile Fayre had snaked her satiny gloved hand up his arm. Brian tried to shake her off. The woman was like his pirate's past hitting him right between the eyes. He'd met her at a cocktail party shortly after Lousia's death. Out of sheer loneliness and grief he'd paid her several calls before meeting Elise Kingsley.

"I'm so glad you're alive and looking well, Brian—that is, except for losing your sight." She purred the comment close to his ear, and he leaned back so he wouldn't get a face full of the red feathers that adorned her elaborate headdress. "I'm ecstatic that you're not marrying Elise, that poor drowned thing."

Behind his dark spectacles, Brian glimpsed the hatred that fell over Benchley's face when Fayre spoke his aunt's name. "Thank you. It's a tragedy about Elise, and I don't take her death—or those of the others aboard, including my own mother—lightly." He meant every word. "I'd appreciate it if you'd do the same."

"Of course, Brian. Welcome home. If you ever need someone

to lead you around town, I'm available. I think you still have the key to my house." She laughed airily. "I know you've got the key to my heart."

He felt Renna stiffen. "I'll have Richard search for your key at once and return it."

Her golden features slid downward. "When did you become so polite?"

"My accident has left me a changed man, Fayre. Perhaps we can tell you about it later." He turned. "Allow me to introduce Miss Renna Fields." He brought her forward. "Renna is a nurse from Chicago. She's my guest tonight, along with her parents, Wendell and Johanna Fields."

"Friends of the family?" Fayre tipped her head in a jerking motion, threatening the beads and feathers covering her flaxen hair.

"Yes. Very, *very* special friends." Brian could see in her eyes that she understood. He had no interest in her anymore.

"It's nice to meet you, Miss Waterford."

Brian felt Renna step back and attempt to pull her hand free, but he grasped her fingertips before she was able.

Fayre's gaze darkened. "Honey," she said to Renna, "I hope you know what you're getting yourself into." She flicked a glance at Brian.

"Yes, thank you."

Again, Brian felt Renna try to tug away, but he refused to let her flee. She was strong and brave and…beautiful. Fayre could hardly compare. He wished Renna would understand that. What's more, Brian wondered what he'd ever seen in Fayre.

Benchley grinned. "Renna, you and I will have to catch up over a glass of punch. Later. When you're not…*on duty.*" With a hooded look at Brian, he took Fayre's elbow and led her away.

Brian leaned over. "Renna, I apologize that you had to witness Fayre's less than respectable behavior. Please believe me when I say that I regret my association with the woman."

Renna had no time to reply. Suddenly the next set of guests was upon them.

~~uuexeuu~~

An hour and a half later, Renna strode toward the refreshments table, relieved the reception line had dwindled. Mum and Da stood with Brian so his secret wouldn't slip, and Renna needed the break. She'd met so many people in such a short time that after a while she gave up trying to keep everyone straight. She doubted she'd recognize any of them if she passed them on the street.

But more than likely she'd never see these people again.

Sadness gripped her. Earlier she'd told Mum that she'd like to return to Chicago as soon as possible. Brian's eyesight worked just fine. He was well on his way to winning his children. Renna and her folks weren't needed here any longer. And Brian's lack of trust in her had shattered their relationship. She should go home, back to the hospital where she belonged.

"Renna..."

She started at the sound of her name and the touch on her sleeve. Turning, she saw Matthew Benchley standing an arm's length away.

"May I get you some punch?"

She drew herself up. "No, thank you."

"It's no trouble." His hand snagged her upper arm. "Come right this way."

Unless she made a scene, Renna felt she had no recourse.

"What do you want with me?" she hissed when they reached the solarium. The room's unheated night air had discouraged most guests.

"I want to know about Sinclair's medical condition. Can he really remember his past and who he is, or is this some game you and your family are playing?"

Renna inhaled sharply. "You know my family. My father is an upstanding man."

"Yes, I suppose you're all on the up and up. And what about Sinclair? Is he expected to make a full recovery?"

Renna crossed her arms. "That's confidential information, Mr. Benchley."

His brows knitted together in anger and frustration. His lip curled. "He has something that belongs to me. This farce of his won't hold up in court. I'll see to that. Memory loss, blindness...bah!"

"You'll have to speak with Brian if you want to know the specifics of his medical ailments." Renna turned away from Benchley and stared through the tall, paned windows. A nearly full moon shone from the inky sky. She stole a few moments to admire the view before casting her gaze back at Benchley.

He'd pulled a flask from the inside pocket of his gray wool jacket. "Tonic for a war injury."

"I'm sure, although in some circles what you're doing is considered *imbibing*."

In the dimly lit room he considered her in two sweeping glances. "In spite of the situation I like you, Renna Fields."

She rolled a shoulder, unaffected by his flattery.

He took a swig from the small bottle. "But I hope you're not a woman so easily bamboozled as my aunt Elise. Our gracious host knows exactly how to play a woman until he gets what he wants. Just ask poor, heartbroken Fayre Waterford." Benchley gave a sad wag of his head and leaned closer to Renna. "He made her promises of marriage and then cast her aside like an old shoe. He did the same to my aunt. And how ironic that Aunt Elise died just after selling *my* shipping company for a fraction of what it's worth."

Her muscles tensed with indignation. "Are you implying that Brian is guilty of murder?"

"Draw your own conclusions, Miss Fields."

She glanced at the doorway and took a step back. She needed to get away.

Benchley caught her elbow.

"Leave her alone, Mister!"

A woman shrieked. Stemware crashed onto the floor. A man shouted, "Stop those rascals!"

Renna gaped as pandemonium broke out in the parlor and quickly spread to the solarium. Gabriel and Michael appeared out of nowhere and rushed toward Benchley, their faces set in determination.

"Slow down, boys!" Renna held out a hand to forestall them. "Where are you going?"

Her tactics failed. Gabriel and Michael slammed into Benchley and knocked the man flat on his back.

Benchley cursed.

A crowd gathered while a couple of gentlemen helped Benchley to his feet. Renna put an arm around each boy's shoulder, guiding them a safe distance away.

"What in the world were you thinking?" She glanced from Gabriel to Michael and then at Gabe again.

"Don't worry," Gabe said. "We're protecting you, Miss Fields."

Michael nodded his dark head.

"Why?"

"Because my dad can't," Michael said, breathless, "cuz he's blind."

Renna swallowed, although when her gaze met Gabe's, an intuitive look passed between them. *He knows the truth…*

"We'll protect you," Michael reiterated.

"Why did you think I needed protecting?" She glanced at Benchley.

"We saw him"—Gabe pointed to Matt—"pull you out here, and he looked like he might hurt you."

"Yeah, and then he grabbed you."

"We were hiding," Gabe confessed. "We saw it."

Renna couldn't help but feel complimented by the boys' actions.

But this was serious business. She straightened Gabe's brown jacket. "Mr. Benchley used to work with my father. He's an acquaintance from Chicago." Renna kept her voice low, her tone soft. "I'm sure there's been a misunderstanding." She tried to sound calm and collected. After all, children shouldn't worry. Righting the collar of Michael's white shirt, she added, "Perhaps you ought to leave the protecting to the police."

"But my dad is trusting me." He brought his shoulders back. "I promised."

Renna didn't know what to say. It wasn't right what they did, tackling a guest, but on the other hand Matt wasn't invited here tonight, and he certainly had a crude way about him.

Maybe she'd been in more danger than she thought.

Sliding an arm around the boys' shoulders, she hugged them to her. "Thank you for wanting to protect me. You're both very brave and very gallant."

They suddenly acted shy, which made Renna laugh softly.

But then a hush fell over the guests. The gathering parted, and Brian stepped into the center of the commotion with Richard guiding him. He made an impressive figure in his black dress coat, white shirt and vest, and black tie. "What's going on here?"

Renna held her tongue, feeling both embarrassed by the moment and confused about how much or how little she could say about Brian's feigned blindness.

"Your children, Captain"—Benchley spit out each word—"are spoiled, uncouth little savages."

"I beg your pardon?"

Renna quickly spoke up. "Brian, the boys thought I was in some kind of danger." She stepped in front of the pair, hoping to shield them from any more of Benchley's hateful words. They were, after all, just children. "Their intentions were noble, albeit somewhat over the top." She glared at Benchley. "And they are not uncouth, spoiled, or savages."

With a toss of his head he dusted off the sleeves of his jacket. Then he swung his gaze at Brian. "Captain, I believe you and I have unfinished business."

Brian dipped his head and arched one brow above his spectacles. "I'm a bit busy at the moment."

Laughter rumbled through the onlookers.

"What's more, I don't believe I ever sent you an invitation, Benchley."

Sudden gasps and murmurs flitted through the crowd.

"I escorted Fayre Waterford this evening." Benchley stood just inches away, his chin raised in defiance. "You remember Fayre, don't you, Captain?"

Renna quickly shooed the boys from the room. They didn't need to hear any ugliness.

"You spoke to her of marriage last spring."

"That's not true."

"But then you met my aunt Elise Kingsley and decided to get your hands on her fortune. After all, it was larger than Fayre Waterford's."

"Get out, Benchley. Get out of my home. *Now.*"

Fayre Waterford pushed her way through until she stood beside Benchley. "Brian, he's right." She pouted. "You treated me badly. You led me to believe you cared."

Benchley sneered. "Shut up, Fayre."

More gasps, but this time at Benchley's venomous reply.

Renna felt herself talking a step backward, longing to be as far away from the man as possible.

Suddenly a pair of warm hands settled on her shoulders. She turned to find Da behind her.

"It's all right, my little wren. Brian wanted to face his past and put rumors to rest. It seems God is answering that prayer."

Renna couldn't imagine having to air such notorious behavior in front of guests. How could Brian take it?

"Great Lakes Shipping was, all along, supposed to be mine. I want it, Sinclair. My uncle willed it to me. Aunt Elise had no right to sell it."

Brian didn't appear frazzled in the least. "You're free to contact my attorney on Monday morning. For now, leave my home at once."

"Oh, no...you're not going to get rid of me that easily. I couldn't care less about your ostentatious social affair." He cleared his throat, behaving as though he held the upper hand. "About Great Lakes Shipping..."

Brian folded his arms. "What about it?"

"I said, I want it."

"It's not for sale." Brian clenched his jaw. "Now, I'm warning you, get out!"

Benchley's face reddened with anger. Richard and another man grabbed hold of his arms and hauled him from the solarium. He blared out every foul word imaginable the entire way to the front door.

Renna stood there feeling the weight of Brian's scrutiny coming at her from behind his dark lenses. She winced. Yes, Matt was in the wrong. But hadn't Brian put him there with his twisted business dealings and manipulative romances?

"Please, everyone." Brian gestured to the elegantly dressed guests surrounding him. "The trouble has left. Let's all continue enjoying ourselves."

He then motioned for her, and Renna stepped forward to take his arm, ever the dutiful nurse. She wouldn't denounce him in front of his friends, but indignation plumed inside of her. Could her pirate ever become a prince?

Just exactly who was Captain Brian Sinclair anyway?

## TWENTY-FOUR

GOODNESS!" LILLIAN LAMONDE CORNERED RENNA minutes later. Brian had gotten distracted with other guests. "Wasn't that...Benchley? Yes, that's his name! Fayre Waterford's escort? Why, he certainly seemed agitated." She gave Renna a sweeping look. "Perhaps he was jealous. Could he be one of your former love interests?"

"Hardly." Renna felt a presence at her side and glanced up to see Brian.

"There are certainly enough of those around here tonight— former love interests, that is." Lillian snorted, turning her scrutiny on him.

He pursed his lips and shrugged as if he couldn't care less.

Lillian tried a different approach. "Your children are up rather late, aren't they, Brian?"

"My children are invited guests tonight. However, you know they almost always make an appearance at social events in my home."

"True, but they're usually accompanied by a governess. Why, those boys are eating up all the hors d'oeuvres. Now they've bowled over a guest. And your housekeeper, Brian...why, she's conversing with the company!" Lillian brought herself up to her full height of all of five feet. "No doubt there are plenty of people who would gladly take advantage of your physical distress."

"Hester is new at housekeeping." Brian sounded a bit terse. "I'll have to speak with her."

Concerned, Renna regarded him. She hoped he wouldn't deal too harshly with poor Hester. The woman tried so hard to please.

"And, as for you, my dear."

Mrs. LaMonde captured Renna's attention.

"It's been a pleasure to meet you—and your parents."

Da gave her a gracious bow.

"However"—she chuckled merrily—"Brian, things do seem topsy-turvy here, if you don't mind my saying so. I hardly expected your latest romantic interest to be of such…average stock. From what I gather, there aren't any fortunes to be won here."

Embarrassment and humiliation coursed through Renna's veins. Her cheeks flamed. She wondered how much longer she could abide this party.

Beside her, she felt the muscles in Brian's arm tense. "You're wrong, Lillian. I've acquired something more precious than gold or silver or banknotes. I have been what the Holy Bible calls 'saved by grace through faith.' Along with salvation came friendship and love. I truly am a rich man."

At another time, Renna's heart would have been stirred. However, at present, her feelings were all jumbled into one great knot of confusion.

However, Mrs. LaMonde didn't seem impressed. "You lost your sight. I should think you'd feel cursed—and many at this reception would agree that you deserved it."

Renna thought she could actually see Brian wrestling with his own emotions.

"That will be another story for another time, Lillian."

"Very well." The woman arched a well-sculpted brow. "I must be off. I have a column to write and a deadline to meet."

Brian dipped his head politely. "Thank you for coming."

Once she'd gone, Da chuckled. "I can't wait to read tomorrow's newspaper."

"Hmm…" Brian clasped his hands behind his back. "Nor can I, Wendell." He inhaled audibly. "Now to find my sons and have a bit of a talk with them." He turned to Renna and offered his arm. "If you'll escort me?"

She hesitated, knowing he didn't need a guide. He could see his way through the house.

"Renna, please?"

Da nodded.

"Oh, all right." She slipped her hand around his elbow. But this was the last time she'd partake in such pretense. After tonight Brian could face his deception all by himself!

~~~~~

The rest of the evening passed without incident, and by ten o'clock all the guests save for Richard and Sarah had departed. The Navises would stay overnight, and Renna hoped for another chance to get to know Sarah better. As for the other company here tonight, Renna was more than glad to see them go. This evening proved the longest, most disheartening four hours of her life!

After helping Hester, Isabelle, and Mum with the cleanup, Renna said her good nights and made her way toward the stairwell. The boys were already upstairs, and Sarah offered to help the girls. But as she reached the first step, Brian stretched his arm out in front of her.

She paused and regarded him askance.

"I'd like a word with you, please."

"I don't feel like talking, Brian."

"Then just listen. I have a lot to explain."

She wished his charm didn't have any effect on her, but it did. She relented.

Taking her hand, Brian led her into his study. "Your father gave me permission to speak with you privately," he said, closing the oak-paneled double doors.

She folded her arms and watched as Brian pulled off his dark spectacles. Hurt and anger enveloped her all over again.

"Now, Renna, don't be upset."

"Upset? Oh, I'm not upset. I'm *incensed*." She inhaled. "How could you, Brian? How could you lie to me all these weeks?" Uncrossing her arms, she moved toward him. "Me? I was your confidant. I prayed for you."

"But you purposely distanced yourself when you learned I'd regained my sight."

She frowned, confused.

"Yes, Renna, your insecurity prompted me to fake a relapse."

"Don't you dare blame me for your bad behavior. You chose to lie."

Brian looked down momentarily. "You're right. But your friendship and devotion were my lifeline. Once I began the deception, there seemed no way out. It rippled. Then this whole thing involving my boating accident and Benchley's determination to own Great Lakes Shipping developed. Authorities here in Milwaukee felt I should continue the charade. So I did."

He sat down on the corner of his wide desk, dangling one leg. They were eye to eye, and Renna felt captivated by his dark scrutiny. *Mr. Blackeyes...*

"I read a passage in the Bible recently that love covers a multitude of sins."

She smiled, somewhat heartened. "Brian, it's not uncommon for men to fall in love with their nurses. Perhaps you have—"

"Blast it all, Renna!" Brian shot to his feet. "Why are you so insistent upon pushing me away?" He opened his arms wide. "Look at all I have to offer. What's more, I see that special adoration in your eyes when you look at me, and the longing on your face. And, yes, you have a beautiful face. I've seen your birthmark nearly every day for the last month, and it has no bearing on my feelings for you."

Her fingertips flew to her cheek while her gaze fell to the imported carpet.

"I sensed it when I kissed you, Renna. You're in love with me. Why don't you allow me to reciprocate?"

She looked at him hard. "And why didn't you feel I was worthy of your trust?"

He pointed at her. "That's not fair, Renna, and you know it."

She pivoted and stood with her back to him now.

Brian exhaled. "Yes, I lied. It's regrettable, and I'm sorry. I wanted to tell you the truth, but the timing never seemed right. Then I thought it could endanger your life—and the lives of my children. I had to keep silent, Renna. Don't you see?"

Renna felt herself melting like butter. His explanation aligned with her reasoning. How many times had she whispered comforting words to a patient, knowing full well his prognosis was grim?

More times than she could count.

Slowly Renna turned to face him.

"You have a marvelous rapport with my children."

*At least they had accepted her as she was.*

"Imagine my sons wanting to protect you from a character like Benchley." Brian chuckled. "Heroes, the both of them."

"You have fine children, Brian." Renna's crinoline rustled as she moved toward the windows, which overlooked the front of the manse. Darkness stretched out as far as she could see except for the sharp stars overhead.

"They adore you, Renna. Even Gabe is fond of you, and he rarely takes to anyone."

A smile tickled her mouth. That boy certainly had a vivid imagination. First came his talk about stowing away, and then tonight he rescued a damsel in distress. Michael went right along with him. Those two needed both nurturing and a firm hand—with the accent on the latter.

Brian came up behind her and placed his hands on her bare shoulders. The warmth of his palms spread down to her toes. "Do you think you could ever love my children, Renna?"

"The way Sarah does?" Renna had heard. Sarah had been the beloved governess.

He paused. "The way only a *mother* could?"

She whirled around, realizing only too late her mistake. How could she be angry, let alone think coherently, with his close proximity? "I'm a nurse..."

"And a good one." Amusement skipped across his swarthy features.

Renna leaned back.

Brian leaned forward.

"I have as much experience as an ornamental showpiece as Hester does being a housekeeper."

"Showpiece?" He brought his chin back sharply. His gaze narrowed. "Is that what you think—that I merely want you as some kind of trinket?"

Renna swallowed hard. Could she speak her fears? "Brian, your determination to change your life is highly commendable. But in the long run, you'd never be happy with a woman like me. Lillian LaMonde was right when she said I come from 'average stock.'"

A muscle worked in his jaw. "Renna Fields, you are the most exasperating woman I have ever encountered."

"Oh, Brian, think about it, will you?"

"As if you're not all I think about?"

His flattery nearly made her head spin. Still, she found the strength to sidestep him. "All right, I'll admit it. I'm the one who'd never be happy, not in this house, not with your lifestyle..."

Faces of the beautiful women she'd seen tonight flitted across her mind.

"You wouldn't be happy with me and my children? Is that what you're really saying?"

It wasn't. Not at all!

But Renna purposely didn't correct him. Her silence would save them both heartache later.

"I told Mum that I'd like leave on the first train Monday morning. I think it's for the best."

"Leave?" Brian quickly reached for her. "You can't leave."

Sadness filled her.

"I won't allow it!"

"What?"

"You made me a promise the other night, Renna. You promised to be patient with me."

"But you deceived me. I thought you were blind, for heaven's sake!"

"Nonetheless, a promise is a promise." His tone mocked her. "Are you or are you not a woman of your word?"

"How dare you threaten me!"

"Hmm…" He stroked his shadowed jaw. "I wonder who your parents will side with, you…or me?"

Renna's jaw slacked. She shook off his hold on her arm. Her gaze never wavered from his. The word *despicable* longed to spring off the tip her tongue, but she saw something other than malice in his eyes. "You're teasing me."

"Press the matter and see."

She weighed her options. Mum and Da were a pair of bleeding hearts. Renna had no doubt that Brian could persuade her father to take his side. And Mum entertained thoughts of her spinster daughter marrying a wealthy man. Of course she'd concede to Brian's wishes to stay on.

Her blood began to boil. "So"—she walked slowly toward the windows—"you're manipulating me just like you manipulated Sarah and Richard."

"I don't see this as manipulation. I call it acting on the truth so you'll come to your senses."

"Oh, I've come to my senses, all right." She whirled around, facing him, her hands clenched at her side. "And you can talk to my parents. Go on and do it. They may well take your side. They may even try to persuade me to stay." She raised her chin in confidence. "But they won't force me to do anything against my will. They never have."

Brian's smug expression vanished, and Renna thought his dark gaze rounded with something that appeared to be hurt. His black eyes bore into her as if he tried to read her thoughts.

Renna stared right back.

"Renna, I love you. Can you blame me for trying to make you stay?"

His words almost touched her heart. Almost. But before she could reply, a large crash rocked the house. Muted sounds of breaking glass reached Renna's ears.

"What in the world?" Brian ran to the door and swung it open. Renna was right behind him, and they met Hester, Isabelle, and Mum in the foyer.

"Must have been a tree that fell on the house, Captain!" Hester exclaimed.

Da and Mr. Navis came running from the men's parlor, wearing worried expressions.

"I think it came from the solarium, Captain."

"I thought so too, Richard. Let's investigate." He turned to Renna. "Take all the ladies upstairs and see that the children are safe."

"All right."

"I'll come for you when I'm sure it's safe."

Renna nodded, and he held her gaze for a long moment before hurrying after the men.

Renna and the three ladies took the wide front staircase. Reaching the top, they found Sarah ready to descend. Her fair features were taut with confusion and concern.

"Something's hit the house," Renna said. "A tree, perhaps."

"Oh, my!" Her hand flew to her throat.

"Where are the girls?" Renna moved to the middle of the upper hallway where there was room to converse.

"They're sleeping."

"Good. What about the boys?"

"Let's find out."

Mum showed Isabelle and Hester into the sitting room adjoined with the bedroom she shared with Da. There they'd wait comfortably. In the meantime, Renna and Sarah proceeded to look in on the boys.

Knocking lightly, they entered when Michael bid them entrance.

"What was that crash?" He frowned then a grin crept over his face. "Was it Granny Hester trying to cook in the kitchen again?" Michael chuckled.

"Your father and others are investigating." Renna tried not to smile. "However, we're certain Granny Hester had nothing to do with it. Good night."

"Good night."

Closing the door, she and Sarah shared a laugh out in the hallway. On to Gabriel's room. They knocked once. No answer. Another knock, this time harder.

"Gabe?" Sarah called to him through. Then she gazed at Renna. "Maybe he's asleep."

Renna turned the knob. A lamp was lit and sat on the bedside table, but Gabriel was nowhere to be found.

"I'll look for him down the hallway near Brian's quarters if you'll look upstairs in the ballroom and Hester's suite."

"Sounds like a good plan to me."

They each collected a lighted lamp and parted.

Renna searched Brian's room, noting its tidiness. Large walnut furniture had been neatly arranged. Burgundy-colored velvet drapes covered the wide windows. The décor was decidedly masculine.

No Gabriel anywhere.

Finally Da came up with the news. "We found Gabriel. Apparently, he crept down for more food and was eating in the hallway between the solarium and the parlor when the crash occurred."

"Praise God!" Relief filled Renna. "When we couldn't find him, I imagined the worst." With a hand on her heart, she expelled another sigh of easement. "What was the source of the crash?"

"An odd-looking metal object, weighing nearly four pounds."

Renna and Sarah both inhaled sharply at the news.

"I'm going to find Richard." Sarah hurried downstairs.

"I'll get back to cleaning up," Hester said. "Are you coming, ladies?" She glanced at Isabelle and Mum.

"Right behind you, Hester." Mum gave Da a quick hug as she passed by.

"I'm still filled with questions." Renna watched the other ladies depart then turned to Da. "What was the object, and why did it come through one of the sunroom's windows?"

His brows knitted together in a deep frown. "Upon closer inspection, Brian identified it as a piece of propeller from a ship. Someone heaved it through one of the glass panes of the solarium." He shook his head sadly. "Such damage. Brian has summoned the police. Meanwhile, Gabriel claims to have seen a man running from the scene." Da paused. "Gabe's sketching the culprit's likeness for the authorities."

Renna swallowed hard. "Brian's suspicions were right, then."

"Yes. There was a note tied around the piece of metal too. A threat."

Fear prickled inside Renna's limbs. "What sort of a threat, Da? Who is the culprit? Benchley?"

"Brian doesn't want you to know the details. He doesn't want you worried."

Renna threw her hands up in exasperation. "Oh, that man! Doesn't he know by know that I'm a very capable woman? I served as a nurse on several battlefields and in an army hospital. A threat won't make me worry. If anything, it'll have me on my knees more often!"

"Oh, don't be too hard on the captain, Renna. He's trying to protect you. The less you know, the better—that's what Brian told me."

"Da, I'm not some swooning little morsel of a woman. During the war there were times I even had to handle a gun. I don't need protecting."

"Maybe not in that sense, Renna. But a man needs to feel that he can protect the woman he loves. So let him. Let Brian protect you."

*The woman he loves?*

Tears sprang to Renna's eyes. "Da, what if Brian only thinks he loves me because I'm the first woman who's really cared about him? Didn't you see all the beauties here tonight? I can't compare. Not with this ugly birthmark on my cheek. And Brian hasn't had the chance to meet other Christians who are serious about their faith." She paused, regarding her father as an errant tear trickled down her marred cheek. "Somewhere in the world there might be a gorgeous woman of faith who'd make Brian the perfect wife. But she's not me."

Da shook his head, looking sorrowful. "Renna, you accept everyone else for who they are and love them. But you don't afford yourself the same courtesy. If we're to love our neighbors as ourselves, then wouldn't you say God expects you to respect yourself?"

"Don't lecture me, Da." She folded her arms.

"God created you with your birthmark, Renna. It's where the angels kissed your cheek."

Renna shook her head. "Not really."

"Brian sees your beauty—even blind he saw it. Why can't you?"

Renna couldn't stand to hear anymore. "I told Brian that we're leaving on Monday morning."

"What?"

"You heard me, Da. I–It's for the b–best." She pushed past him and hurried across the hallway to her bedroom.

"Good night, my little wren," Da called after her.

Renna's sob drowned out his words.

## TWENTY-FIVE

THE FOLLOWING DAY THE SUN SHONE BRIGHTLY THROUGH the bare tree branches. A brisk wind whipped off of Lake Michigan as Renna and her parents traveled with Brian to his mother's home. He still had the matter of her estate to settle, and Brian had asked them along for moral support, while Richard and Sarah were kind enough to stay behind with the children. Everyone sensed a difficult task lay ahead of Brian. But the Navises and Mum and Da were much more eager to help him than Renna. She still felt betrayed and manipulated—by the man she loved and by her own parents as well. What's more, her own heart had betrayed her. Now she regretted her angry declaration that she would be leaving on Monday. Overnight the reality of Brian's situation had sunk in, and she feared for his life.

"Are you sure it's safe for us to inspect your mother's estate?" She sat beside him inside the carriage, her gaze fixed on the passing scenery. They passed small cottages with yards covered by fallen leaves, and now and again she caught glimpses of Lake Michigan. Her parents sat across from them.

"Perfectly safe, Renna." Brian's leather gloved hand covered hers, and he smiled, showing that he read her concern as proof of her love.

She snatched her hand away. "What about the children?" she asked briskly. She would show the concern of a friend. Nothing more.

"They're fine. Richard is a smart, capable man."

*I'm capable as well!* She wanted to scream it. Instead she inhaled deeply.

"Stop fretting, Renna." Da leaned forward and clapped her knee affectionately.

She couldn't seem to help it. A spirit of suspicion taunted her. Brian, Da, and Richard knew something and wouldn't share it. More secrets.

The journey took nearly forty-five minutes, and when they finally arrived, Renna felt chilled. November was doing a good job of making itself known, a mark of winter to be sure. But inside the stately, gray-stone home a cozy fire burned in the parlor's hearth.

The butler greeted them with a mournful grin. "I'm the only staff member left, sir," he told Brian. An older man, he was perhaps the same age as Da. He had white hair and well-groomed white whiskers that came down along his jowls. "I'm so sorry for your loss, sir. I shall miss Mrs. Reil greatly. But I never gave up hope on you," the butler added, his British accent suddenly apparent. "Since your body was never recovered, sir, I just knew you still had to be alive."

"Thank you, Ramsey." Brian shook the man's hand before introducing Renna and her parents. "Ramsey has worked for our family for the past twenty-five years. He's a trustworthy staff member."

"I appreciate it, sir." He paused. "I started gathering up Madam's things. Her clothes and belongings are packed in wooden crates, sir. I left them upstairs until further notice."

"Thank you. We'll give them to charity."

"Yes, sir."

Watching the exchange, Renna sensed the butler's remorse and Brian's gratitude.

"May I take your coats?" Ramsey offered. Turning to Brian, he held out his arm. "Sir?"

Brian nodded and helped Renna off with her woolen cloak

before removing his own. Likewise, Mum and Da handed their winter wear into Ramsey's waiting arms.

The butler smiled. "It's good to be of service again."

"Would you consider coming to work for me, Ramsey?" Brian rubbed his palms together and glanced around the room. "I have a new housekeeper, and I sense I'll soon have need of a butler as well. Hester is not as, um, experienced as Gretchen was."

"I appreciate the offer, sir." He bowed in deference. "I would be honored to work for you."

"Very good. We'll talk business later."

Another bow and Ramsey left the room.

Brian turned his attention to Renna and her parents. "Would you like a tour of my mother's home?"

Da smiled. "I think we'd all enjoy it."

"I grew up in this home, and I'd wager it hasn't changed in years." He went on to explain. "Aurora was married several times during my upbringing. Each time we moved into a different house. Even so, Aurora never sold this place. She loved it. She called it home, and after her last husband died, she moved back here to stay."

Brian showed them outside to the back. As he didn't have to conceal the fact that he could see while in the company of Renna, her folks, and Ramsey, he led the tour. The wide yard gave way to a gently sloping hillside, which led to the sandy shores of Lake Michigan. To the right stood an elaborate stable.

"Aurora loved to ride. Every day at dawn she'd saddle her favorite horse, and with her hair loose and billowing behind her, she'd gallop along the beach." Brian shook his head over the memory. "She didn't sit sidesaddle, either. I used to think that if her socialite friends could see her, they'd be aghast! But Aurora didn't care, and she was an excellent horsewoman. I believe she had my children on a pony by the time they were two years old."

Listening, Renna looked out along the shores and tried to imagine such a woman. So eccentric, she rode like the wind and insisted that her son and grandchildren call her by her first name.

Renna turned, surveying the yard. Except for another small, gray stone cottage, which was Ramsey's home, there wasn't a neighbor for miles. The bustling city seemed so far away with its crowds and clamor.

She noted, then, that evergreens bordered the property, and the terrace looked like a marvelous place for children to play. In the summer, Renna could well imagine moonlit walks along the beach—and, of course, she imagined Brian by her side.

Glancing his way, she caught his gaze. He'd been watching her.

"This home originally belonged to my grandmother, and I hate the thought of parting with it. My grandmother lived with Aurora and me until I was about ten years old. When she died, I missed her terribly. My grandmother was more of a mother to me than Aurora." Brian paused in momentary reflection. "Only now I realize that she had a strong faith and prayed often. I can recall my grandmother reading the Bible and doing all kinds of charity work. She belonged to a local church, although I can't remember which one. I do, however, remember attending services with her from time to time. I have very pleasant childhood memories, and they're a result of my grandmother's nurturing.

"But then, about two years after she died," Brian continued, "I started getting into all kinds of mischief. Aurora packed me off to boarding school and remarried. I never lived in this house again."

In spite of herself, Renna stepped toward him, wondering over his melancholy. But in a flash it vanished.

"Let's move on, shall we?"

Back inside the house, Renna and her parents toured the first floor—kitchen, dining room, sunroom, parlor, and sitting room. The latter, Brian said, once served as his grandfather's study.

As they ambled about, Renna observed that each room opened

to the next, save for the sitting room, which opened only to the foyer. This made the sitting room more private but allowed for easy access to and from the other rooms. The floor plan seemed homey to Renna, and though it was a larger home than her own, it wasn't too different from the one she'd known all her life.

At last the tour concluded, and they ended up back in the parlor. Ramsey prepared hot tea, which he served by the fire. Only then did Brian excuse himself to talk business with his newly acquired butler.

They sipped from the dainty porcelain cups as an awkward silence fell. Finally Mum spoke up. "Renna, your father tells me that you have asked to leave Milwaukee on Monday, and I fear your decision might be partly our fault. Please don't be angry with your father and me. We never meant to keep secrets from you."

"That's right, my little wren." Da looked pained. "We thought we were helping matters."

"And what matters would those happen to be?" Renna stared into the fire, refusing to meet their eyes.

Da let out a slow breath. "Renna, we'd like to see you marry Brian. He has a good heart. A blemished past, yes, but a good heart. He's sensitive to God's Spirit and wants to do the right thing." Da sat forward. "He needs a devoted wife and loving mother for his children."

Renna chafed.

"You'd be set for life, dear," Mum added.

"Marriage and money." Renna stood and walked to the hearth, inspecting the collection of wooden horse figures. Some were brightly painted. "What about love and happiness?" She spun on her heel, giving her parents a glare. "And trust? What about that?"

"Renna..." Da spoke her name on a remorseful sigh.

"As Christians we are to forgive one another." Mum's eyes clouded. "Can't you find it in your heart to forgive your father and me? We only want the best for you."

"Of course I forgive you. Both of you." Renna crossed her arms. "And Brian too." She lifted her chin. "But you'd best know that Brian has not proposed. He's only asked that I be patient." She paused, regretting her reply. "I gave him my promise that I'd do so."

"Reasonable." Da gave an approving nod.

"Yes," Mum agreed. "Now don't you agree that patience is best exercised in close proximity? We've only just arrived in Milwaukee. You've had a trying few days, what with meeting the children, finding out about Brian's sight, and attending that reception, not to mention these threats from a madman. This is hardly the time to be packing up to go. And what would the children think? Have you thought of them?"

"Of course!" Renna had thought of how she didn't want to break their hearts if their father decided she wasn't suited to be his wife. She'd all but decided it would be better if she made the break swift and clean. But her head and her heart both told her now that her parents were right. While her pride and insecurity told her to flee, love and common courtesy told her to stay.

She lifted her hands helplessly. "All right. I'll stay at least a week longer. But no more talk of marriage. With all due respect to you both, that is for Brian and me to decide, not you."

Slowly she turned back to the hearth. Little did they know her promise had enslaved her. It was becoming very clear that her pirate hadn't changed much at all. And her parents were too dazzled by his wealth and charm to see straight. To them he could do no wrong.

She picked up a metal poker and jabbed at the dying fire. Brian's children she could live with and love. His wealth and social status and mansion she could tolerate. But his manipulations and connivings to get his own way at the expense of everyone around him—never.

# Twenty-Six

THE WIND PICKED UP OFF THE LAKE, AND THE CARRIAGE rocked, at times precariously, as they rode home from the late Aurora Reil's estate. Living in Chicago, Renna was accustomed to the gusts. However, she never realized how much the tall buildings in the city broke the force of the wind. Now, with the road running parallel to the shoreline, there was often nothing to shield them from the gale. It felt a bit unsettling, even for a Chicagoan like herself.

"I hope we get home soon." Mum appeared worried.

"Don't fret, dear lady," Brian said. "The wind will die down when the sun sets."

"Is there a storm approaching?" Mum nervously held on to the green felt hat she wore.

"I think not." Brian turned his head and glanced out the conveyance's pane. "It's just nature's way of ridding the trees of their leaves in preparation for winter."

"I marvel at your sense of meteorology," Da said. "Quite a gift from God, I'd say."

"You think so?"

Renna looked in time to see an expression of pleasure spreading across Brian's face.

"A gift from God. How I relish it more now because I know Him."

A smile pulled at Renna's mouth.

"And speaking of the sun setting." Brian cleared his throat. "I just remembered…last night at the reception I was invited to a party tonight. I accepted the invitation, and Renna, I'd like you to accompany me."

Parting her lips, she prepared to reply with a resounding, "No, thank you!" But Brian clutched her hand before she could speak.

"Please, Renna. It's important to me."

"We're happy to watch the children and get the girls washed up and into bed." Mum smiled and gave Renna a hopeful glance.

"You should know that I've invited Richard and Sarah along." Brian pulled his dark gaze away and looked toward Mum and Da. "Please don't mention this yet, but I plan to ask Richard to be my business partner. He's been like a brother to me."

"How generous of you, Brian." Da looked both surprised and impressed.

But Renna crossed her arms and focused on the passing view outside. *More manipulation—this time designed to make Richard stay.* "Richard wants to be a farmer," she finally muttered.

"Yes, I thought so too. Until I tore up our contract from this summer and released him from my employ. Richard told me he'd missed the business and added that in my absence he discovered he enjoyed being in charge and making important decisions." Brian shifted. "In any case, I shall make the offer. It's up to Richard whether to accept it or not."

"No strings attached?" The question flew off Renna's tongue before she could think better of it. She turned to look at him.

Brian met her gaze. "No strings attached. On my honor as a Christian man."

In spite of herself she believed him.

"Will you attend the party with me tonight?"

"Yes." Her heart had replied because apparently her common sense had blown away on the last hearty gust of wind.

~~~~~~~~

Brian heard the rustling of skirts and made a subtle glance toward the door. The sight of Renna standing there in an elegant black velvet dress rendered him momentarily senseless. She looked captivating, and Brian decided it was a good thing that Renna had never realized how beautiful she was. If she had, she might have become another Fayre Waterford!

Johanna Fields stepped forward. "Captain Sinclair, did you hear me?"

He lifted Rachel, who had been sitting on his lap, and stood politely. "Mrs. Fields, I apologize. My thoughts were elsewhere. What did you say?"

"I said, Renna is here and ready for the party tonight. I'll take the baby from you, although Rachel is hardly a baby anymore...are you, darling?"

"Nope, I'm a big girl like Libby." She turned adoring eyes on Brian. "Right, Daddy?"

"Right, kitten." He bent to kiss her rounded cheek.

Johanna took his daughter's hand, and Brian turned his attention to Renna again. The only word to describe the way he felt was *enthralled*.

"Renna, I must say you're stunning."

She walked toward him, and Brian's heart beat a little faster. A teasing gleam entered her green eyes. "Perhaps you really are blind."

He narrowed his gaze at the quip. But she could go ahead with her self-deprecation. At least Brian wouldn't have to worry about her flirting with every man at the party tonight. But he suspected Renna didn't have a disloyal bone in her body anyway.

"I suppose you two should be off." Wendell gave Brian a friendly slap on the back.

His thoughts immediately returned to the present, and Wendell gave him a knowing grin. For the first time in years, Brian felt embarrassed. Why, he'd been gawking like a schoolboy, and no doubt Wendell had noticed.

What in the world was wrong with him?

Brian cleared his throat, hoping to conceal his discomfort. "Yes, I suppose we should leave since Richard and Sarah went on ahead in another of my carriages."

Wendell chuckled. "I dare say the newlyweds are eager to spend every minute they can alone with each other."

Brian's eyes lingered on Renna, and he could imagine being so much in love.

At long last he tore his gaze away. "Thank you both for agreeing to watch the children tonight."

"Oh, we're seasoned grandparents, aren't we, Johanna?"

"Indeed."

He smiled. "Very well. Renna and I shall take our leave, then." After donning his outerwear, Brian put on his dark glasses. Then he offered his arm. "Ready?"

"No. I refuse to play this game a moment longer!"

Brian nearly grinned at the stubborn tilt to her lovely chin. "If it means life or death, will you play along then?"

"Life or death?" She wetted her lips in indecision, and Brian longed to kiss her. "You know I'd do anything to protect you."

"Renna," Da said, "Brian's assailant must believe he's blind."

"Is it Matt Benchley?" Her eyes begged for the truth.

Still, Brian didn't want to tell her. He preferred she stay in blissful ignorance. However, he began to realize Renna was smarter than that.

He gave in. "Yes, it's Benchley, although I can't prove it. Not yet. But I still suspect him."

Her features brightened. "Thank you, Brian. Thank you for trusting me enough to tell me the truth." With that, Renna slid her gloved hand around his elbow.

Something of a thrill passed through him. *God, if this isn't love, I don't know what is.*

They walked out to the carriage, and their driver saw them comfortably settled inside. A slap of the reins, and they were off.

Sitting beside her, Brian lifted her hand and held it between his two palms. "Thank you, Renna."

"For what?"

"For accompanying me tonight. I know it's asking a lot of you to attend a social event two evenings in a row."

She stiffened, and immediately he knew he'd said the wrong thing. "Well, I did make you a promise, and I intend to keep it."

So now she was throwing her promise in his face, letting him know that she was there not on her own account but because he had coerced her. Was there ever such an exasperating woman as this?

"So you're only here out of a sense of duty, is that it?"

"Or something like it."

"You're wrong—and I'll prove it." Brian gathered her into his arms. His lips sought hers gently—so very gently. He had a point to make.

He glimpsed her eyes fluttering closed as he kissed her. Her willing, even enthusiastic response caused him to pull away and grin.

He straightened. "Just duty, eh?"

Reality seemed to slap her. "You're despicable!"

Brian sat back against the leather bench, smiling. "Renna, you're as much of a liar as I am."

"What?" She stiffened.

"You love me. Admit it."

"I'll do no such thing." Only then did she snatch her hand from his and give him a mild shove. "And I'll thank you to mind your manners, *Captain*."

He laughed. And God help him! He couldn't keep from smiling for the next few blocks until they reached the Carpenters' home.

~~~⟋⟍⟋⟍~~~

Renna fumed as the carriage lurched to a halt. Moments later the driver swung open the carriage door, and Brian climbed out.

"Thank you, Wallace. I'll send word when we're ready to leave."

"Yes, Captain." The man bowed respectfully as Brian helped Renna alight from the carriage.

Then he grasped her elbow to keep up the pretense of his blindness. Together they walked to the house, which was lit up brightly. Candles flickered in each of the eight front windows, signaling a welcome.

At the front door, the lanky butler welcomed them with a stiff bow. He took Renna's woolen cape and then ushered them into a large hall. A small quartet played an upbeat tune, and couples waltzed to the music.

They were immediately offered a glass of punch. Renna accepted one and put it into Brian's hand. Then she took another for herself. Taking a sip, she allowed her gaze to roam. The room was nearly filled to capacity, but the object of Renna's attention was, oddly enough, the chandelier.

"It's the most hideous thing I've ever laid eyes on," she whispered. "Why, it looks to be made of wrought iron and…antlers! Have you ever seen anything like it?"

"No, but I imagine it's an original TC." Brian laughed. "Ted Carpenter, whose home we're visiting, is a much sought-after artist. He first made a name for himself in the theater, but lately his forte is unusual artwork. My guess is that before this evening is over, someone will offer him millions for that piece."

"The chandelier? A piece of art?" Renna shook her head in disbelief. "Why, Gabriel's drawings are finer than that horned thing."

"Are you telling me that I had better not purchase it?" Brian asked with a darkly handsome grin.

Renna knew he teased her. "Unlike yourself, I would never tell you what to do. I'm merely voicing my opinion—whether you wanted to hear it this time or not."

He chuckled. "And I suppose I had better get used to it."

"Adjust if you will. But there's no need."

"What are you saying, Renna? That you'd allow your stubbornness to stand in the way of love?"

"Love?" She stood close to him so she wouldn't be overheard. "How dare you speak to me of love! Charm and persuasion are hardly its equal."

Before Brian could counter the remark, a short, slim man appeared and extended his hand.

"Captain, nice to see you here. As I said last night, I'm very glad you're alive." The man chuckled, his gray eyes dancing with amusement. "You're one of my best customers."

"Ted." Brian smiled and blindly reached for his hand, and the other man made the connection. "Good to see you again."

"Likewise, Captain." The man's gaze settled on Renna. He reached for her gloved hand and brought it to his lips. "Miss Fields, isn't it?"

"Yes."

"We met last night, and I never forget a name. Thank you so much for coming tonight."

"My pleasure, sir." Renna vaguely recalled the meeting but smiled all the same.

"Sir?" With a frown, Mr. Carpenter looked at Brian then back at Renna. "I'm not a 'sir.' I'm a 'Ted.' Please call me by my given name. All my friends do."

"Thank you. Then you must call me Renna."

Ted turned to Brian. "The authorities were here this afternoon," he said, seriously now. "They asked about Benchley, and he is invited tonight. However, I told them, as I'll tell you, we're not likely to see him. He owes me money for a sculpture I sold him. I made it from a ship's propeller." Ted beamed. "It was a magnificent thing, Brian. You would have appreciated it."

"I believe I found a piece of it," he replied tersely.

Renna gasped, catching the implication. "Last night, Brian? The solarium?"

He glanced at her. "Yes."

"Ghastly." Ted shook his head. "I heard about the damage to your home. But as for Benchley—"

Brian interrupted and turned to Renna. "My dear, don't concern yourself with this." He faced his friend again. "Ted, let's talk about this in private." Brian disengaged Renna's arm. "I won't leave you for long," he promised.

She bristled. Couldn't he see that she wasn't a child?

He glanced in her direction. Renna looked away.

As her gaze fell on the guests, she noted the ladies' expensive gowns and sparkling jewels around their necks. The men were dressed in handsome, well-tailored suits. Renna felt detached and conspicuous—

Until the Navises appeared.

"Isn't this a marvelous party?" Sarah had a happy smile on her face, and the gray silk dress she wore enhanced the blue of her eyes.

Richard chuckled. "My Sarah enjoys hobnobbing."

Renna grinned at the remark.

"Oh, I can't help it, Richard. Back in Jericho Junction, we never had parties of this magnitude."

"So you've told me." He teasingly rolled his eyes.

Sarah ignored him. "You look beautiful tonight, Miss Fields."

"Please, call me Renna. Your gown is lovely, Sarah."

"Thank you. I purchased it with my first paycheck."

"And your second and third," Richard added.

Sarah gave him a warning jab with her elbow.

Renna laughed. The two were quite a pair. Made for each other.

Looking in Brian's direction, Renna saw him motioning. Then she caught Richard's reply with an incline of his head.

"Please excuse me for a moment, ladies." Richard left their side.

Sarah took her arm. "Come with me. I'll show you the most delicious spread of food."

Together she and Sarah made their way to the other end of the room where a long, white-linen covered table stood cluttered with delectables. Tiny meatballs smothered in gravy, liver pâté, a variety of cheeses, and salmon. Renna shamefully wanted to taste it all.

When her plate was filled, Renna looked up and saw Sarah at the opposite end of the table. They'd gotten separated somehow. As Renna took a step in that direction, she felt a tap on her shoulder.

"Well, well, we meet again."

Renna whirled around, coming face-to-smirking-face with Lillian LaMonde. She felt undignified holding a plate nearly filled to capacity, but held herself in check. "Good evening, Mrs. LaMonde."

An inquiring frown caused her left eyebrow to dip slightly. "What on earth are you doing with a man like Brian Sinclair?"

"I beg your pardon?" Renna had thought the woman might question her large appetite.

"He's a rogue and a rake, and this entire town knows it. Didn't your parents do any kind of a background check?"

"My parents and I are well aware of Brian's background. But, you see—"

"Then there must be something else, another reason you're associating with him. Have you agreed to a marriage of convenience, perhaps—because of the children? Maybe Brian is too frugal to hire another governess. They never stayed long anyway—and you'd make a fine example for his brood." She tipped her coiffured head. "Did I guess correctly?"

"Not even close." Renna squared her shoulders.

"Well, that's what everyone's saying."

Renna refused to be intimidated. The realization hit her then— if Brian had to duel his past, she had to battle her insecurities. Perhaps she and her pirate made a good match after all.

"Mrs. LaMonde, you and everyone else are free to think what you like."

"So it's true?"

"No, but are you really concerned with the truth?" Renna gave her a patient smile. "It probably won't make as good a story as all the gossip."

Lillian LaMonde's countenance cracked into a genuine grin. "You know, I think I like you. Plucky, that's what you are." She paused, narrowing her gaze and scrutinizing Renna. "So, you think you can tame a man like Captain Brian Sinclair, do you?"

"Tame him?" Renna chuckled lightly. "Hardly, Mrs. LaMonde. I don't have that kind of power and influence. Only God can change a man's heart, and that's exactly what He did too. God changed Brian."

"God?" The probing journalist seemed positively stunned. "You're telling me that Brian has found God?"

"Brian will have to tell you about it. It wouldn't be right for me to share."

"Oh, this is delicious." Lillian held her hand in the air, as if penning a headline. "Brian Sinclair Turns From Scoundrel to Saint."

"It does have a nice ring to it." Renna giggled softly behind her gloved hand.

Surprise wafted across the older woman's powdered face. "Tell me more."

"Mrs. LaMonde, as I said, Brian will have to tell you—"

"I'd like to tell Lillian many things."

Renna felt someone take hold of her arm. Brian was at her side.

"But how specifically can I be of service to you this time?" His voice dripped with annoyance.

At the retort, Lillian lifted her chin. "You are so droll, Brian."

Glancing up at him, Renna thought nothing about his expression said he was amused.

"I mentioned that you're a believer now," Renna explained. "But I didn't think it would be right if I said any more. I told Mrs. LaMonde that your testimony would have to come from you."

"Yes, do tell, Brian." A mischievous gleam entered Lillian's blue eyes. "In fact, why don't you tell everyone here what happened to you?" She turned around. "Everyone, listen here!" She clapped her hands, getting all the guests' attention. The musicians stopped playing.

The din in the ballroom slowly ceased while Renna's heart plummeted. How embarrassing! And it was all her fault. "Brian, make her stop," she whispered. "I had no idea she'd go this far so as to humiliate you."

"Renna, I am not humiliated. If these guests want to hear about my conversion, let them hear. I'll gladly tell them."

Every eye was fixed upon Brian now. Renna set down her plate of food and stepped back to allow him room to speak.

"The captain has had some sort of religious experience," Lillian announced. "Can you imagine?" She laughed, as did several others. She turned toward him. "We must hear the story, Brian. Please, tell us."

"My pleasure." He bowed graciously, and Renna thought Brian looked as confident as ever.

As her gaze surveyed the guests, Renna realized affluence packed the room, from politicians to businessmen. Didn't he understand that publicly professing Christ could endanger his reputation with this crowd? She glanced at Brian again. Obviously, he didn't care, and suddenly her heart swelled with admiration. If ever she thought she loved Brian Sinclair before, she was certain of it now.

"As you all know, I was in a boating accident this past summer. I helplessly watched my mother, her escort, and Elise Kingsley fight for their lives in the rain and driving wind, then tragically succumb to the lake. It was a heart-wrenching scene, even for me, a man who has lived something like a..." He cleared his throat. "A pirate."

Renna lowered her head and hid her grin.

"I'm not a stranger to death," Brian continued. "During the war I saw men die bravely and honorably. On the gunner, my crew and I viewed death as a tragedy, of course, but we determined our cause was worth dying for. However, last summer, death was not brave, nor was it honorable. It was swift and mighty. I could do nothing to save anyone, nor could I save myself. I nearly perished too. Worse, I'd been struck in the head by debris from my schooner. It knocked me unconscious."

Sympathetic gasps emanated from many of the women. Some touched gloved fingertips to their lips.

"I would have drowned like the others, except a ship in passing saw me, and its crew pulled me aboard. But I don't remember anything except the dark stormy waters and then waking up in a Chicago hospital. There I was under the care of Miss Lorenna Fields. As some of you know, Renna is a nurse."

As the guests' attention descended on her, Renna resisted the urge to conceal her birthmark.

"While I was in the hospital," Brian continued, "I was saved once more. Just like the crew of that passing ship pulled me from the dark waters of Lake Michigan, Jesus Christ pulled me from the darkness of my transgressions. No one had to point out the fact that I was a sinner. Even suffering from amnesia I remembered pieces of my shameful past. But upon my belief in Christ, who willingly shed His blood for a sinner like me, I was promised eternal life in heaven, where I will be made perfect in the likeness of Him."

Standing beside Renna, Lillian LaMonde laughed cynically. "Brian, if God will let you into heaven, He'll let anyone in."

"You're right...well, almost." Brian stepped over to Renna.

"Help me out. I can't recall. That verse...how anyone can be saved. What it is?"

Renna smiled. "'Whosoever shall call upon the name of the Lord shall be saved.' Is that the one you mean?"

"Yes. Whosoever...that includes anyone here in this room. But you have to want it and believe in it, just as it's laid out in the Bible. Then God will give His salvation to whosoever shall ask. It's a gift, you see. God's given it, and whosoever shall take it will be saved."

The room grew so still that Renna could hear Lillian LaMonde breathing. She glanced over at the woman, who seemed dazed by what she'd just heard.

"I am not saying I am now perfect. In fact, I am far from it." His gaze sought Renna's, and in it she saw every ounce of his remorse. "I've been manipulative, and I've hurt the people I love the most. But with the help of God, I do intend to change my ways."

Renna believed it. She believed him!

Suddenly a shot exploded in the room and hit just above the ugly, horned chandelier, sending it crashing onto the guests. Instantly Brian pushed her and Lillian to the floor. Through the screams, she heard Brian telling them to stay down. Smoke and the acrid smell of gunpowder filled the air. Women screamed, men yelled, the injured moaned.

"Brian?" Renna raised her head, reaching for him. But he wasn't there. "Brian?" He'd been kneeling beside her...but now he was nowhere to be found.

# TWENTY-SEVEN

AGONIZING GROANS CAPTURED RENNA'S ATTENTION. THE wounded needed immediate medical attention. Someone announced that a doctor had been summoned, but in the meantime, Renna was on her own. Several small fires had started as a result of the fallen chandelier, but they were quickly extinguished. Unfortunately, an older gentleman incurred an awful burn to his left hand.

"What can we do to help?

Renna looked over her shoulder and saw Sarah standing above her. Richard was at her side. Both appeared unharmed.

"Fetch a bowl of ice water for this man's hand."

On to the next victim. "Miss Waterford."

She moaned. Upon inspection, Renna saw a nasty gash on the other woman's shoulder. Her expensive gown had been torn irreparably. Taking a strip of it, Renna instructed Lillian LaMonde to hold it firmly to Miss Waterford's wound.

"Pressure will stop the bleeding."

Lillian nodded that she understood what had to be done, so Renna moved on to help a man with a large lump on his forehead. But he was conscious and seemed alert. Grabbing a chunk of ice out of the punch bowl, Renna instructed the man's wife to hold it on his head.

The guests became her patients, and suddenly Renna was in her element. She went from one to the next, triaging in the same manner as when she treated wounded soldiers. But unlike the enlisted men, most of the Carpenters' guests had minor cuts and contusions.

The doctor finally arrived, and Renna helped him stitch Fayre's shoulder. The blonde beauty wailed and cried and begged Dr. Welch not to leave a scar.

Sometime later, after everyone in need had been helped, Renna glanced around the ballroom. What a shambles! Gathering the skirt of her ruined gown, she strode from the room in search of Brian. Where had he disappeared to?

Relief made her knees weak when she spotted him. He stood near the front door with Lillian LaMonde, Ted Carpenter, and a policeman.

"He got away." His mouth formed a grim line.

"He still had his gun," Ted insisted. "I had to let him go."

"You did your best, Ted." Brian clapped the man on his shoulder.

"Do you know who the gunman was?" Renna asked. "A guest?" She swallowed before saying, "Benchley?"

"He wore a mask, so I can't be sure, but I believe so," Ted said.

*Someone's really out to kill Brian.* For the first time the horror of the reality struck Renna. She shuddered.

Brian's arm encircled her waist. "Well, it's late, and you've worked hard tonight. I'm very proud of you. But it's time I brought you home."

She almost chided him right then and there. She wasn't a child like Libby or Rachel. Would he ever learn? What's more, would she come to understand his determination and desire to protect her?

After tonight, Renna thought she'd at least like to try.

The butler brought Renna's cape and Brian's overcoat. The police had no more questions, so they walked out to the awaiting carriage. Brian helped Renna inside then climbed in after her. Wallace, their hired driver, closed the door.

Exhausted from the ordeal, Renna sagged against him. The carriage jerked forward.

Brian's arm tightened around her. "Are you all right, Renna?"

"Yes."

"Good. I thank God Ted spotted the devil and managed to knock into him just as the gun fired. If only we could have caught him at the scene…"

Renna slid a bit closer to him. She hated to admit it. "I'm frightened, Brian."

"Don't be." His voice lost its frustrated edge. "As your father has said, God will protect us. I trust He will—He did tonight."

Renna nodded a reply and then rested her head against his shoulder once more. She sensed there would be no words of love between them until this madman, Benchley, was apprehended.

Until then Renna had no choice but to watch and pray.

⁓ꞈꬵⱺⱦꞈ⁓

The next morning church bells rang throughout the city. Renna and her folks accompanied Brian and the children to church. The largest carriage Brian owned carried six comfortably, and the girls sat on Renna's and Mum's laps.

They rode out of Milwaukee, bracing themselves whenever the conveyance hit a rut in the road, until they reached a quaint country church. A white picket fence bordered its parameter.

"This is the church the Navises attend." Brian disembarked, then extended his hand to Renna. "It's located near their farm, and Sarah brought the children out here all summer long." He helped Mum alight then. "I'm ashamed to say it's the only church my children have ever known."

As if to prove Brian's point, his brood took off, laughing and scampering across the churchyard.

After adjusting her bonnet, Renna accepted Brian's proffered arm. They walked to the structure while other buggies and carriages parked on the gravel lot. Inside the sanctuary Sarah, Richard, and his parents greeted them with smiles and hugs.

They took their places. After hearing the pastor's uplifting sermon, Renna sang the closing hymn, but she couldn't quite capture the joy that usually accompanied song. Last night's near-deadly calamity crowded her thoughts.

The congregation was dismissed. Renna left the church and climbed back into the carriage. The children had insisted upon riding in the Navises' wagon, so just she and Brian and her parents rode to the farm, where they'd enjoy Sunday dinner.

"I have to admit this is only my second visit to the Navises' home." Brian sat directly across from Renna. Da sat beside him. "Although Richard has invited me on numerous occasions."

Renna watched Brian straighten his wine-colored wool coat. Beneath it he wore a white shirt, black waistcoat, and black pantaloons. He stretched his long legs out far enough that his boots met the tips of Renna's shiny black, ankle-high, laced shoes.

"I've listened over the years with envy as Richard described holidays, birthdays, and other family celebrations. I longed to capture that same sense of joyful family unity—but I had no idea how to do it, and certainly Louisa showed no interest. I'm afraid that hired governesses were left with the bulk of the parenting, parties and holidays included."

"That's regrettable, Brian, but it's not too late to change things." Renna smiled at him, and he removed his dark glasses, massaging the bridge of his nose.

"I know." He closed his eyes. "It's just painful to recall." He looked across the coach at her. "Didn't you notice how my children preferred the rough ride of a wagon with the Navises to a comfortable carriage ride with me?"

"Having been a lad myself," Da chuckled, "the back of a wagon seems the more adventurous choice."

Brian's frown lifted.

"You've only been back home a week, Captain," Mum reminded him. "It's going to take time."

"Patience." Renna arched a brow.

Brian regarded her with intent. "Ah, yes, patience. How soon I forget." He moved one foot forward, giving Renna a subtle nudge for her facetiousness.

Smiling, she lowered her gaze.

"We're here to help you, Brian," Da assured him.

"Thank you." The carriage slowed, and Brian donned his spectacles once more. "But I can't really begin to start anew, can I? Not until I'm able to stop living under this pretense of blindness."

"Soon, Brian." Da slid his focus to the carriage's window. "This can't go on forever."

"I should say not!" Mum's hand clasped Renna's. "After last night…"

Renna's heart skipped a beat. Fear reared its ugly head. *Oh, God…please keep us all safe.*

# TWENTY-EIGHT

RENNA YAWNED AND STRETCHED, ALLOWING HERSELF some minutes of luxury in the soft bed. Sunshine beckoned behind the thick draperies, but Renna ignored the call and chose, instead, to stay beneath the soft bedcovers.

She thought back on the pleasant outing yesterday. Dinner at the Navises' farm included the tastiest and tenderest fried chicken Renna ever ate. The children romped, the men talked business, and Brian and Marty Navis shared war stories. In the kitchen, Renna had enjoyed getting to know Beatrice Navis and Sarah as they washed, dried, and put away dishes.

A blush crept across Renna's cheeks as she recalled how she'd entered the dining room, catching Sarah and her husband in a private moment. Mr. Navis had cornered her and tickled and kissed her. Sarah giggled all the while. It wasn't the first time Renna witnessed happy couples. Her sister Elizabeth and her brother-in-law often enjoyed such exchanges.

Renna recalled Brian's kiss yesterday. He certainly knew how to melt a woman's resolve. *The pirate.* And then his testimony in front of the guests, the way his eyes sought her out, the way he'd shown remorse and concern for her welfare, like a husband would.

But would he live to be her husband? She shivered at the thought. She'd almost given him up out of her own pride and insecurity, then she'd almost lost him to a crazy man's bullet. How could she bear it if she were parted from him now?

She shook the gloomy thoughts away, then threw back the covers and climbed out of bed. After washing up, she dressed for the day, selecting an emerald plaid gown with an off-white collar and cuffs.

A knock sounded at her bedroom door. Renna had just finished buttoning the front of her bodice. "Yes?" She smoothed her skirt over her crinoline.

The door squeaked open, and a pair of hazel eyes peeked around the corner.

"Gabriel." Renna smiled. "What can I do for you?"

The door opened wider, and Gabriel slipped in, shutting it behind him. He held something behind his back and then slowly brought it around and into Renna's view.

"What's in the newspaper that you're hiding it?"

"It's the society page." Gabe grinned mischievously.

"You rascal."

He gave a shrug. "I know I'm not supposed to be reading it, but I do anyhow." Gabe's voice lowered to a whisper. "I've been read-ing it since I was nine. That's how I kept up on what my parents were doing."

"Gabriel!"

"Never did read anything good about them, though."

Renna shook her head at the boy's misdeed while marveling at his inquisitiveness.

"It isn't right, is it? My reading the society page when my mother told me not to a long, long time ago?"

"No, it isn't right."

He appeared contrite. "I won't do it again. I promise. But, here, take a look at what it says today. It says my dad's a hero!"

"It does?" Renna took the newspaper from him. Sure enough. Lillian LaMonde had described last night's events and described Brian's attempt to apprehend the shooter. "Despite his disabil-ity," Renna read, "Captain Brian Sinclair managed to save my life when he pushed Nurse Lorenna Fields and me out of the line of fire."

Renna glanced up and grinned. "Hmm…"

"Read what it says about you."

Gabriel stepped in beside her, but she glimpsed his expression, shining with boyish pride. "Miss Renna Fields is an angel of mercy," he read from the newspaper. "She willingly tended to all the wounded at the Carpenters' ill-fated ball." He stumbled over a few words but pressed on. "In addition, Miss Fields has so obviously won the heart of Captain Sinclair and, by her love and devotion, has rendered him a new man!"

Renna rolled her eyes and shook her head. "It's God who rendered your father a new man, not me."

"I know, but don't you see, Miss Fields? This is the best thing I ever read or even heard about my dad. Lillian LaMonde usually writes about what Miss Sarah calls 'sandals.' You know, the stuff children shouldn't hear about."

Renna was hard pressed to conceal her grin. "I think the word is *scandals*, Gabriel."

"Yeah, that's it. My father's name usually appears in one of those articles, along with whatever lady he escorted." Gabe studied the tips of his scuffed boots. "Most times I knew what the newspaper said wasn't true, but it hurt me anyway. I hated my father for it." Gabriel suddenly smiled broadly, looking up at Renna. "But that was before his accident and before he knew Jesus. And before you."

Renna gave him a hug. Gabe returned the gesture in a less than enthusiastic manner, typical of a twelve-year-old boy.

He pulled back. "You could be a mom to us, Miss Fields—a mom who doesn't get written up in the newspaper. And you could help our dad stay out of the society page from now on."

"I'm flattered that you hold me in such high regard." Renna meant it.

"So will you marry my dad?"

She found it difficult to keep from smiling. "I think the

proposal should come from him, Gabe." Striding to the door, Rena opened it.

Gabe followed her. "I guess I'd better go now."

"Mm-hmm."

He paused in the doorway. "You can keep the newspaper. I promise never to read the society page again... unless my dad says I can."

"I'll hold you to it."

He smiled and sauntered off down the hallway.

Renna closed the door and stared at the newspaper in her hand. Feeling almost guilty, she finished reading the column. Her heart stopped when she came to the last paragraph.

> Police won't say who the evildoer is in Saturday's foiled murder attempt, but sources close to the captain have murmured the name Benchley. A middle-class working man from Chicago, Benchley is the nephew of the late Elise Kingsley, who was engaged to marry Captain Sinclair before her tragic death in a boating accident in September. He is disputing the sale of his aunt's shipping company, Great Lakes Shipping, to Captain Sinclair.

Renna worked her lower lip between her teeth. Yes, it was quite the compliment to be featured so favorably in Mrs. LaMonde's column, and yet she wondered if the publicity would provoke Matt Benchley to strike again.

Had Lillian LaMonde just put all their lives in greater danger?

With the newspaper still in hand, Renna set out to find Brian. She descended the stairs and crossed the foyer. Her heels clicked against the dark brown tiled floor. In the dining room, she found her mother sitting at the table, sipping tea.

"Good morning, Mum. Do you know where Brian is?"

"He and your father left on some business."

Renna sat down across from her mother.

"Would you like some breakfast? Isabelle is still in the kitchen with Hester underfoot."

"And the children?"

Mum smiled. "They're playing outside in the backyard. The captain gave them strict orders not to play in the front. Every so often I've glanced out the window. They seem fine out there. It's warmer today."

"A lovely fall day." But Renna's mind didn't linger on the weather. She pushed the newspaper toward her. "Have you seen the society page?"

Mum picked up the newspaper, and Renna watched as her eyes widened while she read the column.

"Oh, my. How shocking!"

"Do you think Brian has seen this morning's paper?"

"I'm sure he has. He and your father were here in the dining room sharing pages over their coffee."

Prickles of unease trickled down Renna's spine. "And you say they're out on business now?"

Clouds of worry filled Mum's light-gray eyes. "Oh, dear, you don't suppose they're—they're up to any heroics."

"Perish the thought, Mum." But it's the exact thought that flitted through Renna's mind too.

Isabelle entered the room. "If there's nothing else, I'll be leaving. I've given Hester instructions for lunch and dinner tonight." She wiped her plump hands on her white apron. "The captain said I could go home early. I've got a husband with a nasty cold, I'm afraid."

Renna twisted around in her chair. "Did Brian say when he'd return?"

"I'm afraid not, ma'am. But you just go on and continue making yourself right at home." She flicked a courteous glance at Mum. "Both of you."

"Thank you, Isabelle."

Renna nodded. "Yes, thank you." After the cook left, she let out a long sigh intended to quell her nerves. She decided on changing the subject so Mum wouldn't begin to fret. "So what will we do today?"

"Well…" Mum's gaze brightened. "There's a tearoom downtown that's said to be quite prestigious."

"Sounds lovely."

"I'd love to tell my friends that I've been there."

"Then we'll have to go."

Suddenly Hester cried out in the kitchen. The sound of a pan clanging to the floor followed.

"Sorry, Granny Hester."

Renna heard Gabriel's voice before she saw him burst into the dining room.

"Miss Fields, it's him! I just saw him—by the stables!"

"Slow down, Gabe." Renna stood to her feet. She intuitively knew whom the boy had just spotted.

Gabe's chest rose and fell in rapid successions. "It's that man, Benchley. The one Mike and me knocked down in the solarium. This time I know he's up to something bad."

"Well, we'd best take care just in case." Renna willed herself to stay calm. "Go and get your brother and sisters."

"I did already. They went upstairs. Mike locked the back door."

"Perfect." Renna hadn't heard the other children come in, but that wasn't so surprising in this large home. "Do you know how to summon the authorities?"

"Yes, ma'am. I'm a fast runner too."

"All right, then. Use the front door. Go."

Gabe dashed off.

"Renna…" Mum rose from her chair and wrung her hands.

"Take Hester and go upstairs with the rest of the children." She swallowed and thought of where the safest, most remote place in the house might be. "Take them into Brian's room. Keep everyone on the floor. Stay away from the windows."

Gabe suddenly returned, startling Renna. Before she could ask, he produced a gun, holding it by the barrel, just as one should.

"Take it. It's my dad's. He doesn't know that I found it in his desk drawer last summer."

Renna blinked.

"It's loaded too."

"Gabriel!"

"But the hammer's on an empty chamber."

"But still..."

"I watched my dad load it. But he always hides his guns from us—except once I saw where he put this one, and, well, I thought I might need it sometime." Turning on a heel, he ran from the room. "I'll be back soon!"

Wide-eyed, Renna marveled at the boy's nonchalance around a loaded weapon.

Her gaze fell to the heavy revolver in her hand. She had to do this. It was up to her!

Mum walked around the table while Renna carefully checked the Colt's chambers. She'd handled this particular gun before while stationed in various Union military hospitals. Just as Gabriel said, the revolver had been loaded. Clicking the hammer into a half-cock position for safety, she looked up and glimpsed her mother's look of horror.

"You're not really going to use that thing."

"Not unless I have to."

"Renna!"

"This is no time for femininities. Go upstairs, Mum. Hurry. Take Hester with you."

Mum didn't waste another moment.

Tucking the gun into the folds of her skirt, Renna strode to the windows and peered out into the now-empty yard. No movement.

Nothing. She ran to the foyer and glanced around, wondering if she ought to hide upstairs in the main hallway or remain down here. She could hear treading footfalls above her and prayed her mother, Hester, and the kids would all be quick about taking cover.

She nibbled her lower lip, deliberating. Would Benchley try to get into the house? If so, through which door would he enter?

Glass suddenly shattered. Renna jumped full circle, guessing it came from the solarium. She quickly pressed her back up against the wall facing the stairs. If Benchley tried to get by her—

Renna couldn't finish her thought. *Lord, I don't want to use this gun!* She held her breath. She couldn't soften now.

Carefully, she cocked the hammer all the way back, praying she didn't shoot her foot off with this fool thing! It locked. With both hands, she held the Colt, barrel up against her shoulder.

*Ready.*

She strained to hear the intruder's moves. A tearing, ripping sound suddenly filled the space and cut the silence. Next a heavy thud. It came from somewhere behind her in the main reception parlor. A vase or some sort of porcelain item crashed to the floor next.

Renna waited.

Then all at once he turned the corner, and there he stood just several feet from her. It happened so fast, Renna gasped.

Hearing her, he spun around. A long blade glinted in his hand.

Renna took aim. "Drop the knife."

He looked about as startled as she'd just felt. And in spite of his dark hood and clothing, she recognized him.

*Matthew Benchley.*

He paused and seemed to gauge the situation. "Renna." He smiled and relaxed his stance.

"Drop it."

"Of course. I really meant no harm. The captain has some of my aunt's jewelry."

"Liar." She didn't believe his ramblings, and she wasn't about to let down her guard.

"Really. I only meant to take back what's rightfully mine."

"Drop it!"

"All right." He wielded the blade, but it didn't leave his hand. Then he narrowed his gaze, and Renna forced herself not to shudder. Evil. Pure evil lurked in the depths of his eyes. "You wouldn't shoot me."

"Don't tempt me, Mr. Benchley." Renna thought she'd do anything to save her mother, the children, Hester—and herself— from this despicable creature!

Seconds ticked by. Determination held her steady.

"What if I told you I'd rather die than be apprehended?"

"I'd say you may get your wish." She swallowed hard. She didn't want to kill him. Her life had been devoted to saving lives, not taking them.

"Tell you what. I'll leave peaceably if you'll put down the gun."

"Drop the knife, Mr. Benchley, I'm warning—"

He lunged at her.

Renna squeezed the trigger. *Click.* Then again. The gun fired with a deafening blast and jammed her shoulders back. She prepared to shoot again, but Benchley's body crumpled to floor.

Frozen in dread, Renna waited as the smoke cleared. She took a cautious step toward her victim, lest he be able enough to retaliate. But one glimpse of the hole in Benchley's chest and she knew her nursing skills would be of no use to him now. Her aim had been right on.

At least he hadn't suffered.

# TWENTY-NINE

Brian heard the shot as he climbed from the buggy. "Wendell, it came from in the house." He took off up the brick walk and pushed open the heavy front door. Running into the foyer he looked to his left then right before he saw the darkly clad figure of a man sprawled near the stairwell. As he neared, he spotted Renna, sagged against the wall.

"Are you all right?"

"Yes."

With his gaze still inspecting Renna for any signs of trauma, he moved near the form on his terrazzo floor. Thinking Renna looked no worse for wear, he peered at the gunshot wound to the left side of the man's chest.

He pursed his lips. *Impressive shot.* Questions swirled in his head. With the tip of his boot he moved the man's head so he could see his face. "Benchley." He looked at Renna. "How'd this happen?"

"He broke in and came at me with a knife, so I...shot him with this gun." She held up the revolver with her thumb and forefinger as though it were a repugnant object.

In a few strides Brian reached her and took the weapon.

"It's loaded," she warned.

Handling the gun with care, he pulled the hammer to the half-cocked position then inspected it. He rubbed his thumb over his engraved initials on the bottom of the handle. "This is my revolver." He frowned, curious. "How did you manage to find it?"

"Gabe gave it to me. He watched you hide it some time ago."

"That rascal! But under the circumstances I'm glad." He

encircled her with one arm and hugged her to him. "Where are the others?"

"Upstairs. Mum, Hester, Michael, and the girls. Gabe went to fetch the authorities." Renna wet her lips. "So you see, Captain, your eldest is really the hero in all this."

"Hero? Hmm...it's really you, Renna, who has saved the day." Brian pulled her close. He expected her to dissolve into tears over the ordeal, but she didn't. Pride and admiration welled inside of him.

Wendell entered the house with Gabe and the police. The boy was the first to run for the body.

"Saints alive! You really did shoot him, Miss Fields, didn't you?"

"Gabriel Sinclair!" Brian cleared his throat and released Renna. He beckoned Gabe with a forefinger, and the youngster sidled up to him. A reprimand formed on his tongue, but when Renna wagged her head ever so slightly, Brian decided on a different approach. "Gabe, I understand I have you to thank for your quick thinking."

"Yessir." He brought himself up to his full height of five feet nothing.

Brian slung his arm around his son's shoulders. "Good job, son." He grinned, seeing Gabe's expression fill with pleasure.

"I said that you could trust me."

"And you've proved it. But we'll talk more later. For now, how about running upstairs and letting everyone know that Renna is fine. Tell them they may come downstairs, but they need to use the back way. Ask Hester to keep the little girls in the kitchen. They don't need to see any of this at their tender ages."

"Right." Gabe was halfway up the stairs already, and Brian realized a little praise went a long way with his son.

He steered his attention to the other side of the foyer. Police surrounded Benchley's body and rolled his lifeless form onto a gurney. The men quickly carried him from the house.

Wendell hugged Renna. "You're a brave woman, my little wren."

Brian agreed. He enfolded her hand in one of his. "Yes, in

fact, you're more courageous than some of the soldiers I've commanded."

"You'll forgive me if I can't feel quite the same about my actions." Sadness rimmed her green eyes. "I hated to kill another human being. But I had no choice. I feared for my life and the lives of my mother, Hester, and the children."

An officer had shuffled over and listened intently.

"We found a Bowie knife under the body, sir." The officer looked at Brian, holding his blue hat in his hands. "This appears to be a clear-cut case of self-defense."

"Of course it is." Wendell looked offended. "My daughter isn't in the habit of shooting people."

Brian grinned. "Easy, Wendell. I know it's been a stressful time for the both of us, but this man's just doing his job."

"You're right." Contrition crawled across the older man's face. "My apologies."

"Accepted." The lanky officer inclined his head.

"As for your daughter, Wendell"—Brian eyed Renna—"I can promise you that I will never take her for granted or treat her like a child again. She's a woman. A very capable woman. Not to mention trustworthy and loyal."

"And quite pretty if I do say so myself," the officer interjected.

Brian turned and sent him his darkest glare.

"But if you'll excuse me, I have work to do." The man scrambled to join his comrades.

A faint grin tugged at his mouth. But as moments passed, Brian realized how close he came to losing Renna.

*Lord, never allow me to take her and my family for granted again.*

"The important thing is, this whole nightmare is over." Wendell put his head back and whispered a quick prayer of thanks. "Matt Benchley will never threaten anyone again, and that means, Brian, you can stop the pretense. You're free to live again. We all are."

# THIRTY

RENNA HELPED HER MOTHER CARRY IN COFFEE AND SLICES of sweet potato pie from the kitchen. This Thanksgiving Day had been a true celebration!

Da prayed before the meal, giving God thanks and praise for all He'd done and for all He promised to do. Then, after eating roast turkey, cranberry sauce, mashed potatoes, and green beans, they transitioned to the main parlor.

Renna set down the large round tray and smiled, seeing Brian and Richard clasp hands near the hearth. Richard had accepted the partnership! She sent a glance at his parents. Their smiles spoke of their own happiness over Richard's decision. As it happened, they had been praying for a similar outcome since they learned Brian survived the accident. Now, after having prayed and considered Brian's offer for the better part of three weeks, Richard took his former boss up on it.

"But I never dreamed of a partnership." Richard sported an ear-to-ear grin. "It's more than I would have imagined."

*How like God to do over, abundantly, and above all we ask or think,* Renna thought.

Sarah clapped her hands, laughing softly. She too was pleased with the decision.

"Well, you've earned it."

Renna caught Brian's earnest expression.

"I just hope you'll allow my family to be part of your family, because that's how I think of you, Richard—like a brother."

"Well, certainly! We're brothers in Christ, to be sure. Brothers in business now also."

"And I hereby adopt you, Captain Brian Sinclair," Marty Navis boomed from his wheelchair, "as my eldest son."

The children stood by and cheered.

"So that makes you our…grandpa." Gabe placed his hand on the older man's shoulder. Renna didn't miss the hopefulness in the boy's gaze.

"That would be Grandpops to you, young man." Richard grinned. "I've called my father 'Pops' for as long as I can recall."

"And I'm Aunt Sarah," Sarah declared, pulling Rachel onto her lap.

Renna's heart swelled to think Richard and Sarah would still be very much a part of the children's lives.

"And now there's just one other thing I must take care of," Brian said.

Renna handed a plate of pie to Mrs. Navis, then turned to look at her beloved—and, yes, Brian Sinclair was the man she loved with all her heart.

"Wendell?"

"Go right ahead, Brian."

Renna straightened, feeling confused. She faced Brian. "Are you leaving?"

"No. *We* are leaving." He stretched out his hand. "Come."

"Was she naughty, Daddy?" Rachel's hazel eyes were wide.

Sarah whispered something to her.

"Oh…" Rachel gave Renna a large smile.

And that got Renna feeling suspicious. She wiped her hands on the apron she wore over a black gown with white pearl buttons and lacy collar and cuffs. Mum stood and took it from her. Then she took Brian's hand. "Where are we going?"

"I need some air after that delicious meal."

Ramsey brought their outerwear. "Everything's all set, sir."

"Thank you."

Before Renna could voice a question, Brian guided her outside to an awaiting carriage.

"I thought you wanted to take a walk."

"No, darling, I have something else in mind."

Their driver helped them inside and then closed the vehicle's door.

"Where are we going?"

"Sit back, Renna. Allow me to hold you close. I want to savor this trip with you here beside me."

Renna did as he bid. No longer insecure around him, she rode silently. With her head on Brian's shoulder, her eyelids grew heavy. It had been a busy day, baking and cooking. Isabelle had the holiday off, so Mum, Hester, and Renna prepared their Thanksgiving Day feast.

Her mind drifted back on the past few weeks. After killing Benchley in self-defense, Renna stayed in Milwaukee with her family. Brian insisted on it, and Renna had never really wanted to cut their holiday short anyway.

With the danger past, Renna had been able to get to know the man she loved and pray about whether it was God's will that they marry. It seemed each time she asked, God used Da to reply, "He's a fine man, Renna." Sometimes the comment came offhandedly, and even Da looked surprised that he'd said it. But Renna knew the Lord gave her direction.

As for herself, she liked getting to know the real Brian Sinclair—and what a blessing it had been allowing his children to get to know her. She sensed they loved her as much as she loved them. When she was with Brian and his kids, Renna felt like they were a family. A happy family...

"Renna?" Brian's voice pulled her from her reverie. Had she fallen asleep?

"Wake up, darling. We're here."

"Oh…" Renna blinked. "Forgive me. I hadn't meant to nap."

Brian hugged her close in reply.

Their driver opened the carriage door, and once they both climbed out, Renna realized they stood in front of his mother's estate. A golden glow coming from the windows made for a welcoming sight.

"Does someone live here now?"

"I should say so." Brian took her hand and led her to the front door.

Renna tamped down her disappointment. She'd been fond of this place and imagined herself living here with Brian and the children. *Silly wishes!* But the fact was, she'd live wherever Brian did. She'd follow him to the ends of the world if need be.

Brian turned the brass knob and let them in. Renna shrugged out of her wool coat and pulled off her gloves. Her velvet bonnet came next. Accepting her outerwear, Brian slung them over the back of a chair in the foyer.

Brian took her hand. "This way, Renna."

He led her into the parlor where a fire in the hearth blazed. Crystal vases containing long-stemmed red roses had been placed on every available tabletop and flat surface.

"They're beautiful," Renna breathed. "This room is beautiful."

"Like you, Renna." Brian sat on the settee and patted the place beside him. He reached into his suede jacket and pulled out a black velvet box.

Renna held her breath as he opened the lid. Diamonds and emeralds sparkled at her.

She gasped.

"A ring. For you. The line of emeralds match the color of your eyes, and the diamonds signify my undying love for you." Brian removed the band from its white satin cradle and slipped it on her finger.

"Oh, Brian…"

"Will you be my wife, Renna? I'm very much in love with you."

"I know." She admired the way the dazzling ring looked on her finger. "And, yes, I'll marry you."

"Because you're pleased with the gift?"

"No, not because of it." She recognized his vulnerability hidden beneath his facetious tone. "I love you too, Brian. And I adore your children."

"You proved you'd do anything for them—and me."

"And it's true. I would. I know you'd do the same for me."

"Without question." He clutched her wrist and pressed a kiss inside her palm. "You have just made me a very happy man. And I swear…no more pretense. Not ever."

"I believe you. You're a pirate no more, Captain Brian Sinclair."

"Well, perhaps…" He arched a sardonic brow. "I'm still just a little bit of a pirate." He stole a kiss.

He'd stolen her heart—long ago.

"We'll live here, raise our children here. I've always been happy in this house."

Renna was overjoyed. "Oh, Brian, that's what I've been hoping!" She glanced around the room. "It almost feels like home already."

"So you approve?"

"I more than approve!" She ran her fingertips along his shadowed jaw. "I feel so blessed right now."

His black eyes darkened even more. "I love you, Renna."

He kissed her again, this time slowly, deliberately. Then he wrapped her in a snug embrace, and Renna never felt more cherished—

And yes, even beautiful.

*Coming in May 2011—*

# Undaunted Faith

**Book 4 in the**
**Seasons of Redemption Series**

# ONE

A KNOCK SOUNDED ONCE. THEN AGAIN, MORE INSISTENT this time.

"Coming." Bethany set down the quill and capped the inkwell. Closing her journal, she stood from where she'd been sitting at the rough-hewn desk Mr. Winters had hammered together for her use. Then, before she could open the door, Millie Winters poked her round, cherubic face into Bethany's bedroom.

"Mama says breakfast is ready."

"Thank you, Millie, I'll be down shortly."

A grin curved the flaxen-haired girl's pink mouth. "Reverend Luke and Reverend Jacob are already here. Sheriff Montano is too."

"I'll be down shortly." Walking to the looking glass, Bethany brushed out her long brown hair. It had dried from her earlier bath in the river.

Thirteen-year-old Millie stepped farther into the room and closed the door behind her. "I'll bet we'll hear some lively conversation. Something about cattle stealing. Papa said the Indians have been causing trouble again."

"Oh, dear." Bethany tried not to show either her discontent with this town or her unease of the natives of this land. She gathered her hair, then twisted it into a coil and pinned it at her nape. "Was anyone killed?"

"I don't know, but I expect we'll find out at breakfast."

With her hair in place, Bethany turned to Millie. "I'm ready."

"Good." The girl strode to the door and paused. "Miss Stafford, who do you think is more handsome, Reverend Luke, Reverend Jacob, or the sheriff?" A conspiratorial expression spread across her face. "I fancy Sheriff Paden Montano is a handsome curiosity, is he not?"

"I don't notice such things," Bethany fibbed. She folded her arms in front of her. If truth be told, only a woman deaf and blind wouldn't notice Paden Montano; however, she wasn't about to encourage Millie. The young lady was one of her pupils, and Bethany wanted to set a good example. "And what would your parents have to say if they heard you talking like this?"

Millie gasped. "You're not going to tell them, are you?"

Bethany raised a contemplative brow. "Well, maybe not this time." She strode earnestly toward the young girl. "But you must stop allowing your thoughts to be consumed by romance. You're going to get hurt."

"Pshaw!"

Bethany gasped. "Millie, really!"

The girl continued unabashed. "Miss Stafford, if you haven't already noticed, you and I are the only eligible women in Silverstone—well, except for Dr. Bryce. But she's too busy to notice men. Even so, you and I can have our pick of any bachelor we want."

"You are not *eligible*." Bethany knew both Mr. and Mrs. Winters wanted their only child to receive an education before she married. "And I am not...interested."

"Are you certain about that?" A taunting glimmer entered Millie's eyes. "You and Reverend Luke seem to spend a lot of time together."

Bethany felt her cheeks flame in a mixture of embarrassment and aggravation. "Millie, I'm a teacher, and Reverend Luke—and Reverend Jake, I might add—are starting a school. It's only natural that we'd spend time together...to plan and organize."

"Well, fine. But *I am* interested—in getting me a husband!"

"You're much too young."

"Am not! My friend Emma got married last year, and she's younger than me!"

"Than I," Bethany corrected. "And every circumstance is different." She knew girls were married off at Millie's age and younger. "But we're talking about you, and you're not ready for marriage. You have a lot of schooling left."

"So I can end up like Dr. Bryce?"

Bethany's jaw tightened. "And what's wrong with Dr. Bryce? She seems like a remarkable woman. She's come all the way from Ohio." Bethany felt a kinship between them, both being women from east of the Mississippi River and two women who had survived the journey along the Santa Fe Trail. But it seemed the physician wasn't interested in making friends, although she was pleasant enough.

"She's a spinster."

Bethany shrank. That shoe could fit her foot as well.

"Besides, no one wants her here. They put an ad in newspapers back East for a male doctor. They thought they were getting one too, until Dr. Bryce arrived in town a month ago."

"Yes, I know about the mix-up." Although Bethany couldn't be sure it was an oversight on Dr. Bryce's part. According to Jake, she'd signed her letter of application *A. L. Bryce*. Everyone just assumed the rest, and since the day she arrived, Dr. Bryce didn't appear to be offering up any explanations, even though plenty of men besides the sheriff and Jake weren't pleased.

"Folks say she's running from something back East, and I just wonder if it's true."

"That's gossip, Millie. Christians ought not indulge in it." Bethany had heard Jake say the sheriff checked Annetta Bryce's background thoroughly—at least as far as the law was concerned. "As for you, young lady, you need to pay attention to your schoolbooks instead of romance and gossip."

Millie gave her foot a stomp. "I'm not a child. Why do you and my parents treat me like one?"

*Could be the tantrums.* Bethany quelled an impatient sigh. Millie Winters was a challenge to be sure.

But in spite of the vexation the girl caused her now and again, Bethany felt determined to befriend her and become her trusted teacher. Perhaps she'd somehow make a difference in Millie's young life. However, she certainly wouldn't accomplish such a feat by arguing with her.

Turning to the looking glass again, Bethany gave her reflection a final inspection. She smoothed down the skirt of her cotton printed dress. The leanness she'd acquired from walking those seemingly endless days on the trail had gone. In the past few weeks she'd put on some weight, so now her clothes fit nicely again. She tugged at her bodice. Perhaps too nicely. In fact, her dresses were almost snug, thanks to Mrs. Winters's good cook, Rosalinda.

Bethany made a mental note to purchase some material and make a few new clothing items.

She whirled back to Millie. "I'm famished. What's for breakfast?"

Millie's countenance brightened. "Omelets with Spanish tomatoes, peppers, and onions…and biscuits, of course. Papa loves biscuits." She paused, looking thoughtful. "Ever wonder why men insist upon biscuits at nearly every meal?"

Bethany laughed lightly. "I suppose the biscuits help to satisfy their voracious appetites." She took Millie's arm. "Come along. Let's go downstairs."

Millie complied, and they strolled into the hallway and to the stairs. "Aren't you the least bit interested in getting married, Miss Stafford?"

She paused on the landing as a vision of Luke McCabe flitted through her mind. "I guess I'd be a liar if I said I never wanted to get married. Doesn't every woman?" She'd marry Luke in a heartbeat. But he treated her like he would another younger sister. Jake did too.

"Then why don't you?"

"Millie, I've learned there are other things in life of greater importance. Serving others, showing them the love of Christ—"

"Yes. I think so too."

"Then steer your thoughts toward reading and arithmetic."

Millie groaned.

They finished descending the stairs, and Bethany felt hopeful. So she was making a difference with Millie…

As they reached the last step, Millie proceeded to flounce into the dining room. Bethany watched in dismay as the girl boldly approached the sheriff and began a conversation. Had she no shame? No fear? Millie was certain to get her heart broken. Bethany sensed it coming like a brewing thunderstorm off in the distance. The men in Silverstone were not exactly refined gentlemen with whom a young lady could trifle in the parlor. No, they were hardworking river men, vaqueros, and former soldiers, and when it came to their land, their horses, and their women, these fellows were serious!

"Well, good mornin', Beth."

Startled from her musing, she looked to her left and found Luke leaning casually against the banister, wearing a rakishly charming smile—one that didn't seem to belong on a reverend's face.

Then again, Luke was always charming, and they were merely friends.

"Morning, Luke."

"You look right pretty today," he drawled. "Can I escort you over to the dining table?"

"Yes, thank you." The compliment carried little weight. She knew Luke was just being his polite self. He'd been raised with the adage "If you can't say something nice, don't say anything at all."

What's more, Bethany knew that if they were in Milwaukee or

even back in Jericho Junction, Luke probably wouldn't give her a second look. He was, after all, a fine-looking man, strong, intelligent, and kind. She, on the other hand, was as plain as a field mouse. Her long hair was a nondescript brown and hung nearly to her waist, although she never wore it down. Her eyes were an average bluish-gray, like the sky on a misty morning, and her lips were just an ordinary shape. A smattering of freckles covered her nose and cheeks—her own fault, since she abhorred wearing a bonnet. She'd likely end up a spinster—a fate worse than death according to Millie Winters. But so be it. Bethany felt sure she could be a respectable part of any community as an unmarried teacher…

Just not this community!

Luke slipped her hand around his elbow and guided her toward the dining room while Bethany gave him a furtive look. His hair was the color of wet sand and his blue eyes were as clear and inviting as Lake Michigan on a hot summer day. Along his well-defined jaw line, a shadow of perpetual whiskers made the good pastor appear more like a shady outlaw; however, his warm, friendly smile disarmed even the worst skeptics. His tall frame included broad shoulders, slim hips, and long legs, and many times during their journey, Bethany found herself admiring God's messenger instead of listening to the message—a sin of which she was forever repenting.

But she'd gotten over that silliness now that they'd arrived in Silverstone. She simply refused to look at Luke while he preached on Sundays and, instead, forced herself to listen closely.

They reached the dining table, and Luke seated her politely before taking his place beside her.

"Good morning, Miz Stafford." Paden Montano stood and smiled at her from across the table.

She inclined her head cordially. "Sheriff." She looked over at Jake, who had also stood when she'd entered. "Good morning."

"Beth." A smile warmed his brown eyes, although it never

made it to his mouth. An onlooker might think Jake McCabe was terse and unfriendly, but Bethany knew from months of traveling with the man that he simply didn't show emotion like other folks. What's more, his bad leg pained him terribly sometimes. But far be it for Jake to let anyone know. He preferred to suffer in silence.

As everyone else took their places, Bethany allowed her gaze to wander around the table until it met the sheriff's brown eyes. He seemed to regard her with interest, and she shifted uncomfortably, lowering her chin and studying the plate in front of her.

"You look very rested, Miz Stafford." The sheriff spoke with a soft Mexican accent that Bethany found quite enchanting. And if she were completely honest, she'd have to agree with Millie. Paden Montano was definitely a "handsome curiosity." Today his shiny, dark hair had been pulled straight back and tied with a piece of leather string. His skin was tanned and clean-shaven, with the exception of his sleek, black mustache. "I trust you are finding your stay here in Silverstone quite comfortable," he added, his dark eyes shining like polished stones.

Bethany hedged, not wanting to lie. She couldn't dare say she hated the Arizona Territory with both Luke and Jake at the table. "Everyone has been very kind to me thus far." She turned a smile on Mrs. Winters.

"Good, good..."

Mr. Winters gave a clap of his hands just then. "Let's ask God's blessing on the food and dig in." He sat at the head of the table and nodded at Jake. "Reverend Jacob, will you do the honors?"

"Of course." Bowing his head in reverence, he began, "Heavenly Father, we thank You for this beautiful day and the appetizing bounty You've placed before us. Thank You for the hands that prepared this meal. Bless it to our bodies, I ask. In Christ's name, amen."

Dishes were immediately passed around the table.

"So, Montano, I hear you had some excitement last night." Mr. Winters forked a large piece of egg into his mouth.

"Excitement, indeed. Cattle rustlers hit the Livermores' ranch. Clayt suspects the Indians, of course."

"Any truth to that?" Ed Winters smacked his thick lips together beneath his long, bushy, light-brown beard. "I heard there's a tribe living just over the eastern ridge."

"*Sí*, but they are a very civilized band. They're not bloodthirsty, nor are they interested in the Livermores' cattle." Sheriff Montano took a long drink of his coffee. He smiled at Doris Winters. "Ah, a good strong brew. Just the way I like it."

The older woman blushed, looking pleased. "I'll be sure to tell Rosalinda," she promised, referring to the grandmotherly Mexican cook.

"About that looting last night, Montano," Mr. Winters continued, "you think us townfolk have to worry?"

"No." He bit into his biscuit.

"Well, what are you going to do about it?"

"Watch. Keep my ears open." He paused to chew his food and then sat back in his chair. "I have a hunch it is the work of outlaws, but they will not get away."

From the sheriff's right side Millie sighed dreamily. "You're so brave."

He gave her an indulgent smile.

"Well, I'd keep my eye on them redskins, if I was you." Mr. Winters snorted. "Can't trust them. I just wish the government would hurry up and take care of them."

Paden Montano's face was devoid of expression, although his next words were deliberate and carried force. "It is a shame that most people feel as you do, señor, because I have known many an Indian to be more trustworthy than a white man." He looked over at Luke. "I'm sure the reverends would agree…God made the Indian as well as the white man. Isn't that right?"

"He did."

"Well, even God makes mistakes," Mr. Winters grumbled.

"No, sir, He does not," Jake quickly replied. Leaning back in his chair, he folded his arms, and Bethany could tell he enjoyed the turn in the conversation. "The God of the Bible is perfect and does not err. He made man in His image. 'For God so loved the world that he gave his only begotten Son, that *whosoever* believeth in him should not perish but have everlasting life.' I reckon the words *world* and *whosoever* includes Indians, Mexicans, and every other kind of people there is."

"Thank you for the sermon." Mr. Winters arched a brow. "And it ain't even Sunday."

"Oh, now, Ed," Doris admonished her husband, looking chagrined. "Birds fly and pastors preach."

Next to Bethany, Luke chuckled. "Amen!"

Paden's mustache switched slightly, indicating his mild amusement. Then he slid his chair backward, scraping its legs against the wooden plank floor, and rose. As usual, he'd dressed in a black shirt and trousers, but he'd tied a red bandana around his neck. "If it is any consolation, Señor Winters," he said, adjusting his gun belt, "I have every intention of finding those cattle rustlers, whoever they are, and I gave Clayt my word."

The man nodded in satisfaction.

Sheriff Montano turned to Mrs. Winters. "Breakfast was delicious, as always. Please compliment Rosalinda for me."

"I shall. Thank you, Sheriff."

With one last nod in Bethany's direction, he strode purposely for the door and out of the boardinghouse, leaving one starry-eyed Millie Winters gazing in his wake.

Bethany expelled a weary sigh. Would she ever be able to convince the girl to look beyond her romantic fantasies before she got hurt?

Just then Ralph Jonas burst into the building wearing a

determined expression that skirted on desperation. His gaze fell on Bethany.

She slowly stood.

"'Scuse me, Miss Stafford." The man sounded breathless. "But I need to speak with you. And Preacher," he added, his gaze hardening and moving to Luke, "I'll thank you to stay out of my way."

Experience the *entertaining* and *inspirational* sagas
of the McCabe family in books one and two of the

# SEASONS OF
# REDEMPTION
### SERIES

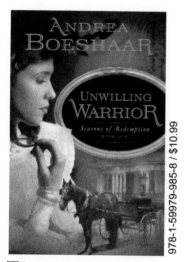

978-1-59979-985-8 / $10.99

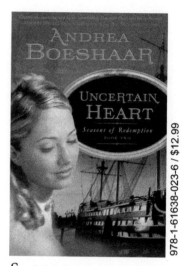

978-1-61638-023-6 / $12.99

The War Between the
States has Valerie Fontaine
frightened about her future.
When her father is arrested,
she is forced to flee the city
or be taken into custody. Will
the war keep her from her
newfound love?

Sarah McCabe's new job
in the city is giving her a
firsthand taste of the life she
has always desired—a life of
luxury, culture, and social
privilege. Sarah knows exactly
what she wants...but what
does God want for her?

## VISIT YOUR
## LOCAL BOOKSTORE.

REALMS